OVER & BACK

Paperback ISBN: 978-1-63337-900-8
Ebook ISBN: 978-1-63337-734-9
LCCN: 2023910528

Printed in the United States of America
1 3 5 7 9 10 8 6 4 2

OVER & BACK

A MYSTERY

LARRY BUTTERMORE

OPENING AUTHOR'S NOTE

I HAVE ALWAYS MADE IT A POINT **to remember things. My memory has served me well in my various careers, as well as in my life in general.**

From my days at college in 1964, to 1991 when I was 48 years old, I worked for a prominent local retail furniture store in Columbus, Ohio. I started as a greeter and ended up as VP of Sales. The store was in the newly opened Northland Mall when I showed up for my very first day on the job. The owner, Gordon, hired me over a simple interview at the store a couple of weeks before the grand opening.

The company had been around for many years, but always in freestanding stores around Columbus. From a very basic four-story building in the 600 block of West Broad Street to the crown of Columbus fashion shopping was quite a journey. That Gordon trusted me after such a brief time—allowing me to be the first impression a new customer would have when entering his fancy new store—still amazes me.

Within the span of just two weeks, I went from head lifeguard/pool manager at Winding Hollow Country Club to greeting hundreds of customers every evening at Northland Mall. My job at the furniture store came about after a conversation I had poolside. It was August, and my job was almost over at the club, as I would be heading back to Otterbein to start my senior year.

Felice and Andy were my best and favorite pool patrons. Andy was seven and loved being at the pool. He took to the water like a fish before the end of that summer. He and I hit it off right away, and I helped him get started as a swimmer and even coaxed him into a dive or two. Felice brought her favorite book and sat by each day, relaxing and working on her tan. She was always nice to me. I mention this only because not every parent/member was.

On my final day at the club, Felice came over to say goodbye.

"Larry," she said with a friendly smile, "thanks for being such a great friend for our Andy this summer. So, what are your plans once you leave here?"

"It's been my pleasure, Felice. I'm heading back to school and hoping to find an extra job to help with my expenses."

"Oh, you're looking for a job? Have you spoken to Gordon?"

"Gordon who?" I asked.

She laughed before saying, "Gordon is my husband. I realize he's hardly been here this summer."

"So, you think he might have a job for me?"

"Yes, we've been talking about needing a person at the store we're opening."

"What kind of store is it?"

"It's a furniture store."

"Would you believe I've never even been in a furniture store, let alone worked at one? I doubt I would be qualified."

"That's pretty funny, Larry, but Gordon and I have talked about this person needing little more than a smile and a personality. You're good on both counts."

I was flattered and quicky realized that the little things I tried to do had been noticed.

"Why don't I go over to the snack bar and see if I can get him on the phone? If he's still looking, maybe I can get you over to see him."

"Thanks so much," I said, unable to believe my luck. Surely it couldn't be this easy to find another job? "Do you want me to wait?"

"Sure."

I made small talk with Andy while I waited for her to return. She gave me a big thumbs-up as she headed back toward me.

"Larry, he wants you to come over now, if you have the time."

I'd only been to one other interview in my life. At that one, I felt like I needed a suit and tie to make a proper impression. So I asked, "Wouldn't I need to go home and change? I'm dressed, as you can see, in jeans and a T-shirt."

She laughed cheerily as she said, "When you get there, you will find that he will be dressed much the same, as he'll be hanging pictures and schlepping furniture around."

"Schlepping" was one of many new slang terms I would soon come to know.

Felice had a way of putting me at ease, and I was eager to meet Gordon. "Well, okay. Tell me how to get there, and I'm on my way."

Several minutes later, I rang the doorbell at the back entrance to White's Fine Furniture. Gordon answered, and after about ten minutes I was hired for a pay that was more than I had been making all summer.

That brief encounter with Felice was fortuitous, as it led to a twenty-seven-year career with the company. I went from being a boy to a man. Gordon became like a second father to me, and I watched Andy grow from a seven-year-old to a teen, seeing him through high school and college. I have since watched him grow into a competent business-man and lifelong friend.

My memory and quick recall served me well on our grand opening Saturday. I spied one of my favorites from the club coming through the door, and I was quick to greet her.

"Hey, Mrs. G, welcome to White's!"

"I'm sorry, young man. Do I know you?"

I smiled and chuckled as I told her, "I'm Larry, from the pool at the club."

"Well, I guess I didn't recognize you with your clothes on."

She was with several people, and there was a crowd around the front entrance when she blurted out those words. I was at full blush, and she was too. In an instant, everyone who heard what she had said started laughing, oohing and aaahing as they began to tease us both.

This relieved both of our momentary embarrassments, and she immediately gave me a big hug. It was not unusual for me to remember names and faces like that. I didn't think of this as an important trait until much later, but it served me well.

My quick recognition that day helped to make a good impression on that particular lady. This quicky got back to Gordon, as she was good friends with the family. I was able to advance in the company through hard work and using my memory to relate to customers and my staff.

Gordon was the master at salesmanship, and I learned a lot from him. I was coached early on to get the name of each customer as quickly as possible. Once obtained, I became a friend and advocate, and the whole process was so much more than the typical salesperson-to-customer conversation. I trained myself to use each person's name as soon and as often as possible.

The reason was simple: say the name back to them a few times and it entered my "memory bank." Repeating it helped drop the preconception that I was purely trying to sell something. This helped the customer relax, instead of feeling on guard against the dreaded salesperson trying to force them to buy something.

It worked well on every level. If I succeeded in making a sale, I could confidently walk them to the office and introduce them so we could complete the process. If I did not make the sale on the first visit, I found it quite easy to exchange names and phone numbers since we had already established a rapport. Then I would also be able to follow up with a thank you.

Later, as a Store and Sales Manager, I taught this technique to hundreds of salespeople over a twenty-five-year period. I present this only to say that this was not as easy for everyone as it was for me.

After 1991, I became an insurance agent. Here again, my memory served me well.

In the beginning, I was on the phone more than I care to mention. As an aside, 1991 was still a great time to be making phone calls, as people actually did answer their phones, which is more than you can say these days.

In order to even gain an appointment to my company, I was required to get over 1,000 "X" dates. An X date was a commitment by a potential customer. The X stood for their "expiration date." It was the time when their bill came due. That, our company had researched, was the best time to make contact with them, as their policy would be front and center in their mind. They would agree to allow me to contact them after my agency opened, and to present a quote to them. I tried hard to get acquainted with each person over the phone. I took meticulous notes of every conversation on 3x5 note cards. When I finally got things opened, these cards became the lifeblood of my success or failure as a new agent. Because I remembered their name (and even more important, something about them) when I called them for the second time, I broke down the typical barriers and made new clients of many.

Over the years, the way my business evolved, I relied on referrals from customers, friends, and trusted business connections. I talked to them on the phone often and met with them only when they desired it. Sometimes the need for a "person-to-person" never felt necessary. Once more, my good memory became a valuable asset.

Another skillset also evolved. I'll call it "voice recognition." I guess I always possessed it, but never realized it as an advantage till then. Many insurance agents let the staff talk to their customers, fielding as many calls as they can get away with. I preferred to answer the phone myself when I was in the office. Being able to recognize a client by their voice helped me in so many ways. I could put a "name with a voice" rather than a "name with a face."

If a client came into the office and I didn't recognize them, I would immediately start up a friendly conversation so I could hear their voice. This bailed me out of many potentially embarrassing moments. On more than one occasion, I had two clients with the same voice. One was a longtime friend from my furniture days named Stu. The other was a newly acquired client. They were approximately the same age and grew up in the Pittsburgh, Pennsylvania, area. If you study accents at all, folks from this area have one. Since I also grew up in that area, I knew instantly that my new client spoke "Pittsburghese." Within a few more moments, I said to myself, *He sounds just like my friend Stu.*

This was the first time I ever experienced such a thing. They were both customers for many years, so I found myself being extra cautious when one of them called, as I didn't want to mix up the "voice with the name."

A few years before I retired, I had a similar encounter. I answered the phone one afternoon, and a pleasant voice came on. "Hi, I'm Laurie from PNC bank. I'd like to see if our mutual client is currently insured with you."

She gave me the name and address, which was in a nearby town called Pataskala, Ohio. I had to laugh out loud as her pronunciation butchered the name of the town. To her, it was "Pata-skalla." At that point, I couldn't help myself, and decided to have a little fun with her.

I said, "I take it you're not from around here?" At the same time, I gave her the correct pronunciation.

"You would be right, Larry, as I'm from right in Pittsburgh."

"Actually, I could tell instantly from your accent. I grew up near there, and it only took a few sentences to indict you."

"Oh, where are you from?" she countered.

"I grew up in a small town called Connellsville."

"You've got to be kidding me! I did too. My dad still lives there."

Soon I learned that I knew her dad, and I even knew a neat story about him. I recounted it to her, and she was beyond pleased and amazed. Before I got off the phone, she asked if I was on Facebook. I replied yes, and she asked if she could send me a friend request.

"Sure, that would be great," I said.

We are friends yet today.

In 2009 I was privileged to write a book. It was called *Switch Hitters*. It took me about a year to write. Once finished, I was beyond elated. I turned it in to the publisher and waited. It was accepted, but with a condition. The publisher asked a question about the characters in the book.

"Are your characters real or made up?"

Early in the writing of this book, I came up with a term for the category for which I felt the book could qualify. I termed it "autobiographical fiction." I used real people with real names but cast some of them in roles that were made up. My publisher was not amused at my category.

"There's no such thing," the publisher told me.

I knew that, but never realized the relevance till that moment. Because the characters were all real people, I had to get written permission to use their names in the story. It took me over a month to reach each "character." In some cases, I needed help. My brother stepped in big time, helping me find several. He was three years younger but spent more time back home than I did. One of my main characters was a real person but in a "made-up" role. To complicate matters, I found that he had passed away. To my surprise, his widow was a person I knew. My brother once again came to the rescue, reminding me that Chuck, a hero in my book, was married to Patty. She was the sister of one of my other characters. Bob paved the way, and when I called him, he was very willing to call his big sis and set us up to chat.

After I told her about her late husband's role, she was thrilled, as his part in the story was heroic. She bought at least ten books and was one of my biggest fans!

As I got this task done, I found it all very fulfilling instead of a royal pain in the ass! I eventually got every one of them on the phone. The conversations were great fun, and I sensed that they were as interested as I was.

As I spoke to each person, I recognized most of the voices of around thirty folks I hadn't seen or heard in almost fifty years. If all of them were presented to me in a lineup, I'm confident that I would not have recognized many of their faces.

The book that you are about to read is also a work of "autobiographical fiction." While the mystery plotline is fictional, many of the characters are inspired by real people, and many more, like my own "character" and those of my family members, are as true-to-life as my memory can make them. My hope is to blend my personal experiences with a little history and mystery for a compelling read. I hope you enjoy the book as much as I enjoyed recording my memories in its writing.

THE CHAPPELEARS

YOU'RE GOING TO GET TO KNOW a guy named Trey pretty quickly and intensely. As you might suspect, Trey is a nickname. It is often given to a member of the third generation with the same name. This particular Trey is the third Bradley Chappelear. His father goes by Brad, while Grandad preferred the more formal name of Bradley.

Trey was born in Ann Arbor, Michigan, in 1943. His sister, Scarlett, was born a few years later. Their parents were recent U of M grads and headed out to seek their careers in business and education.

Father Brad tried to join the service but was thwarted by a heart problem that was discovered during his junior year at Michigan. He was very ambitious and outgoing and was encouraged by his college professors to use the reputation of his Alma Mater to get a foothold in a large company-type management training program.

He coveted the auto industry, as he had always been a "car guy" growing up. It also didn't hurt that the hub of that industry was right in the state of Michigan.

After several failed interviews, he and his wife, Brooke, decided to broaden their horizons and look farther out, always with the plan of a return to Michigan. The children were young, and Brooke and Brad knew the timing was right to relocate for any position that would better their station in life.

Brad secured a great entry-level management stint with Dupont at their home office in Wilmington, Delaware. After five years, he was recruited by The Hershey Chocolate Company in eastern Pennsylvania to head up a new division. His expertise at Dupont and his reputation as a tough-minded but fair manager drew the attention of a corporate headhunter.

After just seven years at Hershey, he had been promoted three times and was managing a packaging plant for them. Though he was pleased with the growth he had managed with the company, he soon realized there were very few opportunities for advancement still in front of him and started looking elsewhere

It wasn't long before he had an interview with The Corning Glass Company in South Central New York. His interviewer, a VP, was impressed with what he saw and knew right away that he wanted Brad on his team. "Easy to see you're our kind of guy, Brad," he said cheerfully. "Corning is a place with a lot of culture. Although it seems like we are in a remote sort of place, we are near many vibrant areas, and not far from The Finger Lakes and Lake Ontario. The Binghamton area is a growing business hub, and places like Ithaca and Syracuse are great college towns."

"Can I stop you right there, George? I know you're just doing your job to try to sell me on coming here. You should know, though, I've already done my research, and you don't need to oversell. It's a beautiful area, and I think Brooke and the children will like it here. My parents are from Petoskey, Michigan, and this area reminds me of Northern Michigan. I also know you have good schools. My children will need that! My wife, Brooke, will also need a teaching job. She's been fortunate to find such a job at each stop along the way so far. Think you can help with that?" "Done. I'm personal friends with the superintendent. He knows how important our schools are, and with the unique alliance our company has with supporting the schools, I can all but guarantee that we can find a good spot for her."

The collateral damage of moving is often not as obvious as one might think. In this case, it came in the form of Trey overhearing his parents. They were excitedly talking about the new position and all the blessings it could bring to their family. What Brad and Brooke did not realize was that their children did not share their joy at the prospect of their father starting a new job. They had moved before and were well aware that they would be forced into a strange new school, neighborhood, and town.

"Sissy, I overheard Mom and Dad talking last night," Trey said, his tone dejected.

"About what?"

"Looks like we're going to move again."

"You've got to be kidding! I like it here. Don't they ever consider our feelings when they do this? I'm set to make the swim team next year. I have a boyfriend. I feel like running away. Please tell me this isn't happening, Trey. We have to do something!"

"I know. This move hurts me more than any other."

"Should we tell them how we feel?"

"Sure, but it won't do any good. If Dad has a new job, we are moving. It's as simple as that, and you know as well as I do that it's already settled."

"It sucks!"

Trey and Scarlett eventually became used to readjusting to new towns. They had to, because no sooner than they got to Corning, the upward trajectory of Brad's career led to an opportunity in my hometown, Connellseville.

CONNELLSVILLE

TREY BLEW INTO OUR TOWN like a winter storm. In all my high school years, we never had a student "move in." Connellsville was not a place conducive to that, as the population had been diminishing for some time. We had an influx of students from the outlying areas because of the creation of a "joint" system, but that was not the same thing as someone coming from out of town. The joint system meant that two or more school systems from our area merged to create a larger one. This was meant to give all students a better opportunity, and that goal was more than met for the kids coming in from our mountain and rural communities.

The arrival of Trey and his sister, Scarlett, was odd because the heyday of Connellsville had long come and gone. When a town suffers economically, people don't usually flock there. Rather, the population dwindles, as folks have no choice but to move on to get jobs in other places.

In the early part of the century, we were a booming town. On a river and in the middle of a rich vein of bituminous coal, Connellsville became the "coke" capital of the world. The coke

I speak of is not Coca-Cola, but rather, the biproduct of coal that became the fuel of choice for the equally booming steel industry centered in the Pittsburgh area. We became a railroad hub as well. At the height of the boom, at least six railroads crisscrossed on one side of the river or the other. The population swelled, and the economy was over the top. We once had more millionaires per capita than any city in the country.

Alas, the coke was later replaced by a new and far less expensive fuel called natural gas. This was devastating for our town, as they had never bothered to come up with a backup plan. The businesses and industries of Connellsville all depended on the success of the coke phenomenon. By the '50s, the last coke ovens had disappeared, and any left would likely be used to provide a residence for a homeless family.

All through my school years, the one industry we still depended on was Anchor Hocking. It thrived and spawned several ancillary businesses. The factory made glass bottles and jars for multiple purposes. The bottles needed caps and lids.

Trey's dad was an executive, and he was selected to take over one of the main divisions of the only business still thriving in our town, The Anchor Hocking Glass Company. The company felt an outside influence was needed, as (like the town) the plant was not exactly on the rise.

The Chappelear family moved near to where I grew up, although theirs was a neighborhood much different from mine. The Chappelears moved to one of the few places in Connellsville where a family with money could reside and feel comfortable. Somehow, I was lucky enough and just ballsy enough to gain a few friends there. I also got to know several families on that street while pursuing spot jobs shoveling snow and mowing grass.

I had one great mowing job that I kept for two summers when I was fourteen and fifteen. I didn't know it at the time, but Dr. Harrison and his wife had the second biggest house and yard in town, and they owned one of only two inground pools on the street. The other pool belonged to my friend Harry, whose parents owned the local Ford dealership. I met him on our summer softball team and was often invited to visit their home and swim in their pool.

My family lived just two streets away. There were no visible barriers between the two streets, but the socio-economic barrier made it unlikely that I would ever be pals with Trey or that my folks and his would ever break bread together at a backyard barbeque. Trey's folks had always lived in bigger cities, as his father had been on the fast track with several big companies before taking the Anchor position.

As such, Trey and his sister had relocated with each promotion, and they were put in private or parochial schools in very small settings within those big cities. With this move, however, Trey's parents decided both of their kids were old enough to need the socialization provided by a public education.

You would think our school would be ideal, as in "small town, small school." You would be wrong. Because of the jointure, we were a big school in a small town. Our average graduating class had just under 400 kids. At some point not long before the Chappelears moved in, students from as far away as 35 miles became part of the same school I attended.

This had a positive effect on everyone coming in from

the outer limits, as they previously would have attended small schools—sometimes even one-room schools—with small budgets and none of the extracurricular activities my school was able to offer. The fact that they had to ride the bus for an extra hour every day was balanced out by the fact that they had every reason to be pleased with their new situation once they arrived at school.

With this new move, Trey would enter as a senior and Scarlett would be a sophomore. They both stood out. Even though Scarlett was young, she didn't look it. She certainly caught the eye of many of the young men in our school, as she was drop-dead gorgeous. She had long, red hair (no doubt the Genesis of her name) and easily filled out every piece of clothing she wore. She was also very smart and athletic. Even though our school was large, there were zero girls' athletic teams. This was symptomatic of the times. Usually only private schools like the one she and Trey attended in Corning had such teams available. She had been on the swim team at her last school and had been destined to be a star at the sport. In the absence of that option at her new school, she became a cheerleader and used her talents that way. Class officer and National Honor Society followed.

While Scarlett was a sweet girl and her ability to fit in was something that came naturally to her, Trey…not so much. Trey looked like a linebacker. He was roughly 5'10" and 200 lbs. He obviously lifted weights, and he was imposing enough that no one wanted to mess with him.

Despite his impressive physical appearance, he was afflicted with something akin to a Napoleon Complex. This would normally be reserved for short people, but in Trey's case, it stemmed from the insecurities of fitting into a completely foreign environment he would never have chosen for himself. His insecurities did not play out well. He acted out in class, got detention, and was sent to see the principal more than once.

If his underlying motive was to get attention, it worked. He soon had a reputation, and everyone knew who he was. He also had a distinctive accent. There was no mistaking that he had spent his entire life farther east. His accent was unlike anything any of us had ever heard before, and I got to know it well, since he and I shared two classes. On top of that, he loved to talk, especially when he wasn't supposed to be talking. His vocabulary included some colorful language that exceeded most kids in our area, and he was never afraid to bring it out for show-and-tell. It both amused me and grated on me. It was unforgettable.

In our school, there were a few "factions." I wouldn't call them "gangs," but each side of town had a group of guys that hung out together. Both boys and girls needed to feel a sense of belonging, and being part of one of these groups was important, since it offered fellowship, protection, and recognition.

Trey's neighborhood had no factions. Quite the opposite, as anyone coming to school from that neighborhood would (right or wrong) be termed a "snob." Trey wasn't about to be called a snob, and he did everything he could to shed that title.

His reputation got him noticed, and he was soon being recruited by the North End Boys. They were definitely a faction known to be rough and tough and not often challenged. To them, Trey would be a prized addition. He took the bait and was seen hanging with them before and after school. He even managed to join them without changing his appearance. It was the early '60s, and the prevailing look was "grease." Slicked-back hair, leather jackets, and engineer boots were in. Smoking was considered the norm. Trey must have really been a special addition, as he had a Marine-type crew cut and would not smoke.

I thought his parents had the upper hand on all of this—more than Trey would ever let on. They likely would put a quick stop to any negative change in Trey's appearance. Nevertheless, there he was, hanging with the North Enders.

THE FIGHT

EACH FACTION HAD its own look and reputation. When there were fights in our town, those fights were between factions. The North End Boys were most often a part of this, because they had an initiation before anyone could be granted full membership. Initiation was simple—get in a fight. Such fights were exciting and well publicized via word of mouth, although they rarely lived up to their billing. The North End Boys couldn't wait to arrange a fight for Trey. The opponent would have to be hand-picked, and only a few seniors, other than current North Enders, would even come close as a worthy challenger.

As it turns out, there was another newish faction that might have the guy. With our joint high school, we started to see a new group of students come in. These were the students who were bused in from over an hour away. "Mountain Boys" was an appropriate name for them, as most of the terrain outside the city limits was mountainous. Where better to find someone to challenge the likes of a streetwise Trey Chappelear?

One fine day, the North Enders and their new recruit, Trey, were sitting at a table just outside the high school. As usual, they were looking rather greasy, smoking, and gawking at every pretty girl who passed by. That is, all except Trey, who looked very out of place.

"What about Will Stone? He's equal in size and stature to Trey, and for sure isn't afraid of him or anyone else," one of the North Enders suggested.

Will was raised in the mountains. If this could be considered a faction, he was from it. He grew up near Camp Wildwood, just outside Normalville. Will was anything but normal, however. He was in my homeroom and sat right behind me. He was friendly enough, but always had an edge, a mystery to him. He looked like a jock, but he never went out for any sport. He probably got his physique from his upbringing. A lot of the kids from the mountains had to go home and work on their parents' farms, logging operations, or sawmills.

Will's parents had a sawmill, from what I understood. He and I touched on such a topic in the only real conversation I ever had with him. We were in Fish and Game Club together, and I was the president and he was the vice president. I'm pretty sure I got elected because no one else wanted to be the president. For me, it was a resume builder, as one of my teachers told me that colleges looked at stuff like that as a plus. It was obvious Will had way more experience in the things our club represented than I ever would.

Once I asked him, "Can you stay after school and help me organize an outing for next weekend?"

His quick answer was, "Nope, got to help Dad at the mill tonight. Maybe another time. Sorry, Butts." That was one of the few pieces of information I knew about Will.

How a fight gets started is always interesting, but it's rarely started by the two combatants. They usually don't even want to fight, nor do they have a problem with each other. In this case, it was a North Ender who started it by asking Trey:

"Hey, Trey. You heard of Will Stone?"

"Can't say I have. Why?"

"Well, he's been bragging around school that he's heard of you and thinks you're soft."

From that fabricated beginning point, the fight of the year got its traction.

Trey shot back, "Bring him on."

The bait worked, and now the same fake news made its way back to Will. One of the North Enders who happened to be in my homeroom was the one who dangled that piece of bait. "Hey, Will. Ever heard of the new guy, Trey Chappelear?"

"Never heard of him."

"Well, he knows who you are. Says he's in your gym class and that you're weak. He wants to fight you!"

"So . . .?"

"So does that mean you're backing down?"

With no other choice, Will fired back, "Bulls*%t, no problem. Just tell me where and when, and I'll be there."

The best time to fight was after school. The best place was anyplace other than school! So, the two factions decided to meet behind the pool hall on North Pittsburgh Street. It had a large parking area off the street far enough, and a security light so the fight could happen on an otherwise dark October evening. Saturday evening at 8:00 was chosen, and word was spread.

Lots of folks would have paid money to see such a fight. I got wind of it and decided to show up. About a hundred other people joined me. The hope was that the cops would not feel so inclined, thus allowing such a fight to materialize.

When I got there, Trey and the North Enders were in full force. It was a warm Indian summer Saturday, perfect for such an event. The fight was scheduled to start in less than five minutes, and Will still wasn't there. The crowd was getting agitated, thinking they had showed up for nothing.

I was at the entrance to the parking lot on Pittsburgh Street, and I saw what looked like a small parade of cars approaching from the south. It was Will and his boys. They came in pickup trucks and loud jalopies, with guys on the running boards and even in the beds. At least a half dozen vehicles showed up, a total of maybe thirty guys. They wheeled into the parking lot, and it was on!

Whatever advantage the North Enders may have envisioned, it was lost, as the mountain guys outnumbered them more than two to one. Soon a huge circle formed. Amid catcalls, taunts, and threats from both sides, the two combatants entered the circle.

Someone from the crowd yelled, "Any rules?"

"Whoever gives up, loses," was the reply.

What I witnessed next was a fight that would go down in history—local history, at least. Neither of the fellas was shy about foreplay, and they just started throwing haymaker after haymaker. This was not a "sanctioned" event. There were no rounds, rest periods, or referees. My guess was that I should pay close attention to every move, as it wouldn't last long. Pretty quickly, Will was getting the best of it. Trey took a few headshots and started bleeding. I don't think he was hurt too badly, but he looked like he was about done in.

Trey's buddies were starting to get anxious, as they had fully expected this fight to be short and sweet and in Trey's favor. One of the North Enders got in the circle and gave Will a kick from behind. That proved to be bad judgement, as two mountain guys grabbed him and started pummeling him. Normally, you'd think an all-out gang fight would ensue. I believe the strength in numbers of the mountain guys made it clear that they would prevail if that were to happen.

Meanwhile, Trey and Will never even saw what was going on outside the circle. They just kept on with their fierce fight. Trey seemed to be getting more desperate and decided to bum-rush his opponent and try to go from boxing to wrestling. Will saw him coming and stepped aside like a bull fighter, leaving Trey face down in the gravel. Will could easily have ended it there, if not for what happened next.

One of the North Enders threw out a five-foot two-by-four to Trey. "Hit him with it. Smack him!" came a call from the crowd that seemed to be weighing in heavily in Trey's favor.

He obligingly grabbed the piece of lumber and charged at Will. The noise it made was sickening—like the crack of a base-ball bat hitting a homerun. Trey let Will have it right across his forehead. I'm sure everyone in attendance felt shocked, as most fights ended before such overt violence took place. I'm also pretty sure everyone thought the fight was over, as Will was literally knocked off his feet and was on the ground. Trey stood over him still wielding the club and looking very much like the victor.

Then two things happened in quick succession. Will got up. First on one knee, then fully upright. He had an ugly crease mark on his forehead and a look in his eyes that let everyone, especially Trey, know that he was not yet finished. He rolled in toward Trey and took the club away and threw it back in the crowd. Trey's demeanor changed, as only seconds had passed since he had been the sure victor. He now looked terrified, as Will was beyond pissed.

I can only speculate what the finish would have looked like, as sirens and screeching tires sent everyone packing. Someone must have alerted the police to the fray.

•　　•　　•

Both guys showed up at school on Monday, and I was shocked to see Will. Sure enough, though, there he was sitting behind me in homeroom. His forehead was black and blue, and I knew it had to hurt.

Trey's homeroom was down the hall. Just before the bell rang, he strutted into our classroom. *Here we go again*, I thought as he walked straight up to Will's desk. Trey faced Will and extended his hand. Will got up from his seat, and they stood toe-to-toe, eyeing each other.

"You are one tough man!" Trey exclaimed. "Sorry about the two-by-four. I just reacted in the heat of the moment. That really could have hurt you bad."

"You're tough too. I guess I have an iron head."

Both laughed as the bell rang. It was as a strange but fitting outcome.

Everyone in school soon heard a version of the fight, and both Trey and Will became superheroes.

During our senior year, Trey and I became pretty good friends. We weren't running in the same circles, but somehow we clicked. There was a mutual respect between us, and we certainly said hi when we passed each other in school.

Trey graduated with us but soon moved again. His dad took a new position in Lancaster, Ohio, with Anchor Hocking. Scarlett was a casualty of moving, and she graduated from Lancaster High instead of CJHS. Even though I figured I'd never see him again, I was glad to count Trey as a friend.

FATE

FATE IS A MYSTERIOUS THING. **I ended up in Ohio after graduating high school, and as fate would have it, Trey did too. I was accepted at Otterbein College (now university) and he at Ohio University.**

Even though our town was trending downward in its economy and population, our schools and teachers were always encouraging. We had a very high percentage of students on a college path. Our teachers allowed us to believe that great things were out there for us.

I had two very good opportunities afforded to me. The coal mine my father worked at was owned by US Steel. I found out about a scholarship they offered and applied during my senior year. I was notified that I was one of the winners!

I also applied for a scholarship to Otterbein. It was the school connected to the church denomination my family was a part of (Evangelical United Brethren). My seventh-grade homeroom teacher, Mr. Witt, was now the assistant dean of admissions there. My cousin Mark was already there and had great things to say about it. I won that scholarship too.

The US Steel scholarship was to Carnegie Tech in Pittsburgh. It was prestigious and covered full tuition. Otterbein offered half tuition. Seemed like a clear choice, until some pesky details came to light. The Tech scholarship would create a path where I had to pursue Mining Engineering as my course of study. After graduation, I would automatically be working for US Steel in that field. At the time, my self-confidence, plus my fear of failing in such a demanding academic area, left me wondering.

My dad, although very proud of me, was adamant about one thing. "I don't want you to ever set foot in a coal mine."

My dad spent his entire adult life working in the bowels of a coal mine. Robena was the biggest underground mine in the world at the time. It was south of us and was at least a 45-mile one- way journey each day. He was already a victim of the industry, as he had the beginning stages of black lung disease and COPD.

It also became apparent that there would be other financial considerations, as my dad and I would still have the expenses of me living in Pittsburgh for four to five years. We sat down, weighed the options, and I was off to Otterbein without a backward glance.

Cousin Mark paved the way for me and for other family members to choose Otterbein. For a five-year period, there would be a family member, or cousin of Mark's, attending Otterbein. Cousin Mark was one year ahead of me. Cousin Craig and Cousin Tom were one year behind me. Cousin Kathy came the following year, and my brother Bob followed her.

Trey and I were both in Ohio while we were in school. Our paths were different, though, since on top of attending different colleges, I was going to be the first college graduate from my family. Trey's parents had both graduated from college, which likely meant he had even more pressure on him. After all, they would expect him to follow in their footsteps.

The probability of us meeting again was small, at best. Fate, however, saw things differently, and Trey and I would soon cross paths.

TREY

FIVE YEARS HAD GONE BY. I had finished college and married a lovely girl named Barb, whom I met while I was attending school. Life was good, but I was a very busy boy. I had just finished my MBA. I had a full-time teaching job, coached tennis, and worked nights and weekends at the furniture store.

Barb and I needed a break! We decided to take a rare weekend off to visit my in-laws in Troy, Ohio. My brother-in-law, Dave, was also there, and he had brought his new girlfriend. He was anxious for his big sister and me to meet her, and even more eager to show us he was no longer the kid we remembered.

He asked us to join them for dinner and drinks at a fancy hotel/restaurant in Dayton. Despite his eagerness to prove his manliness, Dave asked me to drive, which came with two perks. One, I had a fancy convertible that would be a lot more fun to drive around in. Two, he could have a lot more fun with his girlfriend on the drive if they were both in the backseat.

Dayton is about twenty miles south of Troy and a fairly big city. I had heard of the restaurant Dave suggested, but none of us had ever been there. Once we arrived, I quickly confirmed that it wasn't my kind of place. It was decked out in over-the-top, garish décor. Red-velvet booths sat atop patterned carpet, with a piano bar off to one side.

It was a Friday night, and so it came as no surprise that the place was jumping, but luckily we were able to get a booth. There was a piano guy who was doing hokey attempts at Frank Sinatra. Just as our waiter finished taking our drink order, I heard a familiar voice.

"Barb, that voice, I know it," I told her.

"You are always pulling this. So, who is it this time?" she asked.

"I'm positive it's a guy I graduated high school with. I'd never forget his voice. That's him sitting at the bar. It's got to be him. He's even being obnoxious, which seals the deal."

It was Trey, and he was knee-deep in hitting on the bartender. She was doing her best to fend him off, but he was her only customer at the time, making him impossible to ignore.

"So, what are you going to do?" Barb asked, somehow sounding a little miffed and amused at the same time.

"I'm going to sit down next to him and see. I have no idea what he would be doing here, but I'm about to find out."

At the bar, I blurted out, "Trey? Trey Chappelear?"

"Yeah," he fired back. "What the F*&% is it to you?"

Surprised by his attitude, I said, "Hey, it's Butts. We graduated from high school together. Don't you remember?"

"So, what do you want from me? Can't you see I'm busy? That was over four years ago."

"Nothing, I guess," I said, finally disgusted by his attitude. "Just wanted to say hi. Have a nice life."

I abandoned my barstool and went back to my booth. I had accomplished one thing and confirmed another. I was as good at recognizing voices as I'd always been, and Trey hadn't changed much.

•   •   •

The next morning, I decided to call my friend Dave Gillott. He had been our class president, and I figured he might be able to shed some light on my encounter.

"Dave, you'll never believe who I saw last night."

"Tell me."

"Trey Chappelear himself."

"No shit…where? I know he's supposed to be in Ohio."

"Yep, saw him at a bar in Dayton. Do you know anything about what's happened to him since high school?"

"Just enough to be dangerous. I have a cousin who ended up in a few classes at Ohio University where he went. The football coach saw him in the weight room one day as a freshman and was beside himself. The rest is history."

"Sounds like our old friend Hersh! Don Hershberger."

"You're right. Hersh was a total physical specimen in high school. I still can't believe his biggest goal was to be our drum major when he could have easily been a football star. Didn't he end up at Otterbein with you?"

"He sure did. In fact, he was my roommate during his first year. That's a story in itself!" As I began to relay the story to Dave, the memory came back in sharp focus.

33

The very first evening we were together, Don confronted me with his own set of rules of engagement. He was explaining that he didn't want any distractions from his routine of studying. Quiet hours would be from 7:00 p.m. till midnight. Then it was bedtime. He further explained that if I didn't abide by these rules, it would not be pretty. Although I chuckled under my breath, I knew he was all too serious, and decided it would be in my best interest to comply. While we were talking, we heard a huge commotion in the room below us. I could see the veins in Don's neck protruding.

"Larry, do me a favor," he said. "Go down and tell those guys they better be quiet, or I'll personally come down and kick their asses."

I was not fond of the idea, but I did what he asked, mostly because I didn't want him to change his mind and kick *my* ass. The guys were jokers, and I had already met them several times. They laughed out loud at my efforts to get them to quiet down. I warned them and went back upstairs.

A few minutes after I returned to our room, they started up again. This time Don went totally berserk. The desks we had were metal and very heavy. The floor was made of asbestos tile. Don, without even getting up, started picking up and dropping the desk. The tile started breaking and tile shards were flying everywhere. The noise below stopped, and Don jumped up and headed for their room. I was right behind him—there was no way I was going to miss whatever happened next.

One of the guys was trying to leave when we got down there. Don grabbed him by the throat and headed into the room. Another housemate was desperately trying to escape through the window. Don had one in each hand 3.5 seconds later. He lifted them both up against the block wall and quietly lectured them on the error of their ways. He then dropped them in a heap on the floor. We never saw either of them again, and no one replaced them in that room.

Dave chuckled as I finished the story. "Wow, what a story. But it doesn't surprise me, as he and I were best friends in high school. I knew both his funny side and his violent side. Getting back to the Trey story, though," Dave continued, "I heard it played out like this:…"

I settled into Dave's telling of what Trey was like back in the day.

"Where have you been, son?" the coach asked.

Trey shot back, "What do you mean? You ain't my dad."

"I mean, how did you not get noticed by my coaches? Where did you play ball in high school?"

"I spent my senior year in a town called Connellsville, over south of Pittsburgh."

"Hey, I know that school. We went over there to see a guy Woody ended up with up in Columbus."

"Yeah, I knew Bo a little bit. I was only there as a senior and never went out for the team. In fact, I never played football at all."

Coach stared at him in amazement. "You've got to be kidding me. You come out and I'll teach you how to be a linebacker in a heartbeat. How much can you bench press?"

"I got 250 this morning."

"Good God, son, my team needs you. You progress and I'll get you a scholarship."

Dave went on to explain the rest of what he'd heard about Trey. He was an immediate fire starter on the team. He liked to hit and didn't like getting hit. About three weeks in, he laid out the quarterback in a scrimmage. Next thing you know, the entire line took offense and had Trey's number on their mind.

For the next several practices, coaches had to keep the peace, as Trey became like an animal when he donned his pads. He was constantly in fights with his own players. This became more than his teammates could take, or deserved. His stint was short and sweet, as Coach simply decided he was far more trouble than he was worth. On his way out, he flipped off the entire team and headed back to his apartment.

Dave said, "He did graduate on time, Larry, even after his missteps with the football team. Someone said his dad got him a job in Dayton through one of his connections, so it's not surprising you saw him there."

"If he's not in school, how do you suppose he's keeping from getting drafted? You and I are 1-A, and I'm sure he is too," I said.

THE DRAFT AND TREY

"THAT'S THE OTHER THING I heard, Larry. Looks like he is on the run from the draft. He may be on his way to Canada."

"What's in Canada?"

"If he's trying to dodge the draft, that's a place he could go. The Canadian government has allowed their country to become a safe haven for our young men. Right now, lots of guys are doing that."

"So, I guess he won't be showing up for our first reunion!"

Because Lancaster was now home to his parents, Trey enrolled at OU in nearby Athens. Brad and Brooke took him first to their Alma Mater, University of Michigan. He acted out on the visit, and although he wouldn't say it, it became clear to them that he did not want to follow in their rather large footprints.

Once they realized that he wasn't interested, they toured him around Ohio, hoping he would stay. They settled on Miami in Oxford. It was known for strong academics and was close enough to visit frequently, as they felt the urge to keep their son on a short leash. His judgement had never been what you would call good.

Trey had met some frat guys from OU through a nearby neighbor. The guy was likely more interested in Trey's now-not-so-little sister than he was in recruiting Trey to go to OU. On his campus visit, he was introduced to Green Beer and the well-known fact (in the '60s) that OU was "party central." He won over his parents by employing some smokescreen tactics, convincing them with brochures he picked up during his visit to campus that the school would be a benefit to him. The brochures played on the strict campus policies in place to make sure students weren't distracted from the main goal of getting a fine education. After all, the college motto, *Religio, Doctrina Civilitas, Prae Omnibus Vitus* (Religion, Learning, Civility, above all, Virtue), would attract any prospective parent and convince them to allow their child to become part of the school. Trey didn't volunteer that he had firsthand knowledge that OU was known as one of the country's prominent party schools.

After his failed stint on the football team, Trey's parents were understandably disappointed. Athens in the fall is a magical place. The campus and its atmosphere were as special as anyone could find. He remained on campus and pressed on to get his degree. He majored in partying, yet managed to keep a decent 2.8 average in marketing.

As time went on, Trey became aware of the politics of the time. He was on campus when President Johnson came to speak into place what became known as "The Great Society," leading the war on poverty.

Sitting in a quiet booth at a local Athens coffee shop with one of his close friends, Trey asked, "Hey, Drew, what's your take on Vietnam?"

"What do you mean by my take?"

"Well, would you go there? You're an ROTC guy, aren't you?"

"Hell yes, I'd go. We're already involved. If I get the call, I am not going to bitch. Besides, our guys are getting killed already. My feelings aside, what about you, Trey?"

"I'm not sure. From what I've read and studied, this should be a Civil War fought between the North and South. We shouldn't even be over there!"

"But we are, dude."

"I know, Drew. But the other thing is, our government has no clue if we can even win. Seems like every day there's a different opinion on what we should do there."

"What are you saying?"

"I'm saying that I don't support it."

"But you're likely to get drafted anyway, so what's the point of complaining about it?"

"I've been reading that Canada has and is providing a safe haven for guys who object to the war."

"So you would desert and go there?"

"I might. I wouldn't call it deserting, though."

"Well, what then?"

"I still love my country. I just object to the war."

THE DRAFT AND ME

AT THAT TIME, **Vietnam was totally heating up, and lots of guys my age were getting the full attention of the draft board. I was lucky enough to have a teaching job, which allowed for a deferment, though my status remained 1-A. If that deferment were ever rescinded, I would be immediately eligible. Dave was an engineer for Westinghouse, and I'm not sure if he was deferred.**

Almost immediately after Barb and I got married, things changed dramatically. We graduated in June of '65, and we got married in July. This was always our plan after going through the steps of college courting.

We met as freshmen. She was dating my roommate, so I knew who she was. I immediately had her on my radar and thought just maybe she felt the same. Even though I knew she had been dating someone else, I felt we would end up together. At some point, I asked my roomie, "What would happen if I asked Barb out?"

I figured he'd say, "Not going to happen," and that would be the end of it, as I wasn't the type to get in a

fistfight. To my surprise, he said, "Larry, it would only delay the inevitable if I objected. I see how you guys ogle each other. She just picked the wrong roommate. She obviously likes you better than me. Go for it."

So I did! Sparks flew, and soon we were seeing each other all the time. We were both part of the Greek system, and I presented her with my Pi Kappa Phi pin late in our sophomore year.

In my junior year, we both seemed to know that our futures included each other. She had a job in Dayton that summer, and I was slated to go back to being a camp counselor at Camp Conestoga in Pennsylvania. It would be my fifth year on staff, and I would likely be tapped as the Assistant Camp Director. Even though this would have been a great feather in my cap, I wanted to be nearer my sweetie.

I talked things over with my dad, and he was fine with me staying in Ohio. His only stipulation was that I needed a job that would pay as much or more than my camp job. I also talked it over with Barb. She said her parents would welcome me on weekends. The decision was easy! I simply wanted to be closer to her. The thought of her being in Ohio while I was in Pennsylvania was almost too much to bear.

My other freshman roommate was a twin. His sister, Lydia, was friends with Barb and knew of a summer job at the country club she worked at. "Why don't you apply, Larry?" Lydia asked me. "You've run a pool at camp, and running this one should be duck soup, as the most traffic you get in a day is about twenty."

I called the club that day and secured an appointment the following Friday with the club manager, Berndt. He was a first-generation German American. His accent cracked me up, as he sounded like the bumbling officer Colonel Klink on *Hogan's Heroes*.

I showed up early for my interview. I was trying my best to convince him that my Boy Scout Lifeguard Certification was as meaningful as the one from the Red Cross (the standard one desired for most such positions) when Berndt interrupted me mid-sentence.

"I don't give a chit about all dat. I just vant to know one thing!"

"What's that, sir?"

Berndt returned in his broken English, "Can you svim?"

"Of course!"

"Okay den, I have one more question… Can you start Monday?"

This ended my humorous interview and led me to a wonderful one-summer stint. It allowed me to visit my Barb each weekend and still make some nice money for my senior year. It also led me to a meeting with Felice and Andy, which ultimately led me to a 27-year career in the retail fine furnishing industry.

SCARLETT

"SWEETIE, WHAT ARE YOU THINKING **about college?**" Brooke asked her daughter.

"Mom, I really want to go to OSU and be a teacher like you. From what I read, they have a very good program for teachers."

Brooke pretended to be shocked. "What . . . not U of M? I'm totally offended, but not really. Would you want to commute or live on campus?"

"One of my friends I made last year is up there, and she belongs to a sorority. She wants me to come for a visit soon. Can we go together and see the campus?"

"You know you're going to disappoint your father if you go there, don't you?" Brooke teased.

"Mom! Do you think Dad would really care? I know they are the biggest football rivals but . . .?"

"Who's your friend? Did I ever meet her?"

"Her name is Julie. You should have met her. She lives just down the street. She and I jogged together and went to the Ohio State Fair."

"Of course I remember her. She's a sweet girl. What sorority is she in?"

"It's called Pi Beta Phi."

"You've got to be kidding!"

"What? Have you heard something bad about them?"

"No, sweetie, quite the opposite. I was a Beta at U of M. We met some of the girls from OSU when we did a charity blood drive during the week before the big game. I can't believe that. My daughter, a Beta! When can we go visit?"

•　　　•　　　•

A couple of weeks later, Scarlett and her parents carved out the time to tour OSU. Scarlett immediately fell in love, and Brooke felt the same way. Brad pretended to be upset, feigning disbelief, but it was clear he was proud of his wonderful daughter for making her own path.

It didn't take Scarlett long to make the cheerleading squad. She had both athletic abilities and a great personality, always willing to go the extra mile to help someone in any way she could. The judging committee was wowed by her. Just before her Senior Day as a cheerleader, she and Brad were exchanging some friendly banter. He was wrapped from head to foot in maize and blue, of course.

"Dad, did you know that one of my Beta sisters was the co-creator of Brutus Buckeye?"

"Now you're rubbing it in! Are you telling me straight, or just kidding?"

"No, it's true. Last year, she and a guy she knew decided that the 'Nut' should be the basis for the school's mascot. They worked together, and Brutus was born. Dad, I've got to go. I hope we are getting together after we win the game!"

"Now you're really getting to me, sweetie!" Brad teased, though his proud smile spoke louder than words ever could.

After the game, Scarlett met up with Brooke and Brad. She seemed a little nervous as she told them, "I have someone I'd like you guys to meet. He's on the team, so it will be a while before he can join us. I told him we would meet him at Tommy's Pizza."

"Didn't we agree that you couldn't date till you were thirty?" Brad asked, only half-joking.

"Dad!"

A short time later, at Tommy's, Scarlett ran off and came back with a young man in tow.

"Dad, Mom, this is Dick, Dick Kirkland. He's a fifth-year senior. He got to play for a few minutes today. Our team is so good this year."

"Hi, Mr. and Mrs. Chappelear," Dick said, reaching out to firmly shake Brad's hand. "Scarlett talks about you guys all the time. So sorry about the game today. We have a very good team this year. I was lucky to even get in the game. I mostly get in on Special Teams. Today, I actually got in for two downs and made a tackle!"

"Scarlett has already rubbed it in big time about the game, so now you do the same?" Brad said, refusing to let the opportunity to get his quick licks in pass him by.

Dick deflected the comment nicely by saying, "No more about the game. I'm starved! I love Tommy's. Let's eat!"

Later that night, when Scarlett and her parents got a chance to talk, she waited nervously to hear what her father thought of Dick.

"Dick seems like a great guy. What will he be doing once he graduates?" Brooke asked.

"He's already enrolled in OSU's law school. He grew up just across the river in Upper Arlington."

"Wow, that's great, sweetie." Brooke was pleased, even more so than she already had been. She had been silently approving of Scarlett's choice since she saw him for the first time.

•　　　•　　　•

It wasn't long before Scarlett graduated with honors. Not long after that, she accepted a position as a math teacher at Jones Jr. High, located in Upper Arlington. Dick waited until he had his degree, and then he knew it was time to propose.

He knew Scarlett's family was a little old school, so he decided that his first step needed to be to ask for Brad's approval.

"Mr. Chappelear, I've been wanting to talk with you. Now that I've graduated, I would like very much to ask Scarlett to marry me. You and your wife have such a neat bond with her, and I can't imagine asking her without your approval."

Keeping his face and tone serious, Brad replied, "Dick, I've known you since that fateful day at Tommy's Pizza. I had a fit when you showed up in your team jersey. I was decked out in my U of M one. I thought for sure Scarlett was going to insist on a photo of you and me. Bad enough she decided to go to school there. Now you want to seal the deal forever and marry her?"

"I hope you're kidding!" Dick exclaimed in mock horror.

"I am. I've watched my daughter and you from day one. I can see your love for each other, and I do approve!"

"Thanks so much, Mr. C. You had me going there!"

"Oh, I do have one caveat."

"Name it."

"If I pay for the tickets, will you be able to provide four season tickets from now on? Brooke and I will join you guys for every home game and sport our maize and blue for all to see."

"Sir, you are bad," Dick said with a laugh.

• • •

The tenth of that July found Scarlett and Dick welcoming their friends and family to a beautiful outside wedding at The Park of Roses, north of OSU campus. The wedding started out very formal and proper, but it ended quite the opposite. Scarlett chose eight bridesmaids. All, of course, were Beta girls. Dick had a time coming up with eight of his pals to be the groomsmen. He was a football player, but more of a student. He studied quite hard, and his social life was limited by both time and effort.

"Scarlett, sweetheart, the only way I'm coming up with eight guys is if I recruit some of my football buddies. Are you okay with that?"

She spent a few minutes making suggestions of her own, but finally ended with, "Looks like you're in charge of recruiting. I hope you coach them up on the manners side."

"What? You think my friends aren't mannerly?"

"Just pick them out!"

At the rehearsal dinner, the girls were all decked out in summer fare and looked very proper, but the guys showed up in full uniform, including pads. Dick, on the other hand, showed up in a scarlet-and-gray tux.

Aghast, Scarlett asked, "What is going on?"

"My boys won't do this gig unless they can express their colors. They all told me they would bail if they had to dress up."

Scarlett, beside herself, stood there speechless as her parents, along with Dick's, joked about the unexpected situation. "Honey," Brad teased, "didn't I tell you that marrying a Buckeye would come with its own set of problems?"

"Brad, can't you see you're not helping?" Brooke asked.

"Honey, I know just how to add the perfect touch to this soiree," Brad teased further. "You and I will show up at the wedding with our maize and blue outfits. It'll be perfect. The photographer will have a ball recording all this!"

After Scarlett adjusted to the idea, she was able to see that the funny part had become the good part. The wedding day was one for the ages. Eight bridesmaids stood up for her wearing soft yellow gowns. Eight groomsmen stood opposite them in full football uniforms. Dick's parents (also OSU grads) wore scarlet-and-gray formalwear, and Brad and Brooke wore maize and blue. Scarlett and Dick, not to be outdone, also abandoned the traditional. Scarlett decided to wear her cheerleading outfit, while Dick wore his practice jersey.

A great time was had by all.

THE MICHIGAN MOVE

IT WASN'T LONG AFTER **Dick** and **Scarlett** were married that Brad achieved a career dream, accepting an executive position in the automotive industry with the Ford Motor Company.

Brad and Brooke moved from Lancaster to Grosse Pointe, a swanky suburb where most of the auto execs lived. They were thrilled about this move, as they were both Michiganders and made no secret about wanting to return. Brooke Grayson—turned Brooke Chappelear—was from the UP. Brad's parents were from Petoskey.

Brad and Brooke met at U of M. She was a cheerleader, while he was trying to be a walk-on with the Wolverine football team. Brad Chappelear was a high school standout and played on both sides of the ball. He was a pile-driving fullback on offense and a linebacker on defense. He was able to make the team, but things worked against him from two directions. He possessed some of the traits that were ultimately passed down to his son, and he was in trouble with his coaches from the get-go. Then, before his sophomore season, a wrestling physical revealed a heart murmur. As such, he was summarily excluded from the football team, or even from trying out for wrestling. He and his football buddies had thought his misplaced aggression might work in his favor as a wrestler. He was never able to find out.

Brad and Brooke met on a blind date. Her best friend/sorority sister, Beth, was dating a football player, and he was friends with Brad. They went to a bar called The Brown Jug. Brooke was a little hesitant, as she wasn't a big drinker. Brad was still a member of the football team at the time of their date, and he and his buddy were not going to jeopardize any chance they had to make the team. The Brown Jug was well known to the UM coaches, and it wasn't unusual to see one or more of them there on any given night. Being there was not that big a deal. Mere presence by coaches was usually enough of a deterrent for the football players. That's probably why they were frequent visitors.

Drinks were flowing, but not at their table. The evening went by quickly, and even though the place was noisy, Brooke and Brad could feel a spark between them. He called her at her Sorority House the next day and asked her to a dance at The Union. At the dance, she was aware of his glances and wondered if he was really going to ask her to dance, or if he would just spend the rest of the night staring at her.

"Are you okay if we wait for something slower?" Brad finally asked sheepishly. "I'm sure I'll make us fall on our asses if we tried the swing dances. I'm not what you would call light on my feet."

"I'm glad you and I have the same thought," she said, relieved. "The dances of today scare me. We had some lessons during a PE class my senior year in high school, but I have to admit that I have never been any good. I almost said no when you suggested we come to a dance. I hope you aren't disappointed."

"Let's wait for something slower, okay?" Brad repeated, looking relieved himself now that she had revealed her own secret.

In that uncomfortable moment, they became comfortable with each other. Soon they were inseparable. They were married in July of 1942, weeks after their graduation. They had Trey in January of 1943.

WWII was still on, but Brad was never a candidate to be drafted, as his recently discovered congenital heart murmur would make him ineligible. He graduated in Marketing and was soon on the fast track, getting into a management job right out of college. Brooke studied to be an elementary teacher and couldn't wait to get her first classroom.

"Now that we are back in Michigan, I hope we can start using our cabin on Lake Charlevoix," Brooke told Brad one night after they were settled in at their new home. "My folks gave that to us in their will, and we've hardly ever been able to take advantage of it."

Calling it a cabin was sort of a rich person's perspective, as it was on a five-acre plot with a winding, tree-lined drive that led to a prime lakefront spot facing west. The "cabin" was more like a log mansion. It had several wings and a wraparound porch with the front facing the lake.

•   •   •

Brad's parents were both born and raised in Petoskey. They met at The Bayview Association Chautauqua encampment in Petoskey. He was a lifeguard, and she was a server at the inn there. They spent three summers there and simply found they couldn't live without each other. Once out of high school, Brad's dad, Bradley Chappelear, apprenticed at welding, and eventually opened his own shop. He specialized in boat repair and became the go-to guy for the well-to-do boat and yacht owners at Petoskey and Harbor Springs. Mom stayed home, but she was instrumental in the success of the business as Bradley's bookkeeper. They had three children, Brad being the oldest. He was born September 18, 1915.

Brooke's folks were originally from Sault Ste. Marie, Ontario. They came down from Canada before she was born. Her dad, Jimmy Grayson, was a successful real estate broker in Sault Ste. Marie. Belle, his wife, was, as her name implied, quite lovely. Jimmy met her when she came to his office and applied to be his assistant. He hired her on the spot. She had an outgoing personality, and they quickly became a team. Within months they began dating and were soon married. His real estate connections led him to a dilapidated car dealership just over the border in Sault Ste. Marie, Michigan. He bought it strictly for the building and found out only later that it was once a Ford dealership. Smart guys see potential beyond what most folks do. Jimmy was not just smart, but very smart. He inquired around town on a visit to decide what to do with his purchase.

"Why did this business fail?" he asked the shopkeeper next door. "Ford dealerships are usually goldmines."

"Well, sir, it's a long story. The bookkeeper for the firm had been there for a long time. One day a vendor came in the front door, demanding to see the owner. He had just come back from wintering in Florida. In fact, he arrived a week before he was supposed to, making him available to talk with the irate vendor. That's another story, as most of the time he was not there. Anyway, the vendor got to see him and demanded payment for a large outstanding bill. The owner was beside himself and went to the bookkeeper for an explanation. She looked every bit like the little kid with her hand in the cookie jar. The owner settled the matter with the vendor immediately, and then shut himself in the office with the bookkeeper. After some hard questioning, she admitted to several misdeeds. The worst was that she had been embezzling funds and not paying bills. Her plan almost worked, as she planned to drive to Detroit and fly off to Las Vegas with her take the very next day. Had the owner not arrived early, she would have been gone."

The shopkeeper went on to relay the conversation as best as he remembered it.

"What about my obligations to Ford?" the owner asked.

"Sir, I'm so sorry. Those haven't been made since you left in the fall."

"What!? You've got to be kidding! I'm surprised they haven't called."

"Oh, they have. I just don't answer," she replied meekly.

"Wow, what now?"

The shopkeeper proceeded to tell Jimmy the rest of the sad story. After the fateful meeting, the bookkeeper went back to her place and hanged herself. The owner was completely clueless on where to find the stolen money. Sadly, he had no backup funds to pay Ford. Ford canceled their contract with the dealership, and it closed.

Jimmy realized that the entire area had no Ford dealership. No one else had stepped in since. He immediately called his attorney to make a few inquiries on how to become a dealer. Soon he opened Belle's Ford in Sault Ste. Marie, Michigan. He found that his business acumen was easily transferrable to the car business and, again, he was highly successful. Within a short time, he and Belle expanded with dealerships in Rudyard, St. Ignace, and even across the Mackinac Bridge in Cheboygan. He decided the best place to live was Rudyard, which made his commute to any of the dealerships easy.

Jimmy and Belle fell in love with Petoskey and Harbor Springs soon after coming down from Canada. The New England appeal of each was what drew them in. Finding the property on Lake Charlevoix was a fluke. Her dad, on top of being a shrewd businessman, was also an avid card player. He played twice a week with some rich buddies from as far away as Pickford and Barbeau. It wasn't unusual for them to have high stakes games, as all of them were loaded.

One night her dad got into a hand where there was an unusual lot of raising and seeing. Thinking he surely had the winning hand, a doctor friend from Petoskey ran out of cash and raised his five-acre plot on Lake Charlevoix. This was not done without a lot of complaining by the other constituents, as by the time it got made, the only two players left were Brooke's dad and the doctor. Jimmy accepted the bid and called. He had a royal flush. The doctor had a full house (kings over jacks), which would win about 99 percent of the time.

Card games are like that, unpredictable. The doctor shrugged his shoulders, told her dad he'd be in touch about transferring the deed, left the table, and headed home.

"Put that deed in the name of my dealership, Doc. I can better deal with it on my taxes that way."

"You got it. By the way, I'm going to catch some pretty serious hell for losing it!"

When you get something non-monetary sight unseen, it doesn't always work out. But when Jimmy and Belle made their first trip to see the property, they couldn't stop smiling. It was worth much more than the bid Doc was trying to cover on that fateful night.

It was a near perfect rectangle, with the long side having frontage on a prestigious lakeside drive. Also, on the lakefront, it had one of the most prime frontages available. The first visit was at sunset. They became aware of the fact that it faced west, and those beautiful sunsets would be plentiful. Doc had already put in riprap and had roughed out a dock. The lake dropped off dramatically where the dock site was, allowing just about any sized boat. They immediately began planning for their cabin.

By this time, they were quite well off and installed every

up-to-date feature available. The cabin had five bedrooms, each with its own private bath. The kitchen had a double oven and a pantry bigger than most kitchens people use full time. In short, it was deluxe!

Outside, they built a large patio with a fireplace at the end. They also were both tennis buffs, so they cleared trees and put in a red clay court, fencing, lights, and even benches for spectators. They already had a sizeable boat that they kept at a private yacht club on Munuscong Lake. This place was a short drive from their home and allowed them direct access to Canada via Sault Ste. Marie, or they could head east across the lake and land at a 400-acre parcel they owned on St. Joseph Island, Ontario.

They worked on the dock and a large pole building there in anticipation of developing the land as a sportsman club at some point in the future. Such clubs were becoming popular with the elite folks from Detroit and Chicago. They were popping up in Northern Michigan and Southern Ontario by the dozens.

It didn't take them long to realize that Lake Charlevoix had an entrance onto Lake Michigan. Soon they finished off what would be one of the most elaborate private docks on the lake. They began to take the longest boat trip of their lives, from Munuscong Lake to their beautiful new property on Lake Charlevoix. Their boat was a 1967 Egg Harbor 37 Vintage Motor Yacht. It sported twin 270HP Crusader V8 motors, and was suitable for just about any great lake adventure, with a full complement of sleeping, cooking, and bath accessories. The yacht was aptly called *Over and*

Back, as Jimmy and Belle were as often found in Ontario as in Michigan. They realized early on that they wanted to be in both countries without being encumbered by much red tape. Once they moved to Michigan, they took steps to become US citizens. They planned to have a business here and reside here. Both also having full Canadian citizenship, they knew as long as they didn't renounce the Canadian heritage that they would be granted dual citizenship. It would serve them well in the future.

Their beautiful property was very near Boyne City, which was a bonus place to be, as both had become avid skiers. It also solidified their decision to make the cabin a four-seasons home. Great attention was paid to making sure each of the four fireplaces had the most up-to-date Heatilator inserts. The furnace basement was also fitted with two separate heating systems. They had an emergency generator installed for the frigid Michigan winters.

In January of 1944 they had their only child, Brooke. From the beginning she was doted on. She grew up rich but never let it define her. She was kind and generous and made friends easily. She got good grades and was never a rebel of any kind. She had more friends than boyfriends, and therefore kept drama at bay for herself and her parents as a teen. She did cause a stir when she decided to go to college. Her folks knew this might be on the horizon, but you can never be fully prepared for that type of news.

One day, as her high-school graduation rapidly approached, she announced, "Hey, Mom and Dad. At school, we had a special assembly. It was in the gym. All kinds of colleges were in there, recruiting us. Places from even California and Florida. My counselor says I have the kind of grades that would get me in lots of those schools. I really would like to try."

"Sweet girl, this is a surprise," Jimmy said. "Somehow, we thought you'd land right here at home and find a guy, get married, have kids, and eventually take over the business."

"Is that a no?"

"If it were only that easy!" Jimmy said, his tone concerned.

"I suppose some faraway school is what you want?" Belle piped in to ask.

"Actually, no," Brooke said. My first choice is U of M. They had a whole table full of stuff. Would you guys like to read it?"

With a joint sigh of relief, they quickly realized that their only child had grown up. However, she was presenting them with the distinct possibility of staying in-state with her college choice. Once settled into the decision, both Brooke and her folks were thrilled. She would get the college experience, and they would see her often with home visits at least once a month.

Sadly, Jimmy and Belle both passed away in the '80s. Jimmy died first, in 1983, from a rare form of bone cancer. Belle lived six years longer before breast cancer took her down. The properties, the dealerships, and all assets from there went into a trust, in essence, to Brooke. That meant that eventually Brooke and Brad would become quite wealthy, as they would inherit everything.

CANADA, CONNECTIONS, AND MORE

TREY DECIDED TO HEAD TO CANADA. **He did it rather quickly, but not without a lot of soul-searching. He decided that his parents would try to convince him to stay, so he did not inform them of his intentions. Scarlett was another matter. The** two of them had always been close, and he felt he had to tell her face-to-face. He called her, and then met her at her dorm. She didn't fully understand, but she accepted that he wasn't doing this to hate on his country. He shared the many articles he'd read and the conversations he'd had with friends that built into his final decision. When finished, she could clearly see two things: He still loved his country, and he dearly loved her and their parents.

Trey packed up and quickly left the Dayton scene. He found himself settling near Sault Saint Marie, Ontario. He was very familiar with the Michigan side and felt that the possibility of travel back and forth from the US to Canada was a unique feature of the geography. He also knew that his grandparents were from there, but they now lived across the border in Michigan. He couldn't contact them directly, as he was considered a deserter in the US. He found an apartment in town and began his life there. Expatriates were treated well in Canada, and many stayed there permanently.

Trey had no trouble being a success and soon owned his own business. As soon as Jimmy Carter signed the bill in 1977, it meant Trey and all others like him would receive no punishment for what had previously been treated as a crime. He would be free to come and go from Canada to the US. He decided at that time to become a Canadian citizen, since the country had taken him in at the lowest point in his life, and he felt a kinship with them. Since he never really denounced his US citizenship, he became a dual citizen, a feature that would playout significantly in his future.

I ended up teaching at the same junior high school as Scarlett. This irony would serve us both well in the future. I started right out of college, albeit with a slight detour. I took a job at White's Furniture that started part-time at the beginning of my senior year. It went quite well. Mr. Gordon took a liking to me and often asked me about my plans after graduation. I explained that I was getting married in July and that Barb and I expected to be teachers. That's what we had studied for.

"How much do they pay a teacher these days, Larry?" Gordon asked.

"Around five thousand a year, sir."

"If you come on with us, I'll start you as an assistant manager and pay you eight to nine thousand right off the bat. If you do well, there is no end to what you can accomplish!"

"Wow, thanks. Let me talk to Barb, and I'll let you know."

I really liked working for the furniture company and certainly wouldn't mind making considerably more than the starting teacher's salary.

"You know it's for nine months, don't you?" said my Barb.

"Yes, but it's obvious that if I did take a teaching job, I'd probably end up working part time at another job for us to make ends meet. Do you know how much your position at Westerville will be?"

"Forty-nine I think."

"Well, since I've been working at the store, I've liked it a lot. The people seem to like me, and advancing might be more possible than as a teacher."

"Sweetie, I'm okay if you take it. If that's what you want to do, I will support your decision one hundred percent."

With Barb's blessing, I talked to Gordon, and he offered me the job right there at the main store I'd been working in. I was thrilled, as everyone already knew me at that location, and we had just signed a lease for an apartment right across the street on Karl Road. We only had one car, but I could easily walk across the street to the mall to work.

On July 10, Barb and I were married in Troy, Ohio. My dad was pleased that we were staying in Columbus, as the economic climate back home was pretty glum, and he had always encouraged me to go if I found something. I had done just that, and things were looking up.

We spent our honeymoon at Niagara Falls, making a meager budget of fifty bucks last three days! We had borrowed the in-laws' '56 Plymouth Savoy wagon for the trip, as my "Blue Beast" '53 Pontiac was deemed too undependable for such a trip. We got back on a Wednesday, and I started my new career the very next day.

Things went swimmingly well for the first few weeks. We both liked the new apartment. Even though I was working in one of the city's finest furniture stores, we couldn't afford a stick of what was sold there, or at any other furniture store, frankly. Her parents gave us a 29-year-old hide-a-bed. We bought a floral slipcover at Lazarus to cover the faded red nylon frieze cover. We made bookcases from bricks and boards, painted them red, filled them with textbooks, cheap paperbacks, and a few knick-knacks, and made do. We made friends with Phil and Nancy downstairs, who remained lifelong friends.

The day we returned from our honeymoon, we were told that the Blue Beast wasn't acting right. Upon a little investigating, I found out that Barb's younger brother had driven it a time or two after we left. I probably could have driven it for three more years, as I knew little nuances that made it run right. Dave did not, and the Blue Beast paid for his lack of knowledge. I can't, and never did, blame him, but it became pretty obvious on the way home from Troy that we needed a new car.

We began the intoxicating adventure of car shopping immediately. We had opened an account at the Huntington Bank right across from my store. We went in, knowing we would have to have a loan to buy a new car. We were approved for a loan and set out to a Pontiac store in downtown Columbus to find a new '65 Tempest. The price of $2,495 was a lot, but we would both be working, and we needed a good car.

"Why not make it a convertible?" I suggested while we were on our way to the dealership.

"I was thinking the same thing, honey." Barb looked over at me and grinned.

So, the very nice salesperson showed us what we came after. The price was as expected, and he took us to finalize the papers. I have no idea what made me ask the question, but on our way back to the salesman's office, I said, "Sir, do you think we're getting the best car you have for the money we're spending?"

"Not actually," he said, though it seemed to pain him to admit it.

We were, of course, surprised at his answer. Such brutal honesty was not something one might expect from someone in his position, after all.

"Can I show you one more car?" he asked. "I have a very special used car that just came into the dealership. I know you are pretty set on a new car, but let me show you this one before you make a final decision. I won't be offended if you say no."

"Of course. Please show us," we both replied.

He took us into another showroom and showed us a magnificent Bonneville Convertible.

"How can this be the same price?" I asked. "It's two or

three tiers above a Tempest, and from first glance, it looks loaded."

"It is, guys. It's a '64, but it only has 3,000 miles on it. I know the guy who owned it, and he comes back every year, trades his car in, and gets a new one. Oh, by the way, he never skimps. This car is basically one of a kind."

He went on to tell us that the man wanted a deluxe convertible but also wanted leather bucket seats. The Bonneville provided the convertible part, but it didn't have leather bucket seats as an option. He then special ordered the leather buckets from the Grand Prix model (which didn't come as a convertible). The result was this "one-off" beautiful teal-turquoise beauty with customized black leather bucket seats. It turned out that this car listed for more than double what we were about to pay!

Neither of us took longer than thirty seconds to say yes to this new find, despite all the time we had agonized over every detail of the car we had been planning to get. We left with huge smiles on our faces, and no one we ever encountered could deny that we got a wonderful deal!

A NOT-GREAT DAY

ONE DAY, after Barb and I had been married less than a month, I was driving down Morse Road with the radio on when I heard a disturbing announcement.

"As of today, per order of the President of the United States, the marital deferment for young men will be rescinded." That was a loud and clear message from Washington that the Vietnam conflict was truly serious. I went home and told Barb.

I had already been through the draft board and taken my pre-draft physical. My draft board was in Pennsylvania, but I took the physical right in Columbus. I specifically remember two things about that day. One was poignant, while the other still makes me chuckle.

"Any questions?" barked the rough-looking young officer who had just given the forty to fifty of us young guys our orders for the day.

"Yeah!" a strapping guy who stood about 6'4" said. "You really going to draft me? I have to run my folks' farm. I've already got a wife and two kids."

"Sit down, farm boy. I hope you're the first one drafted out of here."

That set the tone for our day. I almost wonder if he was a "plant," to let us all know the possibilities that were awaiting us. The second recollection was when I was at a long table filling out papers and answering questions. I was in total shock, to be truthful.

One of the ladies asked me a question and then asked it a second time. Finally, she said, "I think this one's deaf. Son, step over here."

In retrospect, I was far too honest and didn't fully grasp the opportunity that had presented itself. Had I gone along with it, I would have probably received a 1-F status and avoided ever being drafted. Instead, I told her I could hear perfectly well and was passed through and handed a 1-A status. That meant I could, and probably would, be drafted at some point.

My thoughts immediately turned to confusion and dismay. After talking with Barb, I spoke with my dad and my father-in-law, as well as Mr. Gordon, my new boss. All were veterans. I respected that status and explained that if I had to go, I certainly would. I also told them that there was one possibility that I could pursue that was totally available and legitimate. I had really studied at Otterbein to be a teacher. I held a teaching certificate, and even though I initially decided on a career in retail for financial reasons, another path might be the best for me and my family right then, as it would produce a legitimate deferment. After all, I was the first in my family to go to college and graduate. Wouldn't it be a shame if I got drafted and ended up being denied this opportunity I had worked hard for?

I made myself a special case, but in retrospect, most of the young men of my era were the same. They were also likely to be the first in their families as well. We were born to soldiers either during or just after the Second World War. Because of that, most of our parents didn't graduate from college. From that somewhat selfish perspective, I began to explore the possibility that I could alter my future.

I got no resistance from the men in my life and immediately began in earnest to find a teaching position. I knew two things. If I didn't find one immediately, it would be of no benefit to my status. Second, it was now early August, and schools had, for the most part, selected the new teachers for the upcoming year, as they usually did that at least two months prior. Nevertheless, I struck out immediately with a résumé and a plan.

I spent a day at Otterbein with a counselor made available to all recent graduates. She gave me a list of schools that had favored Otterbein graduates in the past. My first visit was to a local Catholic high school.

You may wonder why that was my first choice when I wasn't even Catholic. The school was right down the road from our apartment. With only one car, still being able to walk to work would be perfect. The fact that the furniture store was so close to home had been one of the best perks.

I stopped at the office and told the young lady at the front desk of my intentions. Getting any kind of job then was much different than it is today. I was very lucky. She excused herself and came back a few minutes later.

"Father will see you in his office. I'll take you back."

"Hello, son," was the greeting from him. Father Baxter sat behind a large desk and was smoking the biggest cigar I had ever seen.

"So, tell me what you can teach," he said, getting the interview started.

"Well, sir, I majored in Math and minored in Chemistry at Otterbein."

With little notice and preparation, I figured I'd need God to be in my corner that day. To my surprise, I heard, "Okay, when can you start?"

Amazed and amused, I asked, "What? That's it? You'd be able to offer me a job just like that?"

"What's the problem.? I'm in charge here, and you're just what we are looking for! It's our lucky day, don't you think?"

"Well, sir, this is my very first interview, so may I ask a question or two?"

"Sure, but I suppose you've already heard we don't pay as much as Columbus, or worse yet, one of the suburban schools."

I really didn't know that, but I did know what Barb was going to make at her new job in Westerville.

So I asked, "How much are we talking, sir?"

"The salary is $3,800."

"Well, that's $1,200 less than my wife will be making."

Sensing my waning interest, he quickly came back with,

"Yeah, yeah. I suppose. Here's what I can kick in. Free lunch every day. Can you coach anything? We can add in a few hundred there."

Hoping it would help, I said, "I did play a little baseball in my youth, and I was on the tennis team at Otterbein."

"If you will make a deal, we can do both. You can be an assistant in baseball, and we can start up a tennis team."

It never dawned on me that this process would be that easy! I explained to him that I had just started and that I wanted to check out a few more schools I had earmarked while talking with my counselor at Otterbein. His reaction was unexpected, as he and I seemed to have hit it off on so many levels.

"Thanks for nothing, pal. I doubt I'll ever see you again."

It occurred to me later that his job as a recruiter was much harder than most, entirely due to his budgetary constraints. But here I was with a solid job offer on my first interview.

"Don't be too sure, sir. I so appreciate you seeing me on the spot. Thanks again!"

I soon went to Worthington, then to Whetstone, two schools that were fairly close by that Otterbein had recommended I talk to. I quickly found out that my success at the first place I tried was going to be the exception and not the rule. No more easy luck. In fact, I couldn't even get a real interview at either school. I had one more stop that I wanted to make on Friday. It was at Upper Arlington. I knew they paid the most out of any local school. I'd already seen the other end of the scale, and thought I had nothing to lose.

I started my day off opening the Northland store, as the manager had a doctor appointment and asked if I would cover for him. He would return around 10:30 and allow me to be at the Arlington office around noon. I was already dressed in a blue blazer and khakis with a button-down shirt and repp tie. I found that to be sort of a uniform at the store.

I felt good about my day until I arrived at the school office. There was a sign that read "closed for lunch" on the glass doors in front. I decided to bang on them anyway, as it was just moments past 12:00 when I arrived. I normally would have been thwarted, but I saw some movement inside the doors. To my surprise, a tall older man came to the door. It was sweltering hot that day, and I was starting to sweat through my stylish outfit in a hurry.

"May I help you?"

At the other schools I visited, I had found a female receptionist who served as my greeter. Unsure what else to say, I blurted out, "Yes, sir. I'm here looking for a job."

"What kind of job?"

"A teaching job."

It seemed like an obvious answer, but it was taken with a strange balance of sarcasm and humor.

"A teaching job. You do realize that it's already August, don't you? Where were you in May and June when we were doing our hiring?"

"Well, sir, circumstances were different for me back

then than they are now, and I'm just now able to begin the process."

Luckily, he did not pursue the reason why, as I would find later that he was once in the military, and an officer himself. I doubt he would have approved of my scheme to keep myself from serving.

"So, what kind of position are you qualified for?"

"Math and Chemistry are the two subjects I'm certified in." I felt like he was playing with me, but answering the question was the only thing I could do in that situation.

"Where'd you go to school?"

"Otterbein," I proudly proclaimed.

"Hummm, well, that's not going to work!"

At this point, I thought I knew where he was going with that and shot back, "I suppose you went to Capital? That makes us archrivals."

"I sure did, and we beat you guys every year I was there. So, back to the business at hand. Hey, Joe, we still looking for any teachers?"

"You know damn well we are," came a voice from the rear office.

"We still haven't hired that math teacher's replacement? Maybe this is your lucky day, son. Let me see if Joe has time to talk with you."

Next thing I knew, I had a real, live interview at one of the best schools in Central Ohio. Turns out, the first guy I talked to was the superintendent, and the second was his assistant in charge of all hiring. They were only there because they voluntarily took lunch off (a Friday tradition) to let the staff out for a lunch break at the Red Door, a popular eatery in Grandview. Looking back, I can assure you, this whole day was a God Thing.

Joe explained that the school system had recently fired a teacher at Jones Jr. High. This was unprecedented, but apparently very necessary, as during the school year, the male teacher had allowed an atmosphere so detrimental to proper learning that he had to go. Jones was an older building with hardwood floors. The final straw came during the last week of school in a large study hall. Ninety ninth-grade boys were in there, and all hell broke loose with fighting so severe that there was soon debris being tossed about the room. The study hall was directly over the principal's office, and the commotion could not be ignored.

When the principal showed up to see what was going on, he found the teacher in the hall reading a paperback and having a smoke.

"We had no choice, Larry," said Joe.

"Boy, I can see that!"

"If you were in such a position, give me one thing in your past that would make me believe you could have handled this group."

"Well, first and foremost, I wouldn't have allowed the ruckus in the first place. I also would not have left the room, and I don't smoke! I'm not a big guy, so I've always made it a point to find ways to deal with both individuals and groups when discipline was necessary. I worked at a large Boy Scout Camp in Pennsylvania for the last four summers. Each week we had a turnover of 300 scouts. I was in charge of the waterfront, and every scout had to come through my area on the first day of camp. They ranged from eleven to fifteen years of age and were from all sorts of backgrounds. I never had a problem, Joe."

"Good answer, Larry. Now, here's what I'm up against. More specifically what *you're* up against. I have no shortage of candidates. Upper Arlington has untold numbers of professors, doctors, and lawyers' wives who have applied, so you've got an uphill fight. No disrespect for their qualifications, which are generally better than yours, but Super and I know how tough the situation created will be for the next teacher we send in. Frankly, I don't want a first-year young lady, or even a not-so-young lady to be subjected to what I think will happen. I know that's probably not something I should even say, but I really believe the wrong hire would be an invitation for disaster. So…it's Friday, and I'm glad you came in. Walt and I will talk over our candidates and let you know."

I thanked them both for seeing me on such short notice and left. I was fully expecting to go back in to my first interview and accept being a teacher who could walk five minutes to school, get free lunch, and coach two sports. Not a bad gig for a rookie. When I got home, Barb said I had a message on the answering machine. The machine was a wedding present, and she reminded me, laughing out loud, that this was the first real message we'd ever gotten. It was the assistant superintendent, Joe, offering me the job if I could start next week, which would be orientation.

God Thing complete.

A CHANGE IN COURSE

MY DRAFT STATUS REMAINED THE SAME—I was still officially 1-A—but I now had a deferment. Unless that changed, I would not get drafted. My dad, Barb's parents, and Mr. Gordon were all pleased, and Barb and I were over the moon with it.

I taught for five years. Upper Arlington had a reciprocal arrangement with OSU. UA allows student teachers to come each year, and our teachers got free tuition at OSU as part of the arrangement. I took full advantage of this and enrolled in the department of education, figuring to get a Masters in School Administration.

I had enrolled, been accepted, and was about four classes in when I was challenged by a friend. This friend helped me make a major change of direction in my grad program.

Lots of weekends, Barb and I would get together for pizza and cards with Phil and Nancy who lived downstairs from us. They were a few years older, but we had a lot in common. Phil was a teacher in Columbus and taught shop. His specialty was small engines. Nancy and

Barb became the best of friends. While Phil and I had a mutual respect for each other, we were like oil and water on most subjects. He often would challenge me on things we discussed.

One night, he asked, "So, you're in grad school now?"

"Yep, I've gotten about four classes in."

"How's it going so far?"

"I love it."

"I figured, but what about grades?"

With my chest bursting, I announced, "Hey, so far I have straight A's."

"Oh really? Did you have straight A's at Otterbein?"

"Only for the last semester. I ended up with about a 2.8 final average."

"Why do you think you're getting straight A's now, then?"

"I guess it's because I'm more mature. I've learned how to study and apply myself."

"Bullshit."

"What's on your mind, Phillip?" I asked, confused and running out of patience.

"Same thing happened to me. I started out in the same department as you. Here's what I saw and perceived: The department is desperate for guys to be in the field. I suppose even their livelihood depends on it. They ply you with grades and suck you in. Once I realized what was happening, I switched out. If you want to test it, figure out who you think is the dimmest bulb in your classes, and ask them what they're getting. Bet it will be straight A's!"

During the next week, I tried his theory. I knew exactly the guy to ask. His answer was just as Phil told me it would be. By week's end, I was convinced, and I went back to Phil for advice on what to do next.

"What did you do when you found this out?" I asked Phil.

"I signed up for an MBA. I figured if I stayed, I'd still get the same bump in pay. If I decide to leave, the MBA will travel lots better. By the way, some of your courses will transfer."

"This all makes sense, Phil. I see myself in the same boat you are in."

I told Barb, and although it would take more time, she agreed. I went into the business college the next week and made the switch. Even though all four classes transferred, I had way more classes, as I basically had to do most of the undergrad business courses as prerequisites.

I also found out that Phil wasn't kidding about the difference in difficulty of the coursework. First things first, I attacked the required courses. I decided that, since I was a math major at Otterbein, the first course to take should be math oriented. I chose Basic Accounting, as it seemed to fit the bill. Soon I learned that Accounting had little to do with math and was much more like a foreign language. I struggled to get a C, which was the minimum grade to move on.

After that, I dreaded taking the follow-up course, Advanced Accounting, which was also required. I solved that by taking some courses where my minimal life experiences might help. I took Marketing and Management. Those came much easier. They were relatable. I decided to take two courses per term so as to not overload. I rolled along nicely this way until I enrolled in Basic Finance.

My professor was different in every way. First, was his appearance. My other professors looked Ivy League. He looked Farm League. He came in on day one and announced, "This class will be hard. In all probability, none of you will get an A. Twenty-five percent of your grade will be determined by your classroom participation. You come in prepared, and I will be your best friend. Otherwise, this class will be pure hell. Do you understand?"

We were in a classroom in Haggerty Hall. It was an old building, and the classrooms had tiered steps in them. We could all see our professor and could also hear him very well. It took us all by surprise. In all the courses so far, the teachers emphasized the class participation part, but it didn't have teeth. Grades were given on quizzes and tests. The quietest person in class could still get an A, just by scores. But this guy seemed to put a special emphasis on participation.

At the end of class, he handed out our assignment for the next class. "All right, folks," he said as he passed out papers. "This is a case. It's a fictional company called the ABC Company. You will find that the company has some issues. Find them out and be ready to discuss them in detail on Monday. Class dismissed."

When Monday arrived, we all thought we were ready. The professor strode to the center of the front.

"Okay, class. Who would like to begin and tell us about the ABC Company and its issues?"

As I figured, everyone began looking down immediately. No one wanted to be the first victim. The professor pointed to the girl next to me in the top row.

"You there, young lady. Stand up and tell us."

"Yes, sir. I'm an Accounting major, and here's what I have discovered."

With that, the professor did something I'm pretty sure would not fly today and would go viral on social media as soon as everyone could get to a safe place to post. He picked up an eraser and threw it directly at her. It crashed off the window behind us and barely missed its mark. I was a close witness, and it could have harmed her (or me) for sure if it had made impact!

"Honey, this is a Finance class. I couldn't care less what you snobs upstairs think. So don't come at me with that kind of BS. That goes for all of you! Now, would someone else please volunteer and tell us about the company's ills?"

As you can imagine, everyone was terrified, and no hand went up to volunteer. Next, he picked a guy two rows down from me. "Stand up, young man, and tell us what she could not."

Meekly, a football-player-sized guy got to his feet. "Well, sir, it appears they have a cash flow problem."

"That's good. Now we're getting somewhere."

A collective sigh came over us all, as most would have come to the same conclusion.

"Well, could you elaborate for us? Details, per chance? Figures, examples?"

The kid thought he had it licked. He was way wrong.

"Well, sir—"

"Well what? You don't have anything, do you?"

"No, sir, but I did recognize the main thing, didn't I?"

Our collective sigh had now been replaced by collective terror.

"Sit down, sir," the professor said. "Now, can anyone stand up and tell the class what I asked?"

As you guessed, no one was up to this task either.

"Here's what I want. Class is dismissed for today. When I told you all about class participation, it seems no one got the message. When/if you come back tomorrow, I want you to be prepared. I want you to be able to discuss the perils of the ABC Company down to a gnat's ass. Do I make myself clear?"

That was a visual that all of us got, for sure!

He dismissed us.

I was one of 50 percent of the class who returned the next day. The girl who had been sitting near me and the football player were among the missing. I was totally intimidated, and I had stayed up nearly all night studying. I felt so prepared. The professor had gotten to me, big time. I made a B- and thought it was an A+. I learned how to study and prepare literally overnight. I became hooked on studying. I soon realized that I never really knew how to study before. His class set the stage for me to succeed in all my classes after his. I thanked him personally after the class was over.

It took three long years, but I finally graduated in 1970. I never achieved a 4.0, but I did finish with a very respectable grade-point average. After graduation, I was offered a store manager position at White's Furniture. I remained there from 1970–1990, when I became an insurance agent. The MBA was valuable for my progression at White's and for my résumé that allowed me to become an agent.

SAULT STE. MARIE

IN 1968, the government in Ottawa announced that as long as a young man crossing the border from the US was seeking permanent residence in Canada, his military status could not come into question. As early as 1965, Canada emerged as a potential refuge for young men to escape the draft. Canada became known as a sympathizer to young people not wanting to be drafted.

There are two popular ways to enter a foreign country. Back then, folks would be coming in as immigrants. The second way would be as a refugee. The 1965 version was when a young man made a conscious decision to leave the USA with the intention of becoming a permanent resident of Canada. This would qualify him as an immigrant. Later, the concept of entering as a refugee became more realistic, as those who were involved felt the US was leaving them no choice concerning their dissention. In Ottawa and other Canadian cities, there were actual "counselors" available to help these young men get established. Canadians in general were quite sympathetic and empathetic with our young men.

One of my own friends, Erwin (I call him "E"), told me of a trip he took with a buddy. They wanted a post-high-school adventure and decided to go up to Canada for a fishing/camping trip. Their first night was at a campground on the Canadian side of Niagara Falls. The whole trip was done on a sparse budget, so hotels were out and tent camping was in. While there, they met a couple with three kids who were from northwest of Toronto. One thing led to another, and the couple started a conversation about the war and the possibility of getting drafted. Both my friend and his buddy knew about this reality but thought it down the road a bit.

They both planned to go to college, and the draft seemed far off. Besides, that's why they were on such a trip, because the draft was several years off in the future. The couple let them know they were offering them a real place to stay if needed.

"We have a large farm in Sudbury," the wife explained. "On it, we have several outbuildings and barns. We already house three young men from New Jersey and are happy to offer the same to you. It's spartan, but clean, warm, and dry. We expect nothing in return. We mean it. Here's a card we've made with our contact info on it. If you decide later that this is something you need, just reach out to us."

My friend kept the card, but he never even considered using it.

•　　•　　•

Trey and I were the same age, but our paths as young adults were quite different. I suppose mine was more typical of the times, as I immediately graduated, got married, got a job, did some post-graduate work, and so on. I had a preconceived notion of what success looked like, and I pursued it relentlessly.

Trey, on the other hand, took a stop, look, and evaluate as cautiously as possible approach to his near future. One thing he decided was that he had no desire to be drafted. At OU, he was somewhat more aware of politics than I was. He knew a lot more about the conflict that was coming of age in Vietnam than most students, and he certainly knew more than I did. When he graduated and moved to Dayton to take his first job, he began to consciously think about his own reality. Would he be going into the service and/or getting drafted? Vietnam was cranking up, big time. He knew he was a prime candidate to be drafted. He also knew that many of his classmates from college were getting drafted, and a few were already in Vietnam. Every day, he read of the carnage that the war was enacting on the young people who were involved.

Some buddies he kept in touch with from OU decided to meet up at a local bar in Dayton. For several hours they got real about their potential futures, based on things brought on by Vietnam. One guy in particular talked about Canada. Trey's ears perked up, as he'd had many experiences being up there because his grandparents had originally lived there.

"Turns out, I personally know two guys who have gone up there to avoid getting drafted. I don't know all the details, but I can definitely tell you guys it should work, and that it's not that hard to accomplish."

Trey was all ears, as this was something he immediately thought could work for him if he wanted it to. He soon decided that this path would offer him a surefire way to avoid the draft. Canada was a foreign country, but not very, which had a rather high level of appeal to him as he thought about it. He realized that he would be able to blend in, and he'd even been there to visit already.

After Trey and I met again briefly in the piano bar that one Friday night in Dayton, he got on the phone with his OU friend. "Trey, the Canadian government is totally on board with letting guys come there and be basically untouchable by their draft boards. Once you get to the border, you just enter like any other tourist. You claim your desire to become a permanent resident and voila, you become one. I've got a buddy who's already up there. He's in Sault Ste. Marie, Ontario. Ever heard of it?"

Trey was astounded by his friend's words.

"Heck yes, my mom's family came down to Michigan from there before she was born. They still live just over the border in the UP. My dad's family grew up in Petoskey. I've been over and back to Canada and Michigan many times. You're telling me that I can go up there to a place I'm both familiar with and would put on a list of my top ten spots to go on a vacation? Piece of cake, sign me up!"

Trey immediately started piecing together a plan, and part of it involved who he planned to tell about it. His sister was the first person he needed to talk to about it.

"Scarlett, you know I don't hate my country, right? I would stay in a heartbeat if I thought we were going to pull out of Vietnam. But they're not, so I'm doing what is right for me. I'll miss you and Dick, Mom and Dad. I hope they know how much I love them."

"What is your plan? You are going to talk to Mom and Dad, aren't you?" Scarlett asked.

Unsure how his parents would react, Trey said, "Sis, I don't think so. I just know they will not be in favor of this. I'm going to hit them with two terrible things at once. First, that I'm planning on leaving, and second, the reason I'm doing this. They will throw a fit and, at minimum, try to talk me out of it. They may even try something more dramatic like turning me in to the authorities."

"Trey, listen, I know they will be upset, but don't you think you owe it to them to let them know what is going on?" Scarlett said.

"I'm not going to be talked out of it, so I don't see what it would accomplish, except a lot of drama I don't want to contend with. My mind is made up. I love you, Sis. I'll try calling you when I get there."

So, with his car packed with his belongings and a load of insecurities, Trey headed off to Canada. His OU friend shared a contact in Ontario and a script to use at the border. He crossed the Mackinac Bridge and headed northeast to Sault Ste. Marie, Michigan. At the border, he told them exactly what he had been coached to say. Once in Ontario, he checked into an inexpensive motel for a few days to buy time to get his bearings.

Safely in his new country, he took stock and made a list of things he needed to figure out at once. Where he would live, work, and how to survive all reared up and took on high-level importance. For a job, he remembered fondly that he had sold cars at a used car place in Athens when he was in school. He decided this would be a good place to start. He also remembered that his mom's parents were from this very town. Even though this was a coincidence, he thought it might come in handy in his job search. He knew they'd eventually moved to Michigan and started a thriving car dealership called Belle's Ford.

After a few weeks he was able to connect with a local car dealer.

"Ever heard of Belle's Ford?" Trey asked the owner.

"Of course. They got started right here. Now I hear they're all over the UP. Do you know them?"

"Yep, they're my grandparents. So, give me a job. I just got up here from Dayton, Ohio, and I need a job as soon as possible."

Cautiously, the dealer responded, "Okay, can I call down to Belle's and get a reference?"

"Don't you dare."

"Why, are you a draft dodger or something?"

"Yeah . . . or something. If you don't hire me, I'll go across the street and become your competition. Yes, or no?"

"Why should I hire you?" the dealer asked, intrigued. "Have you ever even sold a car before?"

"At college I had a part-time job at a popular used car lot in Athens, Ohio, my senior year. Sold all used, and probably moved forty or fifty in my last semester. They wanted me to stay, but I had a job waiting in Dayton. Easy-peasy, selling cars."

Convinced, and hoping he had found a hidden gem, the dealer relented. "Okay, I'll hire you, and you can start Monday. Be here at noon. I will tell you one thing. I'm not impressed with your reason for becoming Canadian. So don't give me a reason to can your ass, understand?"

"Yep, got it. And thanks, sir. I'll be your number one guy in a hurry."

And a success he was. He soon realized that his new employer was an opportunity in the making. The dealership Trey joined was the Burchfield Group. Rick Burchfield was the owner and had been so for many years. Rick had blended two compatible businesses under one roof. They sat side by side on the busiest street in town. The auto dealership was primary and had gained a reputation as *the* place to buy a good used car in Sault Ste. Marie.

Next door was The Garage. Cars needed service, and there was a built-in clientele as every car sold at the dealership carried a 30-day warranty and a special opportunity. Each new owner would get a certificate stating that any future service performed on the car, as long as they owned it, would receive a 10 percent discount. This served two purposes. The warranty ingratiated the place with every customer buying a car, even though few actually got to take advantage of it. It also made the service part of the business flourish to the point that it brought in more revenue than the dealership.

Rick had owned the business for many years. He was in his mid-sixties and quite well off. His health was good, and he wanted to retire, as did his wife, Angie. His daughters, Kaitlyn and Megan, were grown, and neither seemed to have a passion for taking things over.

After a few months, Trey was indeed the best salesperson the Burchfield Group had ever had. He also learned that both sides of the business worked well with each other. He made it a priority to get acquainted with the operation and all the guys and gals working there. After he successfully celebrated his first anniversary in his new job, he was passing Rick's office when he darted in and requested an impromptu meeting.

"Rick, what are you planning to do when you retire?"

"Trey, I think about that a lot these days. I'm not getting any younger. Angie and I really want to move to somewhere warmer—Arizona, we think, as I have allergies aplenty, and the desert weather seems to help that."

"Well, I've been thinking too, Rick."

"Oh you have? And what might that be about?"

"Well, I really like the car business. I take things seriously and have tried my best to represent you well. I've been back and forth between the showroom and the shop and know pretty much what it takes to run things with both. Rick, would you consider selling me the business any time soon?"

"Wow, Trey, this takes me by surprise! Never thought of selling now, but to retire, I have to have some kind of a plan. Let me talk to Angie, and I'll get back to you."

"Well, sir, when you're ready, I do have a plan that might work for both of us."

"You know, son, maybe if you're at all prepared, let's talk about that now. It would help me in talking to the wife and our girls."

"Okay, here goes. First and foremost, I would retain the name, the location, and the staff, for sure. It would keep your great name and reputation in the community, which is worth a lot and worthy of all the hard work you've done to gain it. Your position in this would be to consider a hefty down payment, then let me pay monthly payments to you guys that would be what you would expect to have a lifestyle commensurate with your success. We come up with a final figure that the dealership would ultimately be worth, and when/if we reach that point, I'm free and clear. In the meantime, you would be able to sell your home here, take that profit and any other investments you surely must have, and be off to enjoy your life in someplace a lot warmer than here."

"Wow, you've thought this out pretty well. My first question would be, do you have a hefty down payment?"

"I've squirreled away ten thousand dollars from some savings I brought with me, plus what I've been able to put away from my commissions."

"That's impressive!"

"If you and I can do the deal, I've got lots of ways that you've taught me through osmosis that I'm sure will generate the income you're looking for."

"Well, this whole thing has me going, Trey. I'm sure you know I didn't come here today with a clue this conversation was going to happen. Let me go home and talk to the family. Nothing you say has me believing we can't strike some kind of deal. Talk to you tomorrow."

The conversation was perfect for both parties. Rick was in the right frame of mind and the exact right time of his life to make such a change. Trey had the saved dollars, the ambition, and the talent to make the plan work.

Rick and Trey had several meetings with Rick's attorneys, the bank, and the many connections Rick had locally. When the transaction was complete, both Rick and Trey were satisfied that everything would work out for both parties.

Soon, Rick and Angie were off to sunny Scottsdale. Kaitlyn and Megan couldn't have been more pleased. They had both wanted off the pressurized hook of Dad asking them at least once a year just who and when one of them would step in and take over the business.

Trey was anxious to step in and take over.

Trey had watched the business from the inside out and knew full well that he was the one who had made things pop since coming aboard. Everyone liked him, and he basically was the liaison between the showroom and shop. In the short year Trey had been there, Rick had unknowingly forfeited his control through the faith he had in Trey. Trey was the general manager without ever having the title.

The business flourished, and Trey had no trouble keeping up with the payment arrangement he and Rick had fashioned. At the same time, he became the "face" of the Burchfield Group, and he also became a real player in the town. He joined service clubs and the local version of the Chamber of Commerce. Within a short time, everyone in Sault Ste. Marie knew him. As he was not yet married, he also, by default, became the most eligible bachelor.

One passion Trey picked up from his parents was boating. On his many trips each summer to the Graysons, he became familiar with boats large and small. Once he got some headway with Burchfield, he would start small and eventually have his own fleet of watercrafts. He also knew that his grandparents had land and buildings in both Canada and Michigan. It wasn't lost on him that crossing over into Michigan and back to Ontario was not that hard if you knew what you were doing and where you were going.

In the beginning, he knew going to Michigan was risky, but he was a risk-taker. It was an adventure in the offing. He decided to start with a bass boat. He went right to the newest and most popular brand, Ranger. He paired it with a Mercruiser 150-hp outboard motor and a Rangertrail trailer.

"I can't even begin to hide my excitement!" he told his staff at the shop, as he showed off his new toy. "You'll have to keep me in check, as I'm afraid this is going to be a giant distraction."

The Saint Marys River divides Sault Ste. Marie, Michigan, from Sault Ste. Marie, Ontario. Some places it widens into a lake-like area, while much of the time it's little more than a wide ditch.

Trey soon decided it was time for him to become a property owner as well as a boat owner. He thought that an optimum place to have such a property might be on a narrow channel of the river. He found a very inexpensive lot that he could afford. It was right near the bend at the south end of Park Road, close to where Pointe Charles and Park met up. The land there was beautiful and very cheap. He was able to make a deal on fifty acres, right on the water. Now he had his own boat and access to waterways that wound back and forth between Canada and Michigan.

At this point, Trey had fully embraced the Canadian experience, but he still longed to see his family in Michigan and Ohio. Despite a visit not being in the cards anytime soon, he had hope that would change in the future. Having an easy way to get there gave him a good feeling that a reunion might come sooner rather than later.

Just south and across the river channel from his new property was Michigan. The Graysons had another lot they owned on E. Northshore Dr. on the Michigan side of the water. It covered 100 acres and had a 120-foot frontage on the river. The other side was just a few hundred yards away. A perfect place to get over to Michigan and back to Canada, if one so desired. It could be accomplished in almost any craft.

His grandparents had this property in Michigan as part of a development plan they thought would materialize into something big. It had a boathouse built with a lift, a beautiful setup they expected to develop later into a full-fledged resort. The shoreline there was spectacular, and such sporting clubs were becoming popular in that area. It never happened, but the groundwork was there, and the property remained in the family.

Trey was pleased. He now had his little piece of land, and an easy way to get over to the US side, if and when he wanted to.

A MOVE AND NEW
HOUSEGUESTS

IN 1967, **Barb and I decided to look at a house.** Apartment living was great for the time we did it. Phil and Nancy had become dear friends, and a new set of friends, Mack and Jean, moved right around the corner. Mack and I had a great—albeit a bit dangerous—golf game we played regularly. We lived on Karl Road, which was extremely busy. Between the street and the sidewalk was a row of oak trees. We set up a course and played "tree golf"—9 par 3 holes from my place up to the corner. The trees weren't too far apart, but occasionally we hit an errant shot into the street. Never hit a car, though.

One Saturday, I was looking at the *Dispatch* newspaper. Usually I just checked out the headlines and the sports section. For some reason, a real estate ad caught my eye. "Great ranch in a newer development in Westerville. Payments as low as rent! Open house Sunday afternoon." Barb and I had never talked about buying a house. We were doing okay, but extra money was nonexistent. When I told her, she was less than thrilled, but she agreed to go to the open house. We were already in Westerville that morning for church, and Huber Ridge was less than ten minutes away. We headed to the open house.

In that time, it was the custom to have an open house as a way of selling a property. We pulled up to the place and smiled. It was a brick ranch with a one-car garage and a backyard with a privacy fence and woods behind that.

"No way we can afford this, Larry!"

"You're probably right, but let's go in and check it out."

The house was great! Built in 1963, it was 1,026 square feet. It had three bedrooms and one bath, and of course, a garage! The backyard was unbelievable. The price was $14,500. It might as well have been a million dollars! How could we afford such a great place?

As much as I smile about this now, that was not the feeling I had then. The real estate agent had a finance guy right there with him. We would soon learn that we could buy this house for $750 down and a payment of $105 per month. We still had some wedding present money in the bank, which would be enough to cover the down payment. Believe me, that was the biggest issue, as our rent payment was $5.00 higher than what they were telling us we'd pay monthly for this house. We literally walked out as new homeowners. Much like our car-buying experience, we got very lucky!

We moved in shortly after. I loved the backyard. I fashioned a flagstone patio and bought a red Weber grill. The neighborhood was great, and we were ecstatic.

•   •   •

We wanted a family from the get-go. As we tried, we got a bonus. Less than a year after we moved in, we got Dusty. Phil, our old neighbor, told us that his parents had a farm outside of town. He also told us that they had just had a litter of puppies, and we should go see them. We did, and Dusty became our first "child."

He was totally cute. He had long hair like a collie but was colored like a German Shepherd. I believe he was born as a snot-nosed teenager, as he did everything a puppy could do in his first several days with us to get thrown out of his new home. Somehow, he/we survived, and we had him a total of 17 years.

Two years after we got Dusty, my brother and his wife came to visit.

"Let's take a ride."

We drove out to the east side of Hoover Reservoir. I unconsciously drove us by the farm where we got Dusty.

"Hey, look at the sign on that post. It says free pups."

I told myself to keep going, but I couldn't resist. We pulled in the long drive and could see the mother dog by the open barn door. The puppies were in a large cardboard box just inside. Puppies are irresistible. There were four. Two looked just like Dusty, while the other two were colored more like a collie.

There was a slight problem. It appeared that the house had been abandoned. After three days of feeding them, I called Phil. It turned out his dad had to evict the tenants for not paying their rent. The puppies and their mother were left to fend for themselves. In a very unexpected move, Barb and I put a note on the front door that said we were taking the puppies. We left our number for anyone who might object. All of a sudden, we had Dusty and four of the cutest puppies on the planet.

"It's okay, sweetie, I'll just give them away," I assured Barb.

The first two were easy. A neighbor two doors down took a Dusty lookalike. My friend Mullins from the close by Sohio station came over and picked out the other Dusty clone. Now we had two. Barb talked her parents into taking one. We couldn't believe it, but we just couldn't part with the last one. Dodie joined Dusty, and she was with us for all of her seventeen years.

ADOPTION

AS FRUSTRATION BUILT about not yet having children, Barb and I decided that adoption was a possible option. A friend knew an attorney in Columbus who was the number-one guy to handle this. Adoption was complicated. Attorneys knew all the ins and outs. There were contracts and legal ramifications for all the parties. With a knowledgeable attorney, both sides would be less likely to back out. Also, and just as important, attorneys in this field had a pipeline that linked potential donors to people like us who desired to adopt. We created a case with the attorney immediately. We signed up and were anxiously awaiting word that a child was on the way. Almost simultaneously, two negative things happened.

The first was the start of what would become *Roe v. Wade*. This Supreme Court decision made abortion legal on a state-to-state basis. The second proved to be even more significant. Abortion became legal in New York. The geography of the two states has them touching at Lake Erie. Immediately, young girls from Ohio had the option to seek an abortion in neighboring New York. A great percentage of them chose this somewhat risky option, thus shutting down most opportunities for adoption in Ohio. This was a dark time for us.

I set up a meeting at my attorney's office, as I wanted to hear what this would do to our case. In the beginning, the adoption timetable that was given was mere months. At our meeting, he didn't beat around the bush.

"If you get a baby at all with the way things are now, you'll be lucky!"

He could not have delivered this news with less compassion. I was beyond pissed. I told him so, which was quite uncharacteristic for me. He seethed back. I could see him pulling something out of his desk. He was writing a check. He threw it at me and told me to get the hell out. It was our deposit check! He was cancelling our agreement.

Still reeling from this myself, I now had to go home and tell Barb. On my way down in the elevator, I remembered something. My boss, Gordon, had given me the name of another attorney he knew who was starting up a new practice and was specializing in adoptions. I decided to call him, as having some good news to share along with the bad would make the task ahead—talking to my bride—less painful for us both.

I stepped out of the building and noticed a phone booth. Although I'm famous for not carrying money, I had enough in my pocket to make the call.

"Hello, is Mr. Crane there?"

"Yes, he is. I'm his secretary. May I tell him what this is about?"

After I briefly relayed to her what had just happened, she asked, "Where are you right now, Larry?"

"I'm in a phone booth at Broad and High."

"Well, look up to your left seven stories, and I'll be waving at you. I just got Mr. Crane's attention, and he will see you now if you have time."

I went up immediately, and we had a wonderful meeting. He had been grappling with the same news my other attorney was, but he presented the good side of it instead of the ugly underbelly.

"Larry, I can't promise you anything, but I'm passionate about adoptions, and I'll be trying my best! My wife and I adopted our two children, and we know all the ups and downs the process holds. We'll be in touch."

I was able to go back to Barb with both bad and good news. After some needed tears, we both agreed that Mr. Crane was a Godsend, and that we would remain encouraged.

That was July of 1970. On Christmas Eve of that year, late afternoon, I was working at my new position at White's Furniture. I had just completed the biggest sale of the day, a plastic wastebasket. As I had endured a few previous Christmas Eves at the store, I knew that most people would not be flocking to a furniture store for last-minute gifts. The phone rang, and my stomach sank. I was expecting a phone call from Gordon—more accurately, I was dreading his call. Sales being all but nonexistent for the entire day was not something he would be happy to hear.

Surprisingly, it was Barb on the line.

"Larry, I don't like to bother you at work, but I just got

a call from Bob Crane. We're getting a baby girl! She was born yesterday, honey!"

She started crying, and so did I. What an unexpected Christmas gift. We picked up the baby just five days later on December 28. As you can imagine, between that Christmas Eve call and the 28th, we had a ton of stuff to accomplish. Even though we knew we were getting a baby sometime, we were caught off guard by the timing.

We called Barb's mom and dad right away. They were beyond ecstatic, as this was their first grandchild. They lived in Troy, Ohio, and were at our house the following day, Christmas Day. They brought a crib they had in their basement, so we had that covered. We designated a bedroom as the nursery. I wanted something special, so I made our first purchase from White's. It was a Hitchcock rocker. It would be perfect to rock our new baby to sleep.

My dad and stepmom were equally excited. He and my stepmom wanted to come right away.

"What are you going to name her, Larry?" my dad asked.

"Angie."

"Larry, I'm disappointed."

"Why? It's a beautiful name."

"I thought you'd name her after me."

"Dad, are you kidding? Your name is Ivan. That's not a girl's name."

"Ivy Ann."

I was stunned, unable to understand this conversation.

I was not going to name my daughter Ivy Ann, but he sounded so serious.

I was relieved when he started to chuckle.

"Angie is a beautiful name, son."

The Grands were thrilled. We were thrilled.

• • •

Mr. Crane had us sign up for a second baby immediately, as the abortion option was becoming the norm, by far, and we might have a long time to wait.

We soon got the hang of parenting. Angie was the love of our lives. She was always happy, and her smile would melt me when I got home from work. Barb decided ahead of time that she would not work when we had our children, a decision that I supported 100 percent.

Barb was the best mom. Angie was generally a good baby and easy for both of us to care for. However, one thing became apparent. She did not fall asleep easily. In fact, we had to rock her to asleep, then transfer her to bed. More often than not, the moment she touched the pillow, she would jolt awake, and the whole process would begin again.

We reasoned that every little baby had ups and downs, and we decided she was a keeper!

COUSIN FRED
COMES FOR A VISIT

"BARB, GUESS WHO CALLED?"

"Tell me."

"It's cousin Fred. He's back from the service, married, and traveling through on the way back to Connellsville. He wants to know if he and Sherry could stay a night or two."

Owning a three-bedroom house made it easy to say yes. They soon arrived, and Barb and Sherry hit it off immediately. Luckily, we had an all-purpose room and a living room. The girls, including our baby, Angie, had a place they could sit, play, and talk. That gave Fred and me a chance to catch up on guy stuff. He had been to Vietnam a second time, and now he was in the reserves. I couldn't get enough of hearing about his experiences the first time. Fred and I sequestered ourselves away for a nice long chat.

"Fred, are you out of the Army now? I see you are in civvies and not a uniform."

"Yep, I'm in the reserves now. That will allow me to serve out and later get my retirement."

"That seems like a good gig. Tell me about Sherry," I

said. I'd never met his wife before or even heard about her, for that matter.

"We met when we were both students at IU of PA. Every week, the college put on a sort a mixer/dinner. Believe it or not, we met on Valentine's Day. We had to dress up a bit, as in look decent. She was at my table. We were either right together, or close enough to talk. Hey, she made the first move. I always remind her of that," he said with a chuckle. "I walked her home, then called her the next day. We started dating, but Vietnam got in the way. I went into the Army, and she continued in college.

"Sherry and I actually knew each other for approximately five years before we got married. I was at Fort Lee, Virginia, when I went through officer candidate school. After OCS, I went to Vietnam for one trip, and then, when I came home after that tour, I asked Sherry to marry me."

"So the end of the first tour happens, and you go home for a while?"

"Yes, I had a two-week leave at home, which was a freebie, so to speak. We had thirty days of leave per year. During Vietnam, however, we never got to use our thirty days. So you got home, had that thirty days of leave, and then you went on to your next assignment."

"You went back to Connellsville for that event, correct?"

"Yes, I did."

"Was your dad, my Uncle Paul, still alive then?"

"Yes, he was. In fact, he and I went out and shopped for a new car—my first new car. I was pretty excited about it. I was all hyped up on getting a Camaro. We looked at one, and I was all set to buy it till I opened the trunk. Found out that it was so small I couldn't even think of getting my military gear in there. So, I changed my mind and ended up buying a Chevelle. I had to make a little bit of a trip to get it. I went first to Greensburg. There, I found out they didn't have the car I wanted. They sent me to Donegal, where I was able to buy the car. Quite an adventure just to shop for a car, but I knew what I wanted."

This was such a fun story for me. I had missed Fred, and I was very fond of my Uncle Paul.

"When you came home, did you get engaged or just married?"

"Well, actually, I got engaged that time. Sherry and I had been writing back and forth from Vietnam all the time I was there. In fact, Larry, she wrote me every single day! She would write a letter that was ten or eleven pages long. It was very encouraging to get such letters from this girl I'd been dating. That's probably when I really fell in love with her. I had already liked her very much and thought that I loved her, but as the year in Vietnam went on, her letters were what made me fall in love with her. They made being there bearable. I was thinking I'd meet her in Hawaii, when I was on my R and R, but Cousin Craig invited me to stay with him when I went there. He was married by then, and he and his wife—I think her name was Sandy—housed me and showed me around like wonderful tourist guides. I decided against staying at the military base, since I wanted to just focus on my leave without reminders of the military just then. Interestingly, they knew I was coming, but they didn't know about Sherry, so they had invited a friend from the United States they knew, and she was my constant date while I was there.

"I felt awkward about it from the get-go, but I didn't want to offend my hosts, so I went along with it. Truthfully, it was pretty neat to have somebody at my side when I was doing things with Craig and Sandy, so I could feel less like a loner. It was all very proper, Larry, I assure you.

"I told Sherry about it, and she totally understood. It was nice to be walking around with a 'round eye,' which was something I hadn't seen since leaving for Vietnam. When I got home, I was assigned to Fort Lee, Virginia, again. When that happened, I asked Sherry to marry me, and we planned for a wedding in June. We actually got married at Fort Lee, Virginia, in June. Lots of my friends and family from Pennsylvania came down for the wedding, which made me feel quite good. Tom Boland, a good friend from Ohio who went to Kent State, was my best man. He's still a dear friend."

"So, Fred, you got married before you went back to Vietnam?"

"Yeah, I was actually in the States for fifteen months before I went back to Vietnam the second time. That was a quick turnaround by all accounts. They needed mortuary officers. They were hard to find, and I had done well enough in my first tour as the commander of the 16th mortuary division. I was promoted again, this time to captain. Finally, that accomplished getting some decent pay."

"Was most of that pay needed, or could you send some of it home and save it?"

"Well, during Vietnam, I sent most of it home. Even though we weren't paid that much, there wasn't much a person could spend there, either."

"I understand you had a commissary and a PBX in Vietnam. Those should have been at reasonable prices, right?"

"Oh yeah, even to this day, if you went to the commissary and bought all your groceries, as opposed to buying them in a civilian economy, you'd save at least thirty percent, Larry."

"Did you cook, or did you eat at a mess hall?"

"In Vietnam, we ate at the mess hall three times a day. Stuff you bought at the PBX or the commissary was for eating in the evening or pleasure eating."

"Tell me more about your second tour."

"July of '69 was when I got to Vietnam the second time. When I got off the plane, I called up the mortuary division there and said I needed a ride. When they heard my name, they said, 'Who are you?' I told them I was their new commander, and that was followed by a real long pause. 'We will send a Jeep for you,' they finally said. Well, I got to the mortuary, and I met the commander, but it turned out that poor guy had no idea I was coming to replace him. It was very uncomfortable, Larry.

"He was being relieved, and that was not a good thing. So, he and I went to the headquarters of the 88th general support group, which was responsible for the mortuary. He waited outside while I talked to the executive officer. Through a discussion, I agreed that I would allow this captain, who was more or less blindsided at the mortuary, to still command the mortuary for at least one month, so that he would have six months in command. If that didn't happen, he would look bad because the six-month mark was more or less used as a measuring stick for whether you were successful or not in your job.

"Also, it would look bad on your record if you were relieved of your command. This guy was a good commander, but he didn't have enough schooling in mortuary affairs, and unfortunately, he didn't allow his NCOs to do their jobs. In the Army, an officer commands. He doesn't really run anything. The NCOs run things. If you don't have the knowledge of what the difference is between running and commanding, then you're gonna have a real problem, and this guy really did. If an officer tries to run something, it's gonna get screwed up because we were not taught to run things.

"That was the problem at the mortuary. He thought he ran the unit and didn't understand the difference. Unfortunately, he had the rank, but I had the respect. So, I worked as the mortuary officer of the 88th support group, which meant I could go out to the mortuary anytime I wanted and recommend changes. But I couldn't tell him to or order him to do such and such. However, he was told by his commander, 'If Captain Fred Seese comes out there and asks you to change something, you will change it.' That's how we worked.

"I spent about six weeks in that mode. I was positioned as the S3. The worthy unit executive officer's name was R.A. Hertz. He was very particular. In fact, most of the people in the group hated his guts. They ended up ignoring him when he gave them orders. Turns out, the officer corps of the US Army was not well thought of.

"Larry, I grew up quick in the Army, and the word responsibility took on a whole new meaning. Back in college, I wasn't mature enough to handle responsibility. I learned really quick in the Army. That's why I was such a good officer and such a good commander. I turned my unit at Fort Lee from one of the worst to one of the best in the First Army. It's one of the reasons I got sent directly as a commander. So, for six weeks, I did whatever was necessary. Unfortunately, it involved going down and looking at the battalions. We had two main ones. One was in Chu Lai and the other in Fu Bai. The CO told the people in those battalions that when I came down there, what I spoke was what would happen. So, with that in mind, when I did make those visits, it was tense. I think you can see why, Larry. Here I am, a second lieutenant, telling a colonel or a major what they're supposed to do. That didn't go over very well, Larry. I didn't make many friends in those encounters."

"After those six weeks were up, you took over, right?"

"Yes, I did. The guy I replaced did some sort of duties, because he had six months to go. Anyway, I never saw him again. During the first six weeks I was there, I had made some changes to the mortuary and the staff. There were a couple of NCOs I knew from my assignment in Fort Lee, Virginia. Two of them were deadheads. They had gone to personnel at the mortuary office and suggested changes that had been put in place when I got there. They were not good changes.

Luckily, I had some experience, and those guys got demoted and reassigned out of my unit. When I got to the mortuary, we had a full assignment of NCOs, which was fifty enlisted and supposedly five officers. But what we really had were just two officers. I had a great first sergeant. He happened to be one of our instructors in the school I attended back at Fort Lee, Sergeant Huckleberry. He and I got along really well. He understood that he ran the unit and that I wouldn't step on his toes as the head enlisted man. On the flip side of that, he would never step on my toes as the commanding officer. So, we got along really well. My success at the Mortuary was due, in part, to his success and cooperation with me. When I needed to do something, I went directly through him."

"Now when you were there, what kind of volume did you process through your area?"

"In the whole conflict, there were over fifty-seven thousand who died. I can't really tell you how many men we processed. Never kept track of numbers."

"It was obviously a fairly high volume, right?"

"Yes. One of the first things I did when I took over was express that I wanted a flagpole out in front of the mortuary. We didn't have one, and I thought that was wrong. So, I got some guys to come in and install one. I was presented with a drawing and design, and I approved them easily. A couple of days later, it was installed. We had a flagpole with approaches. We raised the American Flag, Larry. Now, I told them, that flag was not gonna be brought down. It would fly twenty-four hours a day until we had no body in that mortuary. As long as there was one body, that flag should still fly. It was flying every day I was there except one, so that will give you an idea of how many bodies we had to process.

"We ran the mortuary twenty-four hours a day. We didn't have any officers on the night shift, but we had NCOs and enlisted men. There were two shifts, 7:00 a.m. through 7:00 p.m., and then 7:00 p.m. through 7:00 a.m. I always had to tell the sergeant in charge where I was gonna be, so I may as well have been there for every shift. Sometimes I was at the officers' club, and a few times I went to play cards with my buddies in the Marines. Our barracks was actually on a Navy compound. It was also a Marine Air Group, or MAG group. I was on call twenty-four hours a day."

"In your second tour, when you were the commander, I'm guessing you did not get as involved with the actual processing of bodies?"

"During the day, I did get involved in the handling. I didn't really have to do the quote/unquote 'dirty work,' but most of them came in with names identified. The X bodies were the toughest ones. We had to go through a lot of material records. Get fingerprints if we could. That's another gory subject. Also, dental records from those and other information about where the guy was, what was going on in the unit, what happened after the deaths occurred, so that we could identify him correctly. I got involved in that way. Once a person was identified by my soldiers, then the records of what they developed went to civilians, identification officers. They would put a stamp of approval on it, then they would send that to me, and I would put my own stamp of approval on it as the commanding officer. Most of the time they were correct, but once in a while I would find a mistake, and I would disagree with them. When that happened, I had to get in the middle of things. I would point out the problem to them so we could move forward the proper way.

"The biggest problem was the United States Marines. Don't get me wrong, Larry, I always have and always will have the greatest respect for our Marines. It was their protocols that sometimes befuddled me. You could identify a body four different ways. The first was by the ID tags they were wearing. The second was by their fingerprints. Everybody was fingerprinted when they got to Vietnam. Everybody also got a dental inspection when they first arrived. It was supposedly a requirement that we would receive the dental records and the fingerprints. Sometimes we got them, sometimes we didn't, but most of the time, we did. The Marines liked to identify people really quickly. The fourth way you could identify a person was called 'facial recognition.' Two signed statements of facial recognition from two members of the unit. Marines often used this because it was very quick.

"It came to a head one day when they sent the body down with the name of so-and-so on it. I looked at the chart showing where the wounds were on the body and how he was killed. Here was a young man who died as a result of a gunshot wound to the head. I went out and looked at this body, and there was no face, Larry. Yet we had two statements of facial recognition of this guy. It was at this point that I knew it had to stop. Things had gone too far. I immediately made an appointment to talk to the two-star general from the Marines. I went over and discussed the problem with him, and he agreed.

"Up until that point, from my first tour till then, that practice was being used. After that, thankfully, it was suspended. One of the things that disturbed me most during both tours was when a colonel or a general would come into the mortuary and want to see their men. I would say to them, 'Sir, they're not your men. They're mine.'

"When we heard that a colonel or general was coming and we had some very bad remains on a table, we would put them in the back room for them to see firsthand. Most couldn't stand it, and their visit was short. They didn't like what they saw, Larry. Our place was never pleasant, but it was an inescapable reality of war.

"Now, down in Saigon, the area between the backroom and the processing room had a door that swung both ways. My commander down there painted it green. We let those senior officers come in. The major, our major, would brief them. He would call me and say, 'Junior, would you escort the officer into the processing area?'

"Many times, the officer would follow me into the processing area, and many times before I could turn around, he was back in the other area because he didn't wanna face what I was looking at or what I was going to show him. On my second tour, I continued that same practice. When somebody wanted to see their men—same result, they didn't stay long. I liked it that way because I was left to my own. I was allowed to command my area, process my bodies, and give the commander of the general support group what he needed when he wanted it.

"I saw Herts only one time. As it turns out, nobody wanted to hear or see what my unit did. A lot of times I'd go to the club and start talking to somebody, and they'd ask me what exit section I was in. When I would tell them, that would be the end of it. If we had war correspondents in the area, we didn't want them in the mortuary anyway, and we especially didn't want them taking pictures, as that would be a misinterpretation of everything we were trying to accomplish. No pictures of any of the bodies were allowed. That was by regulation. It wasn't my rule."

After this long conversation, we took a break and went to see how the girls were getting along. We found Sherry rocking Angie, and Barb watching over both of them, all smiles. They were obviously not bothered by our absence, so we got back to it.

"All right," I said, once we had returned to the other room, "so that took another year, and basically you stayed in the Army quite a while after that, but in a reserve role, right?"

"Yes, I was an army reservist. I served in many units. Everywhere from the 433rd support group, which was at Oakdale, Pennsylvania, to commanding a psychological operations company. I had a detachment up in Butler, Pennsylvania. It was a personnel administration battalion. Many, many duties, many, many jobs, and I enjoyed them all."

"Being back in the United States, those roles you were in were more like a job, right?"

"Oh, right. Yeah, it was a daily job. Well, actually, it wasn't daily. It was one weekend a month, plus an administration meeting every week. The advertisement says one week a month, but that's not correct. As an officer or senior NCO, you had to attend once a week in the evening for four hours, which was unpaid in most cases, plus two days on a weekend in the month where you were paid four days for two days of work. Every drill you did was a day's pay. I did five and a half years on active duty, and the rest of the time I was in as a reservist. But during that time, I also worked for the Army Reserve. I was at the 99th R-Corp."

"What does 'R-Corp' stand for?"

"I was a recruiter. Actually, I was a civilian recruiter working for the Army. We had our own office in with officers, which we shared with the other services. When I was in Butler, I was actually working with active duty as well. When we went out to schools and so on, the active-duty people would do their spiel, and then I would do mine. I would take a thick magazine with me that I would hold up between my hands and say, 'This is the United States Army. Full-time soldiers, working full time. Soldiers working twenty-four hours a day.' Then I would hold up a hardback book and explain to them that it represented the Army Reserve, the army guard together, which was the backup to the United States Army. There were more people in the reserves than there were in active duty, so we were a bigger backup. That's why I showed them the book, to demonstrate that if you hit the magazine, it would bend, but if I put that book behind the magazine and you hit it, it wouldn't bend anymore. The strength of the book represented the strength of the Army Reserve backing up the United States Army. So, if somebody didn't want to serve in the active Army, then they would certainly have a place in the Army Reserves."

"So, you really liked the Army, right?"

"Yep, I even talked Sherry into it. We were in Butler, Pennsylvania. I was in the 300th transportation group, which meant I attended a lot of admin meetings. When I came home one night, Sherry said to me, 'What in the world do you do there all the time?'

"'Why don't you join and find out?' I said. She looked at me and said, 'Okay, I'm going to. I'm going to join.' We had a program at the time in the Army Reserves that took the expertise of a civilian and converted it to military expertise. She could go to a two-week basic training, then come back to a unit that had agreed to take her. They would finish the basic training, but they already had a skill, so they really didn't have to go to individual training. Sherry's skill was in administration. So, she started out as the clerk typist. She came in as a PFC, not as an E-1e or E-2, but as an E-3, since she already had a skill. The normal soldier would make PFC in about eight to ten months. It was called a civilian-acquired skill program."

"Well, that sounds like a good deal when it comes to that. Will you likely ever get called up again?"

"Nope, and that's a good thing. I'm already feeling some of the aftereffects of being in."

"What do you mean?"

"Like nightmares and lots of anxiety. My last CO told

me that might happen."

"I hate to hear that, but I can understand how it would happen. You probably could stay up all night, but I don't have Army stamina, and I have a long day tomorrow. Let's turn in, okay? I don't have to go in till noon, though, so Barb and I will treat you guys to eggs, bacon, and waffles in the morning. How about that?"

A DISAPPOINTMENT, THEN A BLESSING

TWO YEARS AFTER ANGIE ARRIVED, **we found that we could sell our house at a nice profit, so we began to look for a new place. I had always wanted a wooded lot. Our first house had a nice bit of woods behind it, which made me realize that I wanted that on land of my own more than ever. I found out about a lot that would be available in the nearby suburb of Gahanna. A guy I met at the store was developing twelve acres of woods there. He would sell four lots, create a wide, wooded driveway in between, and keep seven acres behind the four lots as his own estate.**

The lot that I was hoping to purchase would be next to the driveway, and it would back up on his property. To me, that was a dream. We would have an acre of woods and share part of the driveway and his property as well. The lot was level, and at the back, it sloped off into a ravine. The trees on it were massive, and walking it made both of us fall in love with it more than ever.

We decided to make the leap and buy it, then contract and build our dream home there! We put down $1,000

and planned to pay the balance of $9,000 with the profits from our house sale. Soon, we were notified of our closing. We met at a familiar bank, and everything was set, or so we thought.

We were to meet with the banker/attorney who represented us, plus the owner of the property. On the day of the meeting, though, things did not go as smoothly as one might hope in a situation like this. Instead of the owner, three imposing men in dark suits showed up. They asked the banker to step outside, and we were left inside to wonder what was going on. They all finally appeared in the conference room, and we got an explanation.

The property, we were informed, was now in "receivership." The three men were the receivers. This was not what we had planned. We asked if we could have a private moment with our representative, and the three of us went into another office.

"What does all this mean? How will it affect our purchase? What should we do?"

After what seemed an eternity, we weighed all our options and felt it too risky to proceed. The owner had a wonderful plan for the property, which was what drew us in. Would the new owners even care what the plans were? Might they build something commercial next to us? Or, would they throw a trailer park on the rest of the property? We feared the worst.

We couldn't have been more disappointed. Our rep explained that we would risk losing our deposit, but we could still walk away. This was upsetting, but we decided losing the deposit was a better option than the risk we would be taking buying from someone we didn't know.

After a few months of licking our wounds, we started looking again. We talked over the idea of living in a wooded setting versus a developed area. Each made sense, and we were open to both. Barb saw some signs for a new area being developed called Annehurst Village. It was already a popular area, and this would be a new phase opening up. We took Angie and went to look at a model home there the following weekend.

Though it wasn't our original choice, we quickly realized we were both thrilled by the thought of a brand-new home. We soon picked a lot and sat down with the builder to select a model and pick out all the elements to make a house a home. I remember well that the one extra I wanted was a screened-in porch. It added a significant amount to the overall cost, which put it well over our budget. Then a break came our way. The builder noticed that I was very aware of how to pick colors, carpet, paint, and such.

"Where did you learn to decorate so well, Larry?" he asked.

"Well, that's what I do a lot in my job. I learned it, and now I love to do it."

As we got down to the very end of the process, he knew we wanted the porch, but we couldn't put it on the loan we had secured.

"Larry, I'll make you a deal. I'll do you a screened porch if you'll meet with my clients and help them pick their paint, carpet, countertops, and trims. Frankly, that is a chore for me, and I'd be glad to have you do it. You could schedule people on your days off and evenings and weekends."

I couldn't say yes fast enough! So we had a new house in short order and couldn't have been happier. The neighborhood was just starting. We soon met our new neighbors, and lifelong friendships were built.

Three years after we got the call about our Angie, at almost the same time on Christmas Eve, Barb called me again.

"Guess what, Larry, we're getting a baby boy!"

There were tears from all of us, as well as prayers of thanks. Our baby boy would complete our beautiful family. We picked up Drew on the 28th. · He will be fifty this year, and Angie will be fifty-three. Our kids have been a true blessing from the beginning to the present.

Drew was all boy! Unlike Angie, he had no trouble falling asleep. We laughed that we could probably drop him from three feet up, and he would be asleep before he hit the pillow.

The new neighborhood was a blessing in disguise. All the new families moved in at the same time. Everyone had the same motivation it seemed, and making friends was easy. On top of that, everyone had kids. Our children had playmates galore. The first five houses on our side alone had twenty-one kids!

We were blessed. Most of the dads had jobs that were nine to five Monday through Friday. I, on the other hand, still worked in a retail job, which meant that I spent my weekends at the store. I had Thursday off, making me the odd guy out. That got me noticed in the neighborhood, and I easily became everyone's dad that day!

SEGUE

OVER THE YEARS, **Barb and I loved to get in the car and go.** Shortly after our marriage, before we adopted our children, we took two major trips. The first one was out West in the 1964 Bonneville convertible. It had every option possible and was one of the neatest cars you'd ever want to see.

We set off to meet our friends Bill and Jean Hughes at Yellowstone National Park. Bill and I taught math together. Barb and Jean were also teachers. We became fast friends and had so much in common. They were on their own vacation, and we were to meet them a week after they started.

On the way out we had stretches of road that were long and straight and enabled us to open the car up to over 100 miles per hour, which was pretty cool. In the '60s, tires didn't last very long. My father, always the prudent one, thought that recap tires were a good answer when you needed tires. Just before we started our trip, I bought a fancy new set of whitewall tires that were recaps. My feeling was that they were brand-new and would be better than the tires that were on the car, which were wearing thin.

I would soon be proved wrong! Once we got out on the prairies and started getting up to high speeds with high temperatures, the worst possible scenario for recap tires came into play. We had a blowout at eighty miles per hour. The back left tire just delaminated. We were lucky because the road was straight, there was no traffic in front of us or behind us, and we were able to get off the road successfully without wrecking. We did have a spare, and when we got to the next town, I bought a new fourth and had a mechanic change it out for me.

The rest of the trip we did not ever try to get up to speed again. We probably never went over sixty miles per hour the rest of the time. We arrived at Yellowstone and eventually met our friends. At that time, we were camping. We had a beautiful red-and-green tent and lots of equipment that I had either saved from my days in the Boy Scouts or that we had purchased together.

We got there one night before Bill and Jean and set up camp. Yellowstone's an incredible place. It has about everything a tourist would ever want to see. Even though it was mid-summer, the temperature got down below freezing that first night. It didn't snow, but it easily could have. We were unprepared for the temperature, as you might imagine. We had fairly warm sleeping bags for the overnight part, but waking and sitting around in the cold would be another matter. We both agreed that we would move from the tent to the car as soon as we could.

I woke up first at about 5:30. It was already light out, but it was freezing! I suggested that we get ourselves into the

Bonneville, turn the heater on high, and get warm. We did a little driving around and found that there was a beautiful lodge and restaurant about a mile away. The downside was that it didn't open till 8:30. We stayed in our car, probably using up about a quarter tank of gas, but we couldn't have cared less at that point. The only thing that mattered to us right then was that we were warm and doing well by the time the restaurant opened.

We spent as much time as we could at the restaurant, enjoying the ambiance as well as the heat from the over-sized fireplace in the lodge. I think the manager realized our plight and didn't give us any hassle. We stayed there for at least an hour and a half. We finished eating after about fifteen minutes, though in retrospect, it likely would have made more sense if we had dragged the meal out so we could have had a legitimate reason for being there so long.

Our friends came the next day and set up tents next to ours. Bill and I wanted to show off our skills in both boating and fishing, so we rented a boat and went fishing on Yellowstone Lake. The guy who rented us the boat told us of his many fishing exploits on the lake and dubbed it a "can't miss" fishing adventure.

With us, it turned out to be a "can't catch" adventure! We were out for hours without a catch. That would not look good to the girls, and we started scheming. God was obviously in the plan, as He placed a fisherman next to us who was watching us for about an hour. It seemed like every cast he caught a fish, while every cast we didn't.

He looked over and spoke.

"Hey, bet you guys could use a fish or two, am I right?"

"Yeah, you surely are. How much would you charge us?"

"Well, I've got plenty, so you guys just met up with the right person today, and here they are for free. I'm going to give you four, 'cause I have a feeling you guys have wives back at the campground, and two would not look good."

We thanked him profusely and headed back to camp just in time for dinner.

"Hey, looks like you guys did great today," the ladies said in greeting. "Those fish are really pretty. What kind are they?"

"Oh, they're rainbow trout," I replied.

"Were they hard to catch?"

"Nah, we got them pretty easily."

It was hard to keep a straight face, as you can imagine. Over a beautiful fire, we cooked them up and had a few side dishes that the girls had made. It turned out to be a wonderful rustic meal.

Our secret remained somewhat safe, although I think the girls always suspected that we didn't catch those fish. Every time we talked about that trip, one or both would ask, "Did you guys really catch those fish?" After forty-some years of occasional questioning and minor guilt, we finally admitted the ruse.

Each site had a garbage pit. We dutifully put all the scraps in it after the meal. Guess what we didn't read? The "camp rules" clearly stated to take precautions because Yellowstone had bears. Bears like food, even leftover food!

LARRY BUTTERMORE

That night, with our bellies full of our "caught" trout, we were awakened by two hungry bears. We were fortunate that Yellowstone bears were somewhat used to humans. We could hear them rooting around in the trash that we had so generously provided. There was a full moon out that night.

Since the bears were just a few feet away, we soon saw their shadowy forms. They were so close. We looked at each other, and all I could think to do was hold up my index finger and implore Barb to be as quiet as possible. Had they any interest in us, we would have been goners, as tent canvas would not be much of a deterrent for them. Fortunately, they were only interested in our leftovers. Soon we could tell that they had moved on. Guess we weren't the only campers to leave them snacks! We could hear them rooting and rattling trash can lids for at least another half hour. We kept silent, but our fear stayed on. Frightening then, fun memories now, as we lived to tell the tale.

At that point in our lives, Barb and I definitely wanted to start a family soon, so taking another big trip was a high priority before the kids came along. The next summer we carved out ten days and went to New England. Once again, we packed up our camping gear and headed out in the Bonneville. On the first night, we camped just south of Niagara Falls and spent two days reliving our honeymoon there. We did a few things we couldn't afford on our honeymoon, like taking a trip on the *Maid of the Mist* and having a nice dinner in the Seagram's Tower restaurant on the Canadian side. We'd only had $50.00 available for our entire honeymoon, so we had to pick and choose wisely or we wouldn't have made it back to Troy without hitchhiking!

Our second day there, we arrived in Lake George, New York. Someone at my school recommended that we go there. We had never even heard of Lake George, and we were soon pleased to have received the recommendation.

What a beautiful lakeside community it was. We arrived late in the morning and had a chance to look around and get the lay of the land. We saw a sign that read "rent an island." After very little conversation, we decided to stop in the booth and ask what exactly that meant. We found out we could literally rent an island that would be exclusive to us.

The campsite would have the basics. It would have a picnic table, a firepit, and an outhouse. Pretty rustic but unbelievably beautiful. The cost was so low that we decided we would do it. We also had to rent a canoe to get to the island, so we loaded up our stuff and headed out. It didn't take long, maybe 15 or 20 minutes, before we were there. The island was spectacular! We had a 360-degree view of Lake George.

The lake was deep, and many islands were dotted around it. It was one of the most beautiful sights that we'd ever seen. We set up and decided it was going to be easier to go back to the restaurant that we had seen at Lake George and have dinner there. So, we set out about 4:00 to go back to the mainland, assuming it was going to take about fifteen to twenty minutes, just like it did coming in. We were wrong, as we encountered a strong headwind. The trip took a little over an hour, and it was beyond exhausting for me, as I was doing most of the work.

We had our dinner and contemplated staying over in Lake George, as we were both still tired from the trip to the restaurant. Enter one of the best and most creative moments I've ever managed. I told Barb I had an idea. I told her what it was, and she laughed out loud and said it wouldn't work.

Not to be swayed, however, I persisted. I fetched a golf umbrella from the Bonneville and went to the canoe. I had Barb sit in the front, and as I pushed off, she raised the umbrella. When I say it worked beyond perfect, I am accurate. We were able to go back to the island in less than ten minutes, and all I had to do was use the paddle as a rudder to steer. The wind picked up in the umbrella and propelled us so fast we were making a wake. I just wish that cellphone videos were possible then, because footage of that trip would have been one of the best videos of all time for me.

As it was, I was able to take a picture and I still have it. The photo shows Barb with the open umbrella and me in the back of the canoe. We slept well! There were no bears on the island—no critters at all, in fact. We had a nice break-fast and got on our way to the rest of our wonderful New England trip.

Our ultimate goal was to go to Maine, which took a couple of days, of course. Traveling through Vermont next, we touched on Lake Champlain and toured a couple of neat ski resorts. We finished off our Vermont stay with a visit to the L.L.Bean headquarters. We couldn't really afford any of their merchandise, but we had heard the Company Store in Freeport was a must-see.

We did some research and decided on Kennebunkport, Maine. We went there and had an enormous lobster dinner. This was a new experience for both of us, something we had only seen on TV or in movies. Again, I wish we could have recorded this event, as rookies eating lobster is very labor intensive and fun! Each of us had on a giant, white plastic bib with red lobster designs on them. By the time we were finished, we understood why they insisted that we wear them. Those bibs were covered with lobster parts and melted butter we had for dipping.

While there, we stayed in a bed and breakfast, which was a first for us. It turned out to be almost like camping. Because I had a desire to do things in the most economical way possible, I chose a place that cost fifteen dollars per night. The first "B" (bed) was a cot on a sleeping porch. The second "B" (breakfast) was our choice of Cheerios or Wheaties. We did get a great recommendation from our hosts, though. I wanted a true New England experience for our next dinner, and I knew we wanted to end our last day in Boston. We found out that Cape Ann was just north of the city and that it had a can't-miss eatery called Mattie's.

We got to town at 10:00 in the morning, and quickly found that it was quiet with just one main drag. A gas station guy told me that the restaurant would be easy to find, as almost every attraction was on one street. Easy enough, we thought, and we headed out. About a half hour later, we still had not found the place. We went up and down the cobblestone street three times.

"Let's see if we can find a local," I suggested.

When we did, it turned out the restaurant was Hattie's, not Mattie's. We were standing right beside it! The place, appearance-wise, was not five stars. We ventured into the bar area and asked if this was indeed Hattie's, as the sign out on the street was so faded it was hard to read. After what seemed like an eternity, the only guy who even looked up, said, "It's upstairs, and it doesn't open till noon."

The bar was obviously not connected to the restaurant, and the patrons were not interested in fulfilling the PR role for it. As soon as we got outside, we looked up at the entrance to the place. There were already two groups waiting outside. It was 11:30. We got the message and soon found out that our B&B hosts weren't kidding when they told us how popular the place was with the locals. By noon there were people lined up fifty feet down the sidewalk.

I'm glad we persisted, as the food did not disappoint. By the way, I couldn't find the restaurant when I looked for it while writing this chapter. My guess is that it has changed hands, names, and is some fancy Gastropub with no appeal to the locals by now. Right place and right time for us!

DIGGING TO CHINA,
A LITTLE LUCK,
AND AN ADVENTURE

OUR FRIENDS **the Hugheses could also be credited for the fact that we started going to Michigan. Barb and I had been up there with our dog Dusty, before we had Angie, to a campsite that Jean's family owned in the Upper Peninsula on the shore of Lake Huron. It was quite beautiful, and the trip up was as well. We fell in love with northern Michigan. So, as soon as the kids were old enough, we decided to take off up there.**

We were lucky enough to borrow a pop-up camper, once again from Bill and Jean, and off we went. We traveled to a place called Young's State Park. It was in the vicinity of Lake Charlevoix, the town of Charlevoix, and the town of Harbor Springs. This campsite was rugged but so scenic. We were close to the showers (a must for my Barb) and had a great time there.

We stayed a week, and the highlight of our trip was laughing about our son, Drew, "digging to China." From my Boy Scout days, I had a little shovel that flipped. It would be straight and used as a small shovel. It had a feature

of being able to have the blade lock at a ninety-degree angle. As such, it alternately could be used as a shovel or a digger. Drew flipped it into the digger mode, and as soon as we got there, he searched for a spot that looked like it had some soft dirt and took off digging. Pretty soon he had a hole that was two feet wide and three feet deep. We laughed a lot about that.

We also visited the town of Charlevoix and went to a fabulous restaurant there that was right up against the canal that led from Lake Charlevoix to Lake Michigan. There was a drawbridge, and we spent a lot of time just watching the drawbridge open and close (each time with a loud warning bell). Boats small and large came through it from the lake, especially in the evening. The kids loved it, often squealing in delight, and Barb and I did too. I think it set the stage for us to come back to Michigan many times, even after the kids had grown up and stopped traveling with us.

•   •   •

Fast-forward many years. The kids were grown, and I was a busy insurance agent. Barb announced that she was anxious to visit all fifty states. She said the compelling reason was that her parents had done it, and she wanted to be able to say that she had done it as well. Looking back on it, I think she realized that her health was never going to get much better, and that this was something we needed to do sooner rather than later. Fortunately, I was well established in my business at the time, and I could afford to take some extra time and some extra money and put it toward this wonderful project. We had three or four areas of the country that we hadn't really visited, and those were the areas Barb wanted to start with.

Luckily, through some trips that we had taken through awards won in my insurance career, we could cross off Hawaii and Alaska. Those were wonderful trips, and the Alaska one even included a cruise. Many people who try to do all fifty states have trouble with Alaska and Hawaii because they are so remote and require extra time and money to get to. We were thrilled to have already been to those two states.

The four areas that we needed to visit included the southeast, in particular: Mississippi, Alabama, and Arkansas. In order to accomplish that, we flew to New Orleans. Here are a couple of quick highlights that were fun about that trip. We rented a car and drove up to Memphis, Tennessee, with the idea of visiting Graceland. That was a thrill for Barb because she was a big Elvis fan and had actually seen him in Troy, Ohio, as a girl. While we were in that area, we decided to take off across the border into Arkansas just to say we'd been there, so we could cross it off our list. After leaving Memphis, we drove southeast and ended up in the area called Flora-Bama. We thought we were in Alabama, but we didn't watch the signage and ended up in the Panhandle of Florida. We were nowhere near any of our goal destinations, but that was a cool little extra that just cost us a little time and no money.

On the way back, we decided to go to a casino we had heard of in Biloxi, Mississippi. I believe it was called Bell

Terra. Barb was an avid slot-machine gambler and loved to play nickel and penny slot machines. We allowed ourselves twenty dollars each. (As you can see, we were definitely high rollers.) Barb found the machine she wanted, and I simply plopped down beside her, as I wasn't as thrilled to be there as she was.

Just after putting in her coins, she poked me. "Hey, my machine isn't working. Can you get an attendant over here?"

Soon we had one, but the attendant simply said, "There's nothing wrong with your machine. You're actually a big winner."

"What do you mean?" Barb asked.

"Well, if you look up at the top of this machine, you will see a big screen. It says that you hit a jackpot that allows you to just keep playing until you can't play anymore. When that happens, you tally your winnings and celebrate."

So, we did what she said. Pretty soon people were stopping by to cheer us on. For most folks, this would have been a fun moment. To my bride, it was a distraction, as Barb didn't like a crowd. Eventually, she won eighty-seven dollars off of one nickel. It was too bad she wasn't a bit more of a risk taker. If the machine had been a dollar machine, the winnings would have paid for our trip! Pretty cool.

Naturally, I thought she would want to play on house money and keep on playing until we had exhausted our money, which is usually the way it went. Instead, she said, "We're done. I'm through. I can't stand having a machine that does this to me. I don't understand it at all, and I'm not going to play anymore. I would rather have just the plain old slot machine with a handle on it and only be able to match three numbers in order to hit a jackpot. This machine is far too complicated. Let's get out of here."

"Where are we going to go?" I asked.

"Well, I suggest we go to the restaurant and spend the eighty-seven dollars on a nice meal before we head back."

I couldn't disagree with her, and we did just that. We had a great steak dinner and dessert, then headed back to our hotel. That was a pretty good distraction.

The next morning proved to be a little more of an adventure than we had planned. GPS had become a thing, so I ordered it as an extra on our rental car. Being travel tourists, I thought it would be of great benefit. I set our alarm, got us out of our room, and we were on our way to the airport with an hour to spare.

The choice on the screen was clear to me. It said, "Go back to office." So, I turned that on and took off. It didn't take me long to realize that the GPS was not taking me the direction that I thought it would. I was on a freeway and clearly going the opposite direction necessary to get to the airport. Also, I couldn't get turned around as soon as I wanted to. The hour we left to get to the airport on what should have been a fifteen-minute journey was now looking a little tenuous. I finally found a place to turn around, plugged in the actual office address of Enterprise Rent-a-Car, and we took off. It was a race because we (I) had wasted so much time with the bad directions. When we got to the Enterprise "turn-in" location, it wasn't obvious where to turn in. More time was wasted, and by this point, I was getting upset. Barb was getting beyond nervous. Once we finally got to the right place at Enterprise, I told them our dilemma.

"Hey, you've got to flag down somebody to get us over to the airport, ASAP," I said.

They were reluctant but nice enough to hail down a shuttle bus driver and give us the ride we needed. We were the last people to board the plane and were less than one minute from being rejected. Far too much adventure on that little trip.

Our next trip to complete our fifty-state adventure would be to the Pacific Northwest. At the time, Skybus was in business and headquartered right in Columbus. We were able to get these wonderful fares all over the United States. We got tickets that were two hundred dollars round trip that took us to Bellingham, Washington. How Skybus worked was never more than a mystery to me, but I know they took us to airports that weren't the major airport for the area. Bellingham was near Seattle, and rather than go into Seattle, Skybus chose a smaller airport. No big deal. We got there and rented a car and took off on what would be an incredible journey.

We went south immediately to the Seattle area and got a hotel in Bellevue. We went over into Seattle and saw as much of that city as we needed to. It's a great place to visit. We took lots of great pictures at the harbor, and even took a "float plane" ride. That's a form of a sea plane with two slender floats instead of wheels. Our pilot was a grizzled veteran who impressed me but not my bride.

"Is the door supposed to rattle and be loose?"

"Ma'am, I've done this trip hundreds of times, and no one has ever fallen out that door. If you look down to your right, you'll see Bill Gates' house."

From there, we went south to Portland and then headed east across the Columbia River Valley. It was a truly wonderful trip. We crossed into Idaho and went to Coeur D'Alene. It is as beautiful a place as one could ever imagine with the crystal-blue lake and scenery that would be hard to match.

From there we went farther east to Glacier National Park. Once again, we were awestruck by the incredible scenery. We rented a log cabin for the night that was on the east edge of the park, and then we went back into the park and did some sightseeing and picture-taking that I still marvel at, even today.

From there, we went north across the border into Calgary. Calgary and Banff once again offered scenery that you can't see in Ohio, Michigan, or Wisconsin. The Canadian Rockies are gorgeous and didn't disappoint.

After leaving there, we headed west through a village called Kalispell. Eventually, our goal was to end up over at Whistler Ski Resort then head down through Vancouver and back across the border, returning to Bellingham.

The border crossing took a lot longer than we anticipated. Getting across the border into Canada was no big deal. Getting back across into the United States was. We were in a very long line. I'm sure it took over an hour. The booth operator even questioned us. It was hard not to be upset, but we both managed. After 9-11, entry into the

United States became much tougher, but this was totally understandable. We were patient and finally got back into Washington and on a scenic Pacific Coast road.

We could see the San Juan islands from the coastline road we were on. We regretted not being able to tour the islands, but time did not allow for it. Just seeing them from the road, we could tell how magnificent they were. We found a restaurant along the highway that had a coastal view. We had a beautiful dinner and headed back to our hotel in Bellingham to begin our trip back home.

Our next venture to get in all the states took us to Denver as our fly-in destination. We had been there many times before, both in the summer and the winter, but this was just simply the easiest way to get where we were going. We rented a car there and took off north and east, wanting to get into states such as Nebraska, South Dakota, and North Dakota. We had been through those states but never stopped, and therefore couldn't officially cross them off of our itinerary. The highlights were mostly in South Dakota.

We retraced some steps that we had taken earlier in our lives and went to the typical places, like Wall Drug and Mount Rushmore. Once we got to South Dakota we discovered we were missing two important sights that were pretty close together.

One was Custer State Park, which was beautiful and had a wildlife sanctuary. The other was the motorcycle rally at Sturgis. We were there one week after the actual event. This was fine with us because the event was so crazy and the parking even crazier. We probably would not have enjoyed it anyway, and we got the flavor just by being there after it had passed.

There were still plenty of motorcyclists in town, and like us, it seemed they didn't want to encounter the craziness of the event itself. We figured they had just come to see the town and all it had to offer. Sturgis looked like a Western movie set with saloons and taverns in mostly wood-framed buildings in the style of the Old West. I made sure I saw the motorcycle museum there. I never much wanted to be a motorcyclist, but I did appreciate them, and the museum certainly didn't disappoint.

There was a motorcycle in the museum that I had actually owned, or half-owned, at one time. It was called a Harley Hummer. It was from the '50s, and I owned it for a very short period of time with my friend "Uncle Mack," as I called him. I was a senior in college at Otterbein at the time. Mack said he had an opportunity to buy this bike for fifty dollars. He asked me if I wanted to be a partner in it. It sounded like a cool thing to be part of, so I said sure and gave him twenty-five dollars. We had a Harley Hummer almost before I could say "boo."

One day, Uncle Mack suggested we go for a ride on the Harley. Although I'd never even been on it before, he gave me a quick lesson. He took off on another friend's Vespa, and I got to drive the Harley Hummer. We headed out of Westerville. We went up Cleveland Avenue to Hanawalt Road and quickly turned onto Bale Kenyon Road. At that time, Bale Kenyon Road was nothing but farms (today it is lined with expensive homes on large, wooded lots). High hills sat on one side and a big drop-off on the other—clear down to Alum Creek. We were driving along on the road, and all of a sudden, Mack decided to turn left into a farm lane.

I was probably following a little too close and going a little bit too fast. The farm lane and the left turn came up too quickly for me. To make it worse, it had rained the night before, and gravel from the farm road had made its way down onto the road we were on. I tried to make my left turn and ended up sliding about 100 yards with the bike on top of my legs, and it wasn't pretty. I had jeans on, and the jeans were torn away from my bottom leg, which was severely damaged with road rash. Mack finally realized what had happened and came to investigate.

"Hey, Butts, you all right?"

"Yeah, I guess so."

"Are you still up for exploring?"

Once again, I mumbled, "Yeah, I guess."

I brushed myself off, righted the bike, and found out it would still start and run just fine, as if the accident never happened at all. We took off and headed up a very steep farm road that was one lane of mud and gravel. The goal was to get up to the top and see a beautiful farm Mack had heard about. We managed to get up about three-quarters of the hill, and then we stopped for a moment to take a break.

A haunting howling that sounded like coon dogs was suddenly floating on the air. I looked up in the woods, and five or six big, ugly dogs were rushing forward, barking wildly, apparently not happy to see us on their property. So, what to do now? Mack turned around and headed down the hill pretty easily. On the other hand, my inexperience with the Hummer proved to make things more interesting than I wanted them to be. I realized these dogs were going to bite me if I didn't get out of there, so I decided that the best thing to do was flip the bike around, rev it up as high as I could get it, and pray the noise from the straight pipe of the Harley would scare off the critters. As soon as I revved it up, I heard some squealing and looked around to see that the dogs were beating a hasty retreat back up the hill to wherever they came from. Hallelujah was all I could say to myself. I went back down the hill as slowly as I could. I found Mack at the bottom, looking as if he hadn't a care in the world.

In typical fashion, his tone said anything but. "Where the hell have you been, Butts?"

"I survived, but I'm heading back to the frat house, and when I get there, I'm parking the bike. I want my twenty-five dollars back. You can have the bike. I never want to see it again."

When I was in the museum, I learned that the bike was considered quite rare, quite classic, and worth many, many times the fifty dollars we spent on it. Such is life, I suppose.

Our last trip on our fifty-state odyssey was to pick up New Mexico. We flew into Albuquerque, rented a car, and drove north to Santa Fe. We had a hotel there, and while at the hotel, I had to make an interesting call. I'd met up with (on the phone only) a gentleman who was going to meet me back in my hometown and help me with the project of restoring some stone pillars in a local park. He was a world-renowned stone mason and artist.

Once I dialed up his number, I looked and realized that it was the exact same area code of the one that I was now in, in Santa Fe. So, when I finally got him to answer, I said, "Hey, Tom, where do you live?"

"I live in Santa Fe, New Mexico."

I laughed. He asked, "Why?"

"Because that's where I'm at right now. My wife and I are visiting New Mexico, and we're in Santa Fe."

"Well gosh, we should get together."

"Yeah, that would be great. Maybe you could show us some of your work if you have any in the town."

"I have a beautiful public art project that I completed a while back, and it's at a small park here in town."

He gave me the address, and we met him there. It was a truly unique experience. The park he designed was very cool. Since his expertise was as a stonemason, the park had several low stone walls for seating, and a unique stone fountain that was its centerpiece. After we finished visiting, we went to the main part of town where local artists set up and displayed their work. We could have spent a lot of time and money there, as it was different from any other place we had been. It was one of those special blessings that you get sometimes when you're traveling.

On that trip, we also got to go into a few Pueblo areas and experience some of the authentic native culture in New Mexico. At one particular village, I spent about an hour walking around. I was especially drawn to an adobe structure. It looked like a church or school. I saw a sign that warned not to take pictures. I wasn't sure why, but

I complied. As I got closer, there was an open door, so I walked in. I had my camera strapped around my neck. A burly native "guard" immediately pointed at it and shook his finger in a very intimidating fashion. It worked, as any inclination I had to snap a picture vanished. I wasn't sure why they were so strict, but I didn't want to find out! We got to check off our 50th state, and that particular part of our life adventure was complete.

Two other trips after that one come to mind, showing that if you are adventurous, mostly good things happen.

The first one happened around 1994. I was privileged to be awarded a special trip as part of my insurance accomplishments. It was supposed to be a free trip to Paris. Barb and I decided that free is a relative term, and that if we really went to Paris, we would spend more money than we should, as we would be part of a group of older, more experienced insurance agents who were also awarded the trip.

That was not the kind of contest I needed in that part of my career, as I was only in my third year as an agent and still struggling financially. I found out that we had an alternative trip we could sign up for that suited us better. It was to Lake Tahoe. We both smiled and said, "Wow, that's our kind of trip." We loved the outdoors, and we had never experienced Lake Tahoe before, so we signed up as soon as we could.

At the time, I was a tennis player, playing tennis five days a week every morning at 7:00 a.m. I met a lot of neat people along the way. One morning, as I was shaving at the tennis club, getting ready to leave for my office, the guy next to me said, "Hey, you're an insurance agent, aren't you?"

"Guilty as charged," I replied.

I had never seen him before, but he seemed to know a little bit about me.

"Are you going on the big trip they have?"

"I am, but I'm taking an alternative trip because we don't feel comfortable leaving the country and spending so much money to go to Paris."

"Where is the alternative trip?"

"Well, it's to Lake Tahoe."

He lit up and said, "Wow, I have a home there. Why don't you and I meet up tomorrow morning over at the French Market and have breakfast? I'll bring you some info about that area that might make your trip more interesting. Would that work for you?"

He then introduced himself formally and said he was with Safelite Glass. When I went home, I did a quick little bit of research and found out that he was more than just "with them." He was the CEO, recently appointed for the company, which had its headquarters right in Columbus, Ohio. I met with him the next morning, and wow, what a neat thing emerged from that morning meeting. He had a stack of brochures and maps and area attractions for Lake Tahoe.

"Larry, if you can take the time, I will help you have the trip of a lifetime in that particular part of the world."

"Okay, tell me what you mean," I said, all the while thinking, *Wow!*

"Very good. So, I have a house in Lake Tahoe and know every inch of the Lake Tahoe area, and here are some things that you should do while you are there. Now, if you can take the time, I want to propose either a one- or two-day side trip for you guys. I also have a place in San Francisco, which is a good half-day drive, but worth every minute of it if you've never been there. Even if you have, it's a great place to visit again."

Barb and I had been there in our early days of marriage, visiting relatives of mine. But his version of travel was very different than the trip we had taken back in the '60s when we didn't have enough money to go, but we did anyway.

"So, Larry, I have a restaurant there and a condo. I won't be there, but if you want to go to my restaurant, I can tell my maître d' that you're coming and approximately when you'll be there. You just introduce yourself to him when you get there, and he'll have a special table for you. Anything you want will be my treat."

Wow again, I thought.

"Okay then. If you have time—and this is where you'll have to take a little more time—you can either make it a long, long day or somehow make a two-day journey out of it and go to my house, which is in Homestead, California, in wine country. My wife and I have a winery there and also a vineyard, and it's our main residence. Once again, I won't be there, but I have a way to make that visit special. If you stop at the Homestead grocery on your way to my place, I'll leave you directions with my friend Bob Sacamonte at that store. He's the owner, and he'll know who you are if you identify yourselves. I've asked him to pack you a picnic basket and give you the directions to my place. It's about five miles out of Homestead. You can go there to my picnic grove. Hopefully it will be a beautiful evening, and you can watch the sunset over the Napa Valley with just about the best view you could ever imagine."

We were stunned by our good fortune. We were excited to take my new friend up on his offer, and we decided that we were going to do it all in one day because, again, the finances of staying overnight in San Francisco would likely take up more funds than going to Paris. So, we arrived in San Francisco on a Sunday morning. We took off very early to get there by about 9:00 a.m.

We thought we'd be able to cover what we wanted to see in San Francisco within a couple of hours. However, that morning happened to be what I would call a "Chamber of Commerce" morning in San Francisco, and thousands of people had flocked to each of the sites we wanted to see.

The main thing we wanted to do was ride the cable car into the city and back out to where we started. The line for that was going to take us over an hour to get through. Once we got on the cable car and into town, we realized another dilemma. The cable car turned around, and when it did, you had to get off and get back on again, and that required getting in another line. Needless to say, when we got through with the cable car, we had to make a quick decision about our plans for the rest of the day.

We realized we would need to skip lunch at the restaurant that the Safelite CEO had suggested and instead head out of town to Homestead as soon as possible. We did that, and it was a beautiful drive, but it was a little stressful because it was taking too long. Once we finally got to

Homestead, we found the grocery quite easily. It was a very small town and had only one grocery store, so we went in and told Bob who we were.

"You guys are lucky you got here when you did," he said, his tone gracious. "It's Sunday, and we close at five o'clock."

By the time we got there it was 4:45, so with no advance knowledge that they closed at 5:00, we counted that as another "God thing."

Bob packed up the picnic basket that we had been told to expect, and while he was working, we asked him about our host.

"Oh, what a great guy he is. You're lucky to have been acquainted with him. We just love 'em up here."

"Hey, does he have any of his wine in your shop?" I asked.

"Yes, of course. There's a whole row of his stuff over there."

"Can I buy one bottle and take it with our picnic basket?"

"Of course."

Once I went over to look at it, I realized that it was more expensive than all the wine I had ever drunk in my whole life. I bought it anyway, just to say I had, and so that when I got back to Columbus, I could tell the Safelite CEO I had done all the things he had wanted us to except one. On top of that, I would be able to say I was fortunate enough to now be the owner of one of his fine wines. So, instead of drinking it on the picnic, I took it home and saved it for a special occasion much later.

We drove from the grocery store to the property, which started on a paved road, then veered left down a very long gravel road, at the end of which stood his entrance. Once at the entrance, we realized that it had a huge chain across it, and that this would prevent us from driving up his lane.

I looked at Barb and said, "We're not getting stopped by this chain or anything else. This is not something I want to miss, and either we're going to walk or figure out a way to get into this place."

Barb was already having some trouble with walking, and I knew just by looking that this lane went far enough it was not going to be conducive to her jumping out and walking to this picnic grove. My creative instincts kicked in, and I looked at the chain.

"Hey, sweetie. Get out and see if that chain can be held up in the air enough so I can drive the car under it."

"Larry, if we do this, we're going to get caught. There's probably an alarm system, a Doberman, or some such thing that will come charging down on us because we went into the property illegally."

"I don't think so, Barb. Anyhow, hold up the chain."

She did, and sure enough, I was able to get our rental car under the chain. We felt a little sheepish, but we did it just the same, and we were on our way up the lane to the picnic grove, which was up at a bend and featured a huge oak tree along with a picnic table on a little level spot overlooking the lower part of the vineyard. We had our picnic and viewed a beautiful sunset that would be hard to ever duplicate.

We finished our picnic and drove back to Lake Tahoe. We didn't get there until midnight, but we didn't care. It was such a wonderful experience, and as I said from the start, it was one we never would have had if we'd not been a little bit adventurous.

•　　•　　•

Our second trip was a little bit later and had something to do with my insurance career as well. Barb and I wanted to go back to New England. We loved it when we went up there just after we got married. This time, we were going to fly into Portland, Maine, then drive down to Bar Harbor. The plan was to spend time in Bar Harbor, take in Acadia National Park, and drive through New Brunswick and visit Nova Scotia. Aggressive, but doable.

I talked to my brother Bob about the trip, and he had some advice. "Why don't you get ahold of my friend Burt? He's an agent down in Philadelphia whom I really call a good friend. He and I did lots of fundraising things together, and I know he's very familiar with Bar Harbor and actually owns a lot of property up there on a place called Swan Island. If you get ahold of him, I'm sure he will tell you all you need to know about visiting Bar Harbor and what you should do when you're there."

I started emailing to try to connect with Burt, and I found him to be extremely friendly and enthusiastic about getting together once we got to Bar Harbor. That part was unexpected, as all I really wanted was trip ideas from him.

He gave me his cell phone number and said, "Once you guys get up there, give me a call. If my wife and I are there at our place, we can get with you and do a little sightseeing together."

When we got there, I told Barb about this encounter, and she almost nixed it before it got started. I assured her that my new friend Burt was sincere and not being patronizing. He would, if he was there, be our host for at least a day.

"Okay, Larry. I don't like it, but you can do it. Give him a call," Barb said.

I found that he was in the area for the week, and we made arrangements to meet at the dock in Bar Harbor the next morning, and he would be our host. Burt explained that he was going to be on his boat and that another couple would also be there. The other couple was from back in Pennsylvania, and Burt assured us we should not worry, as they would be nice to us, and we would be nice to them. It wouldn't be a problem, just part of the deal.

So, we met up with him in the morning. He had a brand-new replica of a lobster boat. It wasn't fancy, but it was very serviceable, had some comfortable seats, and was big enough for the six of us. He began to explain that he was going to take us up through this area that was called a fjord. He said it was unusual to be in that area, but it was one of the most unique places he'd ever seen, and he wanted us to see it. It was very peaceful, no waves or anything.

"Hey, would you like to see Martha Stewart's house?" he asked.

"Of course we would," Barb and I exclaimed.

She had recently been in the news for a negative reason, and so we knew she would not be at her place. Instead, she would be spending some forced quality time in a prison somewhere in West Virginia. We pulled up close to her dock and yard. Both the dock and the whole area were incredible. Even though she wasn't there, she had ample staff still scurrying around. The grounds were being attended to and were full of summer flowers and greenery that would only befit somebody quite wealthy.

Once we were finished with our sightseeing at Martha Stewarts' house, it was lunchtime. Burt suggested we go to this place he knew about on Cranberry Island. It was a wonderful oceanside restaurant, and he even treated us, which was not what I was expecting. He was our host, and we couldn't complain, so we politely thanked him. After lunch, Burt looked at Barb and me, his gaze darting back and forth.

"Hey, we have the rest of the day to plan. You can do what you want to, and we will be very happy to comply. My first choice is that you come with us and finish the boat tour, and then we'll go to our island and show you around. We can show you our cottages and the rest of the island. Then a ferry boat will come as late as nine o'clock and pick you up and take you back to Bar Harbor. But if you don't want to do that, we can just go back to Bar Harbor now and drop you off, and you can call it a day."

I expected Barb to go for the latter, but she surprised me.

"Hey, if you guys want to do that, that's wonderful," she said. "That's so kind of you. We'd love to spend the rest of the day with you."

Once we got to the island, Burt explained that he had partnered with a guy who was the conductor of the Philadelphia Pops Orchestra. They somehow got connected with Swan Island back in the '60s, and subsequently found that they could buy land there for $100 an acre. They bought as much as they could afford. They bought land that was adjacent to each other's, and Burt and his family built two cottages, one for themselves and one for their kids, as they hoped they would grow fond of the place.

They did, as they came up there every summer during the '60s. As soon as school was out, his wife would load up the station wagon and take the kids up there, and that's where they spent their summers. Burt would then drive or fly up on the weekends and join them. Their cottages were nice, not luxurious. Each had killer views of the bays and inlets that you could see out on the areas around Swan Island.

By the time we visited, he also had bought the lighthouse at Swan Island. We didn't get to see it, but I can only imagine how scenic that place must be. We got off his boat and walked up into this little town area and then hung a left and eventually got to his two cottages. Barb was beat, and I could understand, so she just hung out there with Burt's wife and the friend's wife. Burt asked me if I wanted to see the rest of the island.

"Of course," I said, and his buddy and I took off up the lane.

"How would you like to see my friend's place? It makes mine look like a shack," Burt said.

I assumed he was kidding, after seeing how nice his place was. He wasn't kidding, though! We went down and looked across this incredible peninsula, and I almost had to hold my breath looking at the log mansion, the tennis courts, a saltwater swimming pool, and the most beautiful view on the entire island. Apparently the owner was an avid tennis player, and I told Burt that I was too.

"Well, let's go down and see if he's here; maybe you can play tennis with him," Burt said.

When we got to the courts, only the caretaker was at the place, so we got a good tour but no tennis. We went back to our cottage, spinning through early evening and dinner.

It still boggles my mind to think about the things we experienced and the adventure we had. An adventure that only happened because I took my brother at his word and took his friend Burt to be as friendly as advertised.

OUR RV

IN 2015, **Barb's health began to deteriorate. She had two dif-ferent strokes, and the last one was around July 4. I remem-ber that specifically, because we spent July 4 in Saint Anne's hospital, and I watched the fireworks from the parking lot, which certainly was the highlight of the experience. Barb was inside and wasn't able to join me when I left for the night. After that, she made a recovery, and we were back home again. We were looking into an uncertain future, but so glad that she was home and on the mend.**

Every Thursday I went to a Realtors' Association meet-ing at the Rusty Bucket restaurant in Westerville. I started out using this meeting to network. A dear friend told me about the meeting in my early years as an insurance agent. He was a realtor, and he said that the meeting had recently opened to folks working in businesses that got involved in real estate transactions. Insurance was certainly one of those, along with home inspectors, lenders, title agencies, attorneys, and others.

He explained that when they met, they always started with breakfast and social time, and then they would do

a formal meeting where they "passed the microphone." Instead of talking to one person at a time, this gave us a chance (in less than 2 minutes) to say who we were and what we did. This meeting became a ritual for me and also became the best way for me to secure new customers.

The eighty-five to one hundred people who attended became like family. We got to learn about each other's businesses, and that alone would have made keeping Thursday mornings free for almost twenty years worthwhile. I tried to sit with different people every week, and after a while, I knew most everyone and they knew me. The little two-minute speech for me was key. I always ended it by saying, "Please call me at 882-FARM."

Early on, I was lucky enough to obtain that distinctive phone number. Before even starting as an agent, I was compelled to gather X-Dates by calling people. An X-Date is short for "expiration date." Someone in the industry found that people were more apt to think about their auto and home insurance when it expired or came due. The thought was that if you had their X-date, you could file it away and call them before their insurance came due again. Auto insurance often comes due every six months, so it was the most important date to have.

One evening, when I was hard at this in my basement office, I thought back to Mr. Gordon, my mentor in the 25-year career I had just left. All the furniture stores had distinctive, easy-to-remember phone numbers, for example: 261-1000, 864-6400.

I thought as I toiled that I should at least try to get

a neat number. Gordon would be proud. It hit me immediately: FARM (3276). Now I just needed to add the Westerville exchange and see what happened. Hopefully, I'd find one that was not currently in use. It was 8:30 p.m. or so when I got this brainchild. I dialed up 882-3276. That was the most popular exchange used for Westerville, and if it didn't work, I still had at least two others to try.

"Please work," I said in a quiet prayer as I dialed.

"The number you have reached is currently out of service," said the recording.

"I can't believe it!" I immediately called the service number for the phone company. Now that I had this info, what could I do with it? I wasn't going to officially start as an agent for at least three more months, so the best I could do was see if I could reserve the number until I actually needed it. The young lady who helped that evening was nothing short of my angel.

"Oh, that is a neat number for you and your new agency. What a lucky day this is. Tell you what, I just did a similar request last week, and I know exactly how to lock it down till you need it," she said.

"Hey, I'll even pay the monthly cost if you'll reserve it," I said.

"Better yet, sir, there will be no cost to you. Your thank you will suffice."

"Can I at least get your name so I can send you flowers or something?" I asked.

"You are so nice, but I can't do that. Company policy."

All of a sudden, I had as good of a phone number as a

State Farm agent could ask for. As soon as I became official, I confirmed the number and opened my agency. I made the number an intrinsic part of every communication. I put it on my answering machine. I put it on my business cards. I was even able to work it onto my outside signage. When asked, I would tell people to call me, not at 882-3276, but 882-FARM. I would have the same number for the next twenty-seven years, and it became like a trademark of sorts.

The real estate meeting is where it paid off the most. After some initial announcements, the pass the mike part would begin. Each person could take a minute or two to introduce themselves, what company they represented, and to give any info they wanted everyone to know. I can't tell you how easily my new phone number rolled off my tongue. It was easy to say and so easy to remember. After a year or two, I asked if I could sponsor a meeting. This was something I thought would work to further deepen the members' recognition of my business. I brought so much giveaway stuff, and all of it had my phone number emblazoned on it. Always up for a little fun, I had a giveaway with a gift card as the prize. I announced this in the form of a trivia question. It was always the same. "Hey guys, what's my phone number?" Hands would go up, and shouts would go out: "882-FARM!" After about the second such meeting, as soon as my audience sensed that I was going to ask my trivia question, I would get the answer blurted out before I even asked.

As time went on, these people provided the referrals that made doing business so much easier. It made taking the two hours every Thursday morning more of a privilege than an obligation. These same folks became my customers as well, and many became close personal friends—lifetime friends.

I saw one member every single week because he was the treasurer and money taker at the front desk when we arrived. Rick Meyer always asked me how Barb was doing because he knew of her situation. One particular day, he just said, "How's Barb doing?"

I said, "She's getting along pretty well as far as I'm concerned. She uses a walker, and we basically can go anywhere we want, either a short trip with a walker or longer trips with a portable wheelchair that we have."

"Why don't you guys just get out of Dodge?" he asked.

"What do you mean?"

"Well, have you ever thought of getting an RV?"

He didn't know it, but a few years before we had this conversation, Barb and I had looked at RVs as a possibility. At the time, I was still in the very busy stage of my agency career, and we went as far as stopping at an RV superstore in Indiana, but that was as far as we got in the process.

Looking at luxury RVs can be intoxicating! It wasn't until I learned that it would take the price of a house to buy such a rig that the rush wore off. While we were still in the showroom and Barb was taking a bathroom break, I came upon a more reasonably priced alternative. Open for inspection was a thirty-three-foot travel trailer. It had a feature that made me drool. In the rear were "opposing" slide outs that, when fully open, made a great room with a forty-six-inch flatscreen TV and two power recliners. On the outside was a full power awning. Instead of $250K plus, it was under $50K. *Perfect*, I thought. I showed it to Barb and was surprised that she loved it too.

In the next few weeks, I studied the specs on this model and tried every way I could to come up with a viable plan. I wanted it, and Barb was on the team. However, as she and I had become a well-oiled machine, I always played the part of the accelerator and she the brakes.

"Larry, our Jeep probably won't pull such a big trailer, right?"

"Sadly, you are right. I've been checking, and it will likely take either the biggest, most powerful SUV, or better yet, an HD truck."

"How much do those cost?"

"They're sixty thousand and up."

"Then we can stop the process right there, dear. I do our money, and we would be pushed just to buy the trailer, let alone a new vehicle to tow it with."

Crestfallen, I made one last attempt to find a tow vehicle that was more reasonably priced. I looked everywhere and found a dually truck at a dealership in the north end of Newark. I talked Barb into joining me. The truck was an HD diesel. Barb and I climbed (no exaggeration) into the cab and started it up. It already had 254K miles on it, but the dealer said that was not a problem, as the diesel motor could easily double that and still be a great vehicle.

"What year is it?" Barb asked.

I could tell that she was quickly accumulating the data needed to apply the brakes and say no.

"Sir . . . and ma'am, I have one more vehicle I'd like to

show you. I just took it in on trade yesterday. It's newer, has far fewer miles, and is much more comfortable to drive."

"Come on, Larry, let's get on with our day," Barb said, starting to sound testy. "The truck was going to cost thirty-five thousand and was eight years old. This one will still be used, and I'm quite sure I won't like it."

"Please, dear. Let's look at it, and I won't press unless it's perfect."

The salesman pointed across the lot. "It's a Ford Expedition. See it over there? It's the Eddie Bauer edition, which is top of the line. It has a Cummins diesel and a heavy-duty suspension and four-wheel drive. It only has seventy-five thousand miles on it and is also only five years old."

"How much?" I asked.

"Just thirty thousand, and I think I can talk the boss down a little. Let me show it to you guys. I'm sure it's what you've been looking for."

"You can go. I'll be in the car," my wife announced.

"Honey! Sorry for your trouble, sir, but our day here is done," I said.

"No worries. If you change your mind, here's my card. It won't last long, though."

Our first look at RVs had plenty of ups and downs. It was not quite right for us then, but we both loved the idea.

While Barb wasn't completely well, Rick mentioning an RV to me at the meeting that morning got my wheels turning. As soon as I got home, I said something to Barb about it, and she was surprisingly very positive.

"If I could get into one successfully, I'm sure I would love the travel part. Find us one with easy steps, and I might really be on board."

I immediately started going online and doing my research, finding out how much they cost and what you could get for the money. I found out in a hurry that they were expensive, but at this point in our lives, we could at least consider doing something like that. We had navigated the hard years at the beginning of my agency, and now we could afford such a vehicle if we wanted one. What made this all the more interesting was that Barb was on board. It was something that we could do together, and the uncertain future was the one thing that drove me to want to do this the most. I didn't know if we had one year or twenty left together, but I knew that doing something we really enjoyed was the best way to spend whatever time we had.

I quickly found an RV that was located in Zanesville. It was pretty amazing. It was called a Fleetwood Bounder, and it was a thirty-seven-foot monster but really had some cool features. Barb and I had listed some things that we might want in an RV, and this one seemed to have them all. Not only did it have a largeness to it because it was thirty-seven feet long, but it had three slides.

Slides are the neatest things. From the inside, you can just push a button, and a part of the side of the RV is designed to slide out, thus expanding the space inside. This can only be done when the rig is parked, as driving with a slide out would be quite dangerous. The Bounder had one slide on the driver's side that made a narrow booth into a spacious dining table. Then there were two in the back that were called opposing slides. They formed a master bedroom when pulled out together that sported a king-size bed and a full-size bathroom with a shower that a wheelchair could easily get into, or that Barb could navigate well with her walker. It had a large closet and was laid out super well, period.

Up front, another slide opened up and became a dinette, and it was easy to imagine sitting there when we were stopped. The additional feature up front was a half bath that could be used when we were traveling. I figured Barb would have to make several stops, and getting back to that master bath would have been a real problem because the slides, when closed, had very narrow openings if you needed to make your way to the very back. Having this one in the middle made it easy to stop, have Barb use it, and then get back on the road in a hurry. That was perfect.

Before we actually went to Zanesville, we stopped at a local RV store. I had a good experience there, but I didn't find anything that seemed to match the features that the one in Zanesville had. We did establish that the price on the Zanesville one was fair, and that was one thing that I certainly wanted to accomplish. The ones at the local lot would all be pretty hard for Barb to get in and out of. Our goal was to find one that would work for her.

After that visit, it was set in our minds which one we needed, so we simply drove over to Zanesville where we had an appointment with the people who were selling it. They met us at Dillon State Park, and they actually had staged the RV with a tablecloth and wine before we arrived.

I have to say that it was beyond cool. We found it hard to resist. Barb got in it very easily because the steps were actually laid out and easy for her to get up and down. The people had added a safety device because they often traveled with one of their moms, and she was elderly and needed that assistance. This was a plus for us once they showed us how to use it.

We were smitten and made an offer on the spot. We drove home recounting how easily we had made a very expensive decision. It seemed serendipitous! I decided to come the next week with the money to pick up our new prize.

I got my "office wife" and wonderful staff person, Nan, to join me to pick it up. She drove me over and made sure I got everything accomplished, and then she drove back to the office in my car while I was left to drive my thirty-seven-foot monster.

I insisted that the owner give me a brief lesson, and believe me when I tell you it was *brief*. We maneuvered it around the parking lot at Dillon State Park, which was not all that hard. I bravely got on the road and headed back to my office. The first 95 percent of the trip went extremely well because I was on wide, straight roads that were easy to maneuver. On the last 5 percent, I quickly learned that my new toy was very large and very hard to maneuver in tight places. My office was on Central College Road, which was narrow, bumpy, and had very little clearance on either side of it. Then I encountered the driveway to my office where I was going to keep it. Making a right angle turn off a narrow road to an even narrower driveway in a vehicle that big...

not easy! Next was another right turn to the smaller drive in front of my garage. I knew my parking lot would be great, but maneuvering back to it with a thirty-seven-foot, bus-like vehicle never crossed my mind when designing it. It had just rained, and I was pretty sure parking it on the grassy area to the west would be a disaster.

I made my right turn as wide as I possibly could, and I thought I had it made. But I quickly realized how wrong I was. I found out that I had managed to get the back right tire in the culvert that was beside the driveway. Even though this was potentially a bad move, I was able to power it out of there and got back to my driveway. After fifteen minutes consisting of many small turns, I finally got it parked. I was exhausted by this time, but I was also realizing that I did this all by myself. With mixed feelings, ranging from exhilaration to nausea, I got out and stood with the monster in full view.

"This damn thing is huge," was all I could utter.

I took a look at any damage that I might have done in the ill-fated turn. It was minimal, but I did realize that I had torn the side off of the outside back tire. No problem—I'd just get it fixed. Well, $660 later, I got a new tire on it, and that was my first inkling that incidents/mistakes with this vehicle were going to be costly. But I laughed it off as a good experience, and Barb and I were soon on our first trip.

We headed to Petoskey, Michigan. My friend Don Gardner told me about a place he had seen there on his travels called the Petoskey Motor Coach Resort. Getting there was a bit of an adventure, of course, because it was my initial foray in the RV on a major trip.

Barb and I did have a bit of a maiden run to a place called Cardinal Campground just north of Columbus. We invited all the kids, and this was the first time they had ever seen the vehicle. As you might imagine, everybody was very curious and excited, and while we were there, we stayed overnight, had a campfire, enjoyed each other's company, and then the kids got to drive home and sleep in their own beds. Barb and I had a wonderful time, found that everything on the RV worked as advertised, and we were soon ready to take our first big trip.

Getting to Michigan proved to be quite an adventure. Route 23 near Findlay, all the way over and up to Ann Arbor, Michigan, was under construction. There I was, driving down a road at sixty-five to seventy miles per hour in what was essentially a bus. On my right, seemingly inches away from the vehicle, was a cement barrier about two-and-a-half to three-feet wide. On the left, inches away, was the passing lane, or truck lane as you might call it. In that lane, it seemed like every two seconds an eighteen-wheeler was whizzing by going seventy-five to eighty miles per hour. It was terrifying, as you might imagine, and I prayed out loud. Barb could hear me call upon the Lord to get me through that portion of the trip. It seemed never-ending, and we spent almost two hours making it through that kind of driving.

Once we got north of this construction zone, things opened up, and the rest of the drive was incredibly nice. It was on a boulevard-type highway where there was nobody in your lane except you. In the middle, you couldn't even see the other lane. The median was pine-covered, and the southbound lanes were never even visible.

We finally got to our destination, and it was just as nice, if not nicer, than Don thought it might be. We were on a late check-in, so we got our check-in packet from an after-hours box and headed to our site.

Backing up a vehicle like that RV is a task I don't recommend for beginners. In a normal camping situation, there would be a co-pilot/passenger to exit and help guide you on the back-in. My Barb couldn't do that, so I was on my own. I tried to use the mirrors and the backup camera, everything to make sure that I didn't hit anything. I had plenty of room to back into our driveway, which was actually a cement drive, and yet I managed to clip off a light that was there, put up by the management to light the way in the evenings, and also to warn people like me not to get too far off the track. I bent it over good!

It was late but still light out. Campers were outside enjoying the beautiful autumn weather. A guy in the next bay over saw my dilemma, came over, and banged on my window and alerted me that he would help me back in. Fortunately, I found that (with help) it's not very hard to back in, and I was able to do that pretty quickly. I got out and assessed the damage and found it was mostly damage to the light, with only about 1 percent to the vehicle. Nothing I would ever, ever even think about fixing; it was just a little scrape. This was the first of many "incidents" that I managed to have in my travels with this vehicle. I took a cellphone photo of the damage to the light, and in the morning, I walked over to the office and was greeted by a very pleasant lady in charge. I showed her the damage to the light.

"Oh, don't worry about it," she said. "This happens all the time. It's our pleasure to let you pass on this one."

I thanked her profusely and got on my way. We couldn't have had a better trip. We rented a car the next morning from Enterprise. They came and picked us up, and we were able to begin to look at the area with fondness. Seeing it through eyes that weren't concerned about a young family was refreshing, since on previous trips we were tent camping with small kids. I was able to golf once at a beautiful golf course called Little Traverse Bay Golf Club. It was unbelievable with both the golf and the view of Little Traverse Bay. We fell in love with northern Michigan all over again and couldn't wait to get back.

Heading back south to get home, I was so terrified about the construction area that I asked for directions to see if I could get around that area and go home a different way. I did manage to find an alternate route, and although the drive back was not much fun because we had to go through Detroit, we did avoid that construction area. What mattered most was that we made it home with everything in one piece.

PENNSYLVANIA VISIT

SINCE I GREW UP in southwestern Pennsylvania, I wanted to take my new rig there as soon as possible. Connellsville was less than a four-hour drive, and there were some scenic parks to go to. I could show off the RV to Dave and Carol, our long-time friends from high school, my sister, Linda, and her husband, Roger, and anyone else I could think of.

I made arrangements to stay at the Yogi Bear campground in Mill Run. I had two reasons for choosing it. First, I knew the area from my childhood and wanted to show that off to Barb. Second, it was owned by a family I knew. Randy, his sister, and their parents bought the property years before for a ridiculously low price. The campground part came as they learned of the Yogi Bear franchise, and 90-plus percent of the owners were uber successful.

I met with Randy when we got there. I asked him if his sister Glenda ever got up there. She and I were friends from way back in grade school. Interestingly, our mothers were the best of friends when they were little.

"Glenda is up here right now, helping me with our

busy time. How about I have her stop over for a visit?"

"How great is that?" I said to Barb happily.

Glenda came over and stayed for two hours. What a bonus opportunity. When we started talking about our moms, a sad discrepancy in our lives came up. My mom died at age thirty-eight. Her mom was still alive. She got to spend over fifty more years with her mom than I did with mine. Good for her. Not so good for me.

The other thing Barb and I got to do was visit Connellsville. Linda came up and got us, as unhooking the beast for a drive down the mountains was not a good option. It probably took me at least a half hour to get the motorhome all hooked up and ready to be used. I had to hook up the water supply, the electric connection, and the sewer piping. Easy for an expert, but not so much for a rookie like me. The campsite was not quite level, so I had to use the built-in levelers. Just pulling in was hard enough. Also, if we unhooked it for such a visit, the return trip would be made in the dark, making the whole process much harder.

Turns out, lots of my cousins were in town. Fred lived at his mom's place on Franklin Avenue. Craig was visiting from Hawaii. Mark was in from Maryland. Linda arranged some time together at our Aunt Betty's place. We were all gathered around the big kitchen table reminiscing. It was special, as our two remaining aunts were there, several cousins, plus my little sister.

Afterward, I asked Fred and Sherry if they wanted to do a two-fer. They could drive us back up the mountain and stay for the evening, giving us the rare chance to catch up with each other. Since we lived in Ohio, we didn't get to see them that often. On the way, I gave them an earful of what was happening with us and our kids.

Then I asked Fred to give us an update on their lives, since we hadn't seen them since their pop-in visit back in the seventies. "It's sad but true, Larry. He we are, first cousins. We have sent each other Christmas cards all these years and talked on the phone a time or two, but we really haven't visited face-to-face since then!"

I was amazed, but what he said was true. I then made a half-hearted attempt at adding humor to the moment. "Do we have a day or two, Barb?"

We all laughed, but we knew that it would take that long if we really got into talking about our lives.

"All right, Larry. We'll do the highlights for sure, how about that?"

"Fred, I remember a lot from our last visit, but how about you help Barb and me out, starting from when Sherry was with you in your reserve unit."

"I was hoping you would get us to a point where I wasn't repeating our story. I'll start there. Sherry's skill was in administration. I gave her the oath of office in the commander's office, with Greg sitting on the desk and Sherry standing beside it near the American flag, her hand raised. I got a nice picture of that, with her and Greg together—pretty special. Greg was probably only about three years old. A couple weeks later, she went to her two-week training. Mom came up and watched Greg during the day. Sherry would come home, and then she would start coming to our unit. She did quite well. She decided that she wanted to become an officer.

"Shortly after she got in, she was in a meeting and was told that because she had college experience, she could have enlisted as an officer. Sherry then was told by her officer that she could have become one, and he asked her why she wasn't enrolled. 'Well, it's because my husband didn't tell me I could be enrolled as an officer,' she said. So, I told her she'd become an officer when I told her. I made her take three command courses and learn certain things before I'd let her apply to become an officer. Because of her experience in college, with time, she was commissioned as a captain in the US Army. Actually, she was made a first lieutenant. That's when we couldn't always be in the same unit. The military tried to keep couples in the same unit. Even when they joined the active army, they were guaranteed their first assignment would at least be together. In the reserves, they tried to keep them together as much as possible. Most of the time we had such different skills that we would be in different units. Every time she was interviewed, she held her own for sure and was easily given new positions. She did well for twenty-two years."

"Did you also have a civilian job during this time, Fred?" I asked.

"All during this time, I worked for the 99th Arkham. Right toward the end, I opened up my computer store and got out of the military. That was the time when I already had my twenty years in. About a year after that, I got completely out of the Army Reserve and retired. That was 1989—I served from 1965 to 1989."

"When you were getting army pay toward the end of your career, would you consider that good money?"

"Larry, I retired as a lieutenant colonel, and the decent money started coming when I made major. Yes, I would say I did make decent pay. As a civilian, I went from a GS7 to a GS9. Yeah, it was decent. We got decent raises also."

"Would you say it was comparable to an experienced teacher, or better?"

"I would say certainly equivalent to, if not a little bit better."

"Also, wouldn't benefits be very good?"

"Yes, when you reached age sixty, you could draw your military retirement. So, we didn't have to necessarily save into individual accounts like IRAs and things like that. The money we had saved up in various ways, we decided to take it in one lump sum when we got out. Because of the number of years and the ranks we attained, our retirements were very good."

"You guys deserved it!"

"Sometimes I think that the benefits should have been even better. One of the things that the US Army says, is if you serve twenty years and retire honorably, you have medical the rest of your life. Well, what they meant was you have basic medical. We're not covered under vision or dental. That was a misunderstanding of young soldiers. Being a combat veteran, I was able to get eye coverage. Sherry is not a combat veteran, so she doesn't get vision. Also, Sherry is not eligible for VA because she wasn't a twenty-year plus combat veteran."

"Fred, I have a question about something. Did you get exposed to Agent Orange when you were in Vietnam?"

"Everybody in Vietnam was exposed to Agent Orange. Yeah, all bases were sprayed around perimeters. Each base had to have an area where no enemy could come into it with short-range weapons and attack directly. Onan Air Force Base, the field of fire, was about half a mile. To create that, and clear all that vegetation, they used Agent Orange. So, if you were in or about an Air Force Base, you definitely got the effects of Agent Orange. Both of my tours in Vietnam were in and about Air Force bases, so I definitely was exposed, Larry. Also, I was exposed when I did a sortie into the Asho Valley. That was a mission I haven't told you about, but I will. That was a mission to recover bodies. All the vegetation was destroyed in that area, and everything had dust on it, and if you brushed any of the vegetation, everything was blown up into the air, so unless you were the first man through the vegetation, you were gonna breathe it."

"Would you wanna elaborate on that mission or not?"

"Larry, after I got PTSD, I could hardly talk about anything like that. I still go once a month and talk to a psychiatrist. Anyway, when I was at the US Army Mortuary, the second trip we had to go out on search-and-recovery missions. It required an officer and an NCO and a couple of other soldiers. With only two officers underneath me instead of four, if we had recovery missions, every other time one of those officers had to go. I felt that wasn't quite fair, so we set up a schedule where they would go out twice, alternating normally, and then I would go out, then they would go out twice and I would go out. So I went on quite a few recovery missions. We probably had half a dozen a month of those."

"What were they like, Fred? Were you going into an area that was totally unknown to you, finding bodies haphazardly, or did you already know where they were?"

"We already knew where they were, roughly. This one mission was to recover the body of two pilots who had been in a Cobra helicopter. They had gone into the jungle. They were shot down in 1966 and were never found until this small unit of Vietnamese soldiers came across the site. They marked on their maps where it was and reported it through channels. It came down to us that we would have to go into the Asho Valley and recover these bodies and return them.

"Asho Valley was not a place to be, no matter where or when. It was totally controlled by the Vietcong and North Vietnamese regulars. So we were sent out in a helicopter. Right before we got there, a ground unit of security was flown to set up security for us when we landed. Then, after we landed, another group of engineers was brought out. They had to set explosives on the Cobra to totally destroy it so it couldn't be used by the enemy. We got there and were led by the Vietnamese who had actually found the place. We had to hike up this mountain. This is in a triple canopy jungle, which most of Vietnam was. So, we trekked up this mountainside.

"We didn't have to search too much because the Vietnamese soldier was fairly close to where the site was. Now, the Cobra helicopter that had crashed actually crashed upside down, on its head. So it was lying on its top, belly up. We had to break through the belly to the cockpit and bring out the remains. But, as you can imagine, Larry, by this time, the remains were all bones and nothing else. Now, when you go out on a search-and-recovery, you have to make a map of the area. While the NCO and the soldiers were getting through the belly, I was getting drawings of the area, making markings of where the helicopter lay and where we had to break through it and bring the bones up. The NCO and the two soldiers retrieved all the bones. We placed them in sandbag sacks. That's how we recovered them. Now, when you handle any remains, you handle them with gentleness and with reverence. Believe me, it might sound crude that we put them in sandbag sacks, but that was just the way it was."

"What else could you do?"

"Right, each pilot was put into two sacks. One sack couldn't hold one body. After this was done, the engineers set explosives in order to destroy the helicopter. This Cobra helicopter still had two pods of active rockets on each side of it, so we couldn't allow those to be left in place. That was one of the main things that had to be exploded. Once the charges were set, we had to run like hell down that mountainside so we didn't get blown up. There's only so much time that you can put on those charges, so we did not have the leisurely walk down. We got ourselves down, jumped behind some fallen trees, and we just managed to do that before the explosion went off.

"Boy, bits and pieces of that craft went flying everywhere. Debris was landing all around us. That was a day that I didn't like at all, Larry. We got it done. The security team had their own choppers. Half the security team was sitting there at the mouth of the Asho Valley—light infantry security and no helicopter. We needed two helicopters to really handle the amount of people we had. It wasn't one of those big Chinook helicopters, it was really just a small chopper. One Huey showed up. We all got in, barely, but we were definitely overloading it. So, when we left, it was just turning dark, we're in an overloaded helicopter, and flying barely over the tops of the trees. That was an anxious time for me and all the guys who were with me. They managed to make a funny light moment from it. We usually tried to do that. As we were riding out of the valley, I look at the soldier handling the door gun. I noticed that he had a second lieutenant bar on his shoulder, so I said, 'Oh, shit, that tells me that the door gunner is flying the helicopter. Turns out the helicopter pilots like to handle the guns, and here we are being flown out, and we really have a sergeant flying our Huey."

"The other light moment was when we landed at Phu Bai. We had to get on a plane to take us down to Saigon. We were always the first on board when we were handling military remains. Our flight was called. We headed out to the aircraft, and we were loading out. The pilot in charge said to us, 'Wait a minute, you guys were supposed to be taking out human remains. Where are the stretchers? Where are the remains?' The two soldiers handling the sandbags held them up and said, 'Here they are.' The pilot says, 'Oh shit, get on the plane.'"

"Sorry I asked, right?"

"That was definitely the worst mission I ever went on."

"I understand. You've seen a lot. Fred, will you tell me about the effects of PTSD?"

"Give me a moment, Larry. I'm trying to get it together. That's a reality that I've rarely liked to talk about."

"I think it's important."

"I do too, Larry, but I don't normally discuss this with non-military personnel."

"Sure, I can understand that."

"That's why I'm hesitating. Well, actually, I can go back to when I first got out. That's when I had some really bad dreams. I had nightmares every night. When I would go on my reserve weekends, which were two weeks each, I would get really bad dreams and wake up thinking I was back in Vietnam. I found out that what I was dreaming about was very common to soldiers. I dreamed that I was captured, that I was being held captive, tortured. Even though I was in a position where I had not experienced true combat, I did see many things I didn't ever want to. I didn't tell you some of the things that happened to me on my first tour, where I was actually shot at. But right now, that's inconsequential. Those first dreams were about being captured. After a while, they went away, but it took a couple of years. I would have them especially during the weekends.

"A lot of times we weren't out in the field. We were in the reserve centers. Mostly, these dreams happened when I was out on bivouacs. We did that routine more and more as time went on, because they wanted us to get more involved with outdoor activities, which was outdoor training, or bivouacs."

"What exactly is a bivouac?"

"Sorry, a little military jargon there. It's like a temporary campsite, but almost never with any kind of tent or shelter."

"Thanks, sir. I probably should have known that. Please continue."

"There, training was more extensive. We did that in mock gear, but that gear was very uncomfortable and heavy. During the most intense periods, you might not eat for eight hours. You'd only have water. When I retired in 1989, the dreams stopped after a while. Then, when I was around sixty-eight, they started back again. My psychiatrist and I agreed that they weren't happening previously mostly because I wasn't put in any kind of position where I would be remembering anything about Vietnam. I cannot watch many movies about Vietnam. So, I just stayed away from them. Nevertheless, even some episodes of *M*A*S*H* would trigger stuff for me. Twice a month, I go to group meetings with other folks who have PTSD. With those people, you find out what's common and what's not. For sure what I had was very common. My dreams really got worse at this time. I would see mangled, almost zombielike soldiers chasing me. That would wake me up in the middle of the night screaming. Especially when I first got out. These dreams would drive Sherry up the wall, as you can imagine."

"How awful, Fred!"

"My other dream was about all the bloody uniforms that we had to burn in the personal property depot. I would dream about the limbs of the soldiers that we would have to burn because at the mortuary we had an incinerator. We got bodies that were in pieces. They came in on stretchers and in body bags in most cases. We would take the human remains out of the body bags and put them on a table. And as I say, there were lots of times that arms and legs were separated. They would be removed and put into separate bags and marked with the same number that we had for the soldier we were processing. Once we got enough of those parts, as they were called, we would have to incinerate them. When the hospitals would amputate limbs, they would put them in coolers, and we would put them in bags. Then we would, in a lighthearted way, on something that shouldn't have been treated that way, call them 'spare parts.' Once, we had a commander come in and we were counting bags. The bags would have numbers on them: X-5, X-27, etc. He was counting the names on the board, and he kept coming up with one extra. First, I couldn't figure out the difference. Finally, it dawned on me what it was, and I said, 'Oh, this is the bag of spare parts.' The commander about fainted. He said, 'What do you mean, spare parts?'

"'My apologies, sir, but that's what we call them. There are spare limbs that come from the hospital when amputations are made.' So I'd have dreams about that. It got to the point where I could hardly do anything during the day because of those dreams I was having at night.

"I became very upset. Our son Brian was down visiting one day. He and I took a walk, just to keep me calm. Just one street off of Virginia Street, where I live, this lady came out of her house and asked what we were doing. I think she thought we were casing her area. I read her up one side, down the other, and scared the crap out of her."

"Wow!"

"After we got back to the house, we were in the back, sitting on the patio. Brian could tell I was upset, as I was shaking like hell and feeling really bad. Mostly it was because of what I said to that woman. It really hit me how rude I had been once I got back home, and that really upset me. I told Brian, 'I'm gonna go back up and talk to that lady, explain who I am and what just happened.'

"'No, no, let's not do that. Let's not go back there.'

"I told him we had to. So, we went back up. I knocked on her door, introduced myself properly, and apologized. I showed her my US Army ID card. I told her that I was so sorry about what I had done. I also tried to school her on what she had done wrong. I decided to tell her, 'The sad thing is, if I had been armed, I probably would have shot you. That's certainly not what we would want to have happened, but if you ever find somebody you can't identify in your yard, please just call the police. Let them handle it.' She accepted my apologies. I felt so much better after that."

"Fred, I can't tell you how proud I am as I hear all of this. I'm sure she understood, as it was a wonderful gesture that you went back and spoke with her. I'm guessing it also made Brian more understanding of what was going on."

"Yes. As it turned out, Brian did understand. Shortly after that, our older son, Greg, came up and visited. I think he came because Brian called him. When he got there, I told him I wanted him to take my pistol. Greg said, 'Dad, you shouldn't necessarily have to do that.' I said, 'No, you take it. I'm telling you right now, you take it.' I was in such a bad state that I thought I might injure myself with it. I was afraid I was gonna kill myself. Larry, I wasn't planning on hurting anybody else, but I sure could have hurt myself. So, he took my pistol. I went to my VA right after that and said I needed help. That's when they started treating me for PTSD and anxiety. They wouldn't just call it PTSD. They had to add the anxiety part on as well. The VA still doesn't truly understand PTSD, even though they probably wouldn't admit that."

"I'd say you're right on that. So, Fred, now that you've received official treatment, do you think it's been helping you?"

"Oh, most definitely, most definitely! Besides that, I've gotten into a group that's called Healing Waters. It's a fishing-themed group. They first started by teaching us to tie flies. When you're sitting there doing that, your mind just goes blank. You don't think about anything except tying that fly. They take us on trips on the weekends, fishing trips. We fish and enjoy each other's company. It's very calming, very healing, very great. They've done as much as the group therapy and the psychiatry have done together. It calms me down so much. I'm at the point right now that when I can get together with other soldiers who have had PTSD, and with my fly-tying buddies, that's all I need."

"Fred, that's great! In fact, very great!"

"I started taking medication, and then it took me about a year before I could really tell my psychiatrist about all the things that happened to me. Talking with you today,

I probably haven't told you even a third of what really happened to me. I'll admit to you that I still have one thing that I haven't discussed with my psychiatrist. I'm not gonna tell you. Greg doesn't even know. Funny thing about it is that I talked to Greg— because he's already a soldier—about some of these things before I even talked to the psychiatrist about them. He's another military man, so we can get together. The psychiatrist I have never served in the military, so he really can't be fully qualified. But he's worked a lot with soldiers with PTSD, so he's gonna help as much as anybody can. He served for twenty years. He has also talked to soldiers who have come back from Afghanistan. One of the first things he did to me was apologize for never being in the service. I told him immediately not to ever apologize. You have no reason to. You're doing more to help the soldiers now then you could have if you had served in active military."

"Absolutely, Fred, that's a great point. So, what has the Agent Orange done to your body?"

"Well, I have diabetes. Which has also given me neuropathy. I have tingling in my legs and my feet all the time, constantly. When I got the neuropathy, it was very difficult to drive. I had to learn real quick, mentally, that my foot's on the accelerator. And we're going at a certain speed, and honestly, Larry, I can't feel my foot on the accelerator. I had to learn when to push my foot forward, even though I couldn't feel it. And when to switch from the accelerator to the brake. So, I drive much differently than I used to when I was younger. I try to know where I'm at and what

I'm doing at all times. Funny thing about it, this happened to my friend, the sergeant major I met in Connellsville. He even stopped driving for a while. I didn't understand that until I got neuropathy myself. It was down for a while, but it's getting really intense more recently. Monday, I have an appointment with my dietitian. I've got my medicine increased temporarily until I can get this neuropathy down to a manageable level. It's not dangerous, but it's too high. I take two medicines a day for my diabetes, and I don't have to take insulin, thankfully."

"What about cancer, Fred?"

"I had a test last year, and they found no cancer in me. There was really no reason to give me the test, but I felt it was necessary. They thought it was the proper thing to do as well, so I took the test, and I'm very relieved to tell you that I'm cancer free! I felt very good about that. I certainly want to keep it that way. I've got many friends who do have it. I'm of the opinion, as well as most of my friends, that if it ever got that bad, and the doctors could give me drugs to prolong my life for another year and a half or so, I would not take the medicine."

"Fred, I understand, and I totally agree with you that if I have that fate myself, I wanna do the same thing. I consider you one hundred percent a hero, Fred. I respect that I got a chance to talk to you again."

"Larry, there were some really good times too. Those good times kept me going. I feel very good about the service that I performed. Getting the soldiers to their correct next of kin was so important. I can tell you a few instances where it was possible that we were going to make a mistake. I sent notes ahead that I would not be satisfied completely until the FBI could make an identification through prints. Any time that happened and a mistake was made, the news would get a hold of it, and they would certainly use it to create ill will between the public and the service sector. Which I did not want, of course. I'm happy to say that no one left Vietnam misidentified under my command. I feel very good that everyone who got buried by their next of kin was the correct person."

"Fred, I could continue for hours more," I said, realizing how long I had kept him talking and worrying that I was wearing him out, and that the girls were most likely getting tired. "All the stuff we have been talking about has been great for me. I hope it was for you, as well. Let's see if the girls are still awake."

"Larry, I don't get many opportunities to open up like this, so thank you, for sure. I appreciate you listening to me for so long."

We soon realized the girls had gone outside and had a glass of wine, and they were busy enjoying the crisp fall evening.

"Guys, this has been so great," I said to Fred and Sherry. "Barb and I appreciate the ride back and all the catching up we got to do. Hope we can keep in touch better! Have a safe trip down the mountain."

A MYSTERY

THE NEXT YEAR, after having taken many more trips in the RV, we decided to go back to Michigan. This time we chose to go to a campsite on the opposite side of Petoskey that we'd read about online. The website made the camp look beautiful, and it had everything we were looking for. We loved the motor resort, but we wanted a place that would allow a wood fire, and the motor resort did not. They allowed propane fire, but we did not have a propane fire pit. So we signed up for a promising week and went on to the new campsite. We also began what would become the adventure of our lives.

We rented a car and began exploring. One of the places we found was a beautiful restaurant that was close to a small lake outside of Petoskey in Harbor Springs. At that restaurant, we sat in a booth that had a high wooden back. It was very private for each couple, except that you could hear any conversation that was going on near you. The couple in the next booth was having a heated discussion. I couldn't tell what it was about, but I instantly recognized the voice.

How could that be? I hadn't heard that voice for probably fifty years. I whispered to Barb to tell her who I thought I was hearing. Naturally, she shook her head and rolled her eyes, because she knew that I had done this before with uncanny success.

"Barb, that's him. It's the same guy who was in the restaurant in Dayton when we were there with your brother."

Once again, I got eye rolls and sighs.

"I've got to check this out," I said. I got up and walked to the other end of the aisle. I turned around and there he was, my old friend Trey Chappelear, sitting next to a lady. I said something right away, and I got pretty much the same result I got fifty years ago, though with a slightly different twist.

"Hey, Trey," I said with a casual wave.

"Who are you talking about? And what the f*** is it to you, anyway?"

The difference in encounters was that this time he denied being Trey. I decided to go one step further, as I was sure I was right. He stared me down with a look that could kill.

"You're mistaken! That's not my name—now, get the hell outta here. Get out of my face or I'll pop you," he snarled.

I wasn't surprised by his attitude, but I wasn't sure why he would deny who he was. I was just an innocent tourist making a chance meeting with an old acquaintance. I certainly wouldn't be able to do anything for him or against him.

I decided I would back up a little bit and nonchalantly take a picture of him. Once again, I had plans to reminisce with Dave, and I wanted a picture so I could send it to him.

So I took the picture, and Trey jumped up in my face.

"Hey, why are you taking that picture? Nobody takes a picture of me! Give me your phone."

He was scaring me now, just like he did when we were in high school. A much bigger and stronger guy than I had ever been, Trey was still intimidating all these years later. However, I'd always felt that I could take care of myself if ever provoked. In a rare moment of belief in myself, I came up with a comeback.

"Don't flatter yourself, pal. I was taking a picture of myself, a selfie, so I could get in the scenery behind me. Can you see the scenery there behind me?"

I walked away, still unsure why he was so insistent that I should not take a picture of him. I was just relieved that he hadn't popped me, as I was, uncharacteristically, being the jerk this time. Barb gave me another "look" as I sat back down. I could hear Trey talking to his lady friend. They abruptly got up and took off. I heard the waitress yelling at them, "You forgot to pay your bill."

"Screw you!" was his response, and they headed straight out the door. After a minute or so, we heard wheels squealing as they beat a hasty retreat. I was turned the wrong way, so I had Barb look and see if she saw them.

"Larry, I didn't see them and probably wouldn't have recognized them anyway."

"Could you tell what he was driving, just in case we ever need to know?"

"Why in the world would we ever need to know something like that? It was a red pickup truck, though. Whatever the emblem is that looks like a keystone, that's the kind it is."

"I just have a hunch that we should know what vehicle he drives. It was such a strange encounter. Sorry if I'm being paranoid."

Upon leaving, we found out by listening to the wait staff that Trey and his friend had left abruptly without paying. I asked if anybody knew who they were, hoping to get a positive ID and satisfy my curiosity. Because they didn't pay, they didn't use a card, and nobody knew who they were, as they had never been in before.

After we left, I pretty much brushed off the encounter and decided it was just that; an encounter. We decided to go around the lake and hit Young State Park. It was a place near and dear to us, as it was where we camped with our kids many, many years ago. When we were over there, just driving around, Barb noticed a red pickup truck.

"Could that be your friend?"

They had a nice camp set up with a tent and everything.

"I'm guessing not, because most of the time, jerks don't camp. Campers are typically pretty nice folks, so I'm guessing that's not our friend."

We found our old campsite. We took a picture of it, got out, and tromped over the land and imagined the spot where our son, Drew, dug to China when we were there all those years ago. What fun we'd had building those memories with our children!

Later, we got back to our RV after a good day of sightseeing that left us tired but happy. I got our camp chairs out and built a fire in the fire pit, which was behind our unit and facing away from the driveway. We could see all sorts of activities going on. Kids were playing, and adults were chatting it up with each other.

It appeared that the people who were near us were all friends. They kept interacting with each other, their kids were playing together, and everybody seemed to be having a great time. It almost looked like a big family reunion. I spotted a young man who was closest to us. He happened to be behind his unit, very near to us, and hanging up some wet clothing from their day at the lake.

As with all camping adventures, I wanted to get acquainted with everybody near us. It's amazing how friendly people are and how much they let their guard down when they're out camping. It's one of the neatest things that we've experienced in our lifetime, and I expected this time to be no different.

"Hey, how are you doing?" I asked.

"I'm great, how about you?"

"I see you guys all seem to be friends here at the camp-site. What's going on? I'm just curious."

"Well, we're all from Canada, and we come down here about every three weeks to spend long weekends. Our shifts are such that we get to have a three- or four-day weekend every once in a while, and what better place to come than this?"

"Where in Canada are you from?"

"A place called Sault Ste Marie."

"I've heard of that. There is also a Sault Ste Marie in Michigan, right?"

"Yep, they're right across the border from each other. Getting down here only takes a few hours, and we just love coming here."

"So you're all friends?"

"Yep."

"Do you all work at the same place?"

I was trying not to pry too much, but I found this to be interesting stuff, and as long as I wasn't getting any resistance, I figured I'd keep going.

"Yep, we're law enforcement. We work for the Canadian police. Some of us are local, and some of us are provincial. We are all about the same age. We've known each other for years, and we have kiddos the same age. They like coming here with each other."

I liked the way this was proceeding, very friendly. "How many kids do you have?" I asked.

"I have three, but only two of them are here."

"What about the other one?"

"He is off in the Philadelphia area right now on a trip with the Canadian junior hockey team."

"Wow, how old is he?"

"He's sixteen. He's a really good hockey player, probably capable of getting a scholarship, and then we'll hopefully see him on a farm team, and maybe, crossing my fingers here, someday in the NHL."

"Wow, that's great. Did you play hockey?"

"Yes, I did too. I went to Laureation, back home in Ontario. I had a tryout and brief stint with the pros, but I got injured and couldn't make it. That was many years ago, and I'm happy to be where I'm at right now. Got a nice wife and family for sure."

"Do you have a picture of your son?"

I always liked to ask to see pictures, because it set a friendly tone, almost to the point of going overboard perhaps, but people liked to show off their families. My new friend got out his cell phone and showed me a picture of his son.

"What a handsome young man he is. You must be very proud of him, as you should be."

"We are definitely very proud of him. Well, enough about my family. How about you, sir? What's your situation? I see you're married. At least, that's either your wife or your girlfriend over there relaxing."

"That's my dear wife, Barb, and we've been married for a long time. We have two children and six grandchildren. One of them, my beautiful granddaughter, happens to be the same age as your son. We should fix them up. What fun that would be, huh? Wanna see a picture of her?"

"Absolutely, and if she's beautiful, I'll work out a deal with you. We can fix our kids up, and then someday you can come up to Canada and I can come down to wherever you're from."

"Well, I'm from Columbus, Ohio, more specifically Westerville. We've been coming up here for several years, and especially the last two with our RV."

I got out my cell phone and started looking for a picture of my granddaughter Kaitlyn. As I was flipping through photos, I happened upon the picture I had just taken of my old pal Trey.

My new friend, looking over my shoulder, spotted the picture of Trey, and the look on his face suddenly darkened.

"Hold on a second. Who is that? Where'd that picture come from?"

"Oh, it's a guy I saw at the restaurant we were at yesterday for lunch."

"Why did you take a picture of him?"

"Well, he graduated from high school with me back in the day, and this is the second time I've run into him since we graduated. The other time was fifty years ago. This time I recognized him by his voice. It's unmistakable when you're from Pennsylvania. It's hard to miss the accent, but more importantly, I heard him talk so many times in my youth that I'm one hundred percent sure it was my former friend."

"I see," he said. "Now let me see a picture of your granddaughter, if you will. I'm curious about Miss Kaitlyn."

I found a few pictures and showed him. He understood immediately why I was so proud of her.

"She's beautiful and certainly would make a worthy girlfriend for any young man."

"You have good taste!" I said. "It's good to know you."

"I'm Cole," he said, stammering just a bit, as if he was nervous to be identified. "My wife's name is Barb, and my two daughters are Gracie and Evie. My son is also named Cole. We call him Junior, as you might guess."

"And I'm Larry. We have two names in common. My wife is also Barb. Our youngest granddaughter is Evie as well. Her real name is Evalynn Grace. How about that?"

"Wow! How about that! Listen, Larry, it was good

to meet you, but I better get back to my group. They are expecting some grub from me."

"No worries, as Barb and I are just going to chill, then make a few steaks ourselves. Have a great evening."

Once I made my way back over to Barb and our camp chairs, she said, "How is it that you always have such an easy time making new friends? I envy that. Since I'm so shy, it works out well that you can get us into the mix when we go places. I don't think I ever told you, but I really think you're so great at that."

"Thanks, sweetie. I love you."

"I love you too, LPB."

"Well, my conversation this time was quite interesting."

"How so?"

"We talked about his family, and he mentioned that he has a son who is a hockey player. He's down in the United States right now, playing for a youth team from Canada, and he might even be NHL material in the future. He's sixteen, so I mentioned that we have Kaitlyn who is also sixteen. I suggested, just in a lighthearted way, that they might become friends sometime. He asked me to show him a picture of her.

"When I did, I had to scroll past the picture of Trey that I took at the restaurant. He immediately jumped on that, and I absolutely think he knows Trey as well, because of the way he reacted. Not sure how, but he knows him."

"Here we are up in northern Michigan, and not only did we find somebody you know, but now we find somebody who also knows Trey. Interesting," Barb said.

When the next morning rolled around, my neighbor Cole was busy behind the camper chopping wood, and as soon as he saw me, he engaged me in some conversation.

"Hey, do you mind talking to me about the guy in that picture?"

"No, not really."

"I know him," he admitted.

"I sort of surmised that because of the way you reacted when you saw the picture. So, what's the deal?"

"Well, my friends and I are actually a task force. We are combining business with pleasure this week. We need to find this gentleman and the lady with him. He has a warrant out in Canada and Michigan. We are trying desperately to locate him, arrest him, and extradite him back to Canada."

"Wow, what's he done that requires such a major effort?"

"I'm afraid I can't tell you what he's done or why we are after him, but we are, and that's a fact. I just wanted you to know that because I know you were taken by surprise when I took such an interest in the picture. Also because taking pictures of a guy like that could be dangerous for you."

"I hope there's not going to be friction between us. Barb and I are strictly on vacation and don't need any drama! I know nothing about Trey, as I haven't seen him for more than fifty years. The two things I do remember still seem to ring true. He still has the same voice, and he still seems like an arrogant jerk."

"Well, interesting you should say that. He's always been a real jerk around me, and that doesn't seem to make much difference to him. Have a good day, Larry. I must be off. My friends and I will be in and out of the campsite a lot, so just get used to that, and hopefully we'll see you every evening and get together. Maybe even sometimes share a campfire with you and have some s'mores. How about that?"

"Campfires and s'mores, what could be better? We'll look forward to it, Cole."

I couldn't wait to get back to Barb and tell her about the conversation I'd just had. I hurried back to our campsite.

"Barb, do you know what Cole said about our friend Trey?"

"He's your friend, not mine, Larry. I've never even met the man. What did Cole say?"

"I told you I thought he was familiar with Trey, and sure enough, he and his friends know him. These people are law enforcement from Canada, and they are here looking for Trey. They wanna arrest him and extradite him back to Canada for something. Cole wouldn't tell me what it is or what he's up to, but I find it very, very interesting, don't you?"

"Yeah, for sure. Who knew we'd be involved in a crime story adventure? But it seems best that we don't get involved in the goings-on. So, what are we going to do today, sweetie?"

"One of the things I'd like to do is head on over to Young State Park and see the place where we used to camp again. There was one part of it that I missed the other day, and I wanted to see if it was still the same. There is a pond over there that is in the back. I'd like to see if there are any fish in it. Since it's a state park, there shouldn't be any problem fishing in it. Is that okay with you? In the meantime, we'll have a nice breakfast and look forward to the day in front of us."

"Sounds good to me," Barb said.

After breakfast, off we went to Young State Park. Almost immediately after we arrived, Barb said, "Hey, look at that red pickup truck back in the corner there. I think that's the truck I saw your friend Trey squeal off in yesterday."

"Hmm, wonder if we should investigate?" I said.

"Well, I don't think he knows what we're driving, and frankly, I doubt if he'd recognize us inside of a car, so let's just drive over there and see if we see him. If we do, perhaps we can go back and tell Cole and his buddies, and they can close in on him."

Sure enough, we drove over there, and there was a couple cooking up breakfast. There were no other campers nearby, so when we drove up, they both looked our way. I turned my head immediately because I didn't want to encounter him.

"Can't tell for sure, sweetie, but that sure looks like them from a distance," I said.

At this point, I didn't know if he was a dangerous person or not, but I was certainly planning on treating him as more of a risk than usual given what Cole had said. So we drove away and found the pond that I was looking for.

•   •   •

Barb and I had special plans that evening. We were dining at a restaurant we'd been to before, but never without the kids.

It sat right on a causeway that led from Lake Charlevoix out to Lake Michigan. If we got a table on the outside deck, we could see the boat traffic coming back into the lake. The drawbridge right near the restaurant was constantly busy at that time of day, and the noise (some would find it annoying) was music to our ears. After a forty-five-minute wait, we got exactly what we wanted: the perfect table on a perfect evening.

By the time we returned to the campsite, it was almost dark. We drove by our new friends, and Cole waved at me. He called out, "Hey, why don't you guys come over tonight and join us at the campfire? I'll introduce you to all my friends."

This sounded like a good idea to both of us. We could see the campfire glowing next to us, so we sauntered over and joined the crowd, just as darkness set in.

"Hey, everybody. These are my new friends, Larry and Barb. Tell us a little bit about yourselves, if you will," Cole said.

I quickly spoke up and said, "Hey, we're from down in Westerville, Ohio, which is near Columbus. We fell in love with this place, and we've been up here several times, but this is the first time we've been to this particular campsite in our RV. We couldn't be happier. It's such a beautiful place. Everything about it is appealing to us. We took off today and visited Young State Park, then had dinner over by the drawbridge at Lake Charlevoix."

"Thanks, guys, and let me just go around the room here and tell you who we've got."

That took about five minutes because there were eight or nine other families there. They all seemed to be happy and getting along just fine. I asked Cole if he'd made any progress in looking for Trey, and he said, "No, we really didn't do much today. We considered this a play day. We've been over at Little Traverse Bay, swimming and kayaking."

I couldn't wait to tell him about our morning experience. "You might find this interesting, Cole. I'm almost sure I saw Trey today with his companion."

Cold replied immediately, "Oh, you've got to be kidding me! Tell me more." Everyone else heard, and we instantly became the center of attention.

I said, "Well, I think he was over at Young State Park, camping in a tent. We happened to see a red pickup truck that we thought was probably his. I nonchalantly drove by. I'm sure he noticed me, but I don't think he's seen me enough times to realize who I was. As soon as I saw him, I turned around and hightailed it out of there. But that's interesting, isn't it?"

"Wow, thanks, Larry. I appreciate it. Maybe we can follow up on that tomorrow. I'll let you know how it goes," Cole said.

We stayed at their beautiful campsite for over an hour. Tired and relaxed, we decided to turn in. "Thanks to you all for inviting us over. We had a really good time," I said as we prepared to leave. Barb and I walked back to our camper and got ready for bed.

Unbeknownst to us, after we left, families put their kids to bed and then Cole called an impromptu meeting with all his guys.

"Guys, we may be getting the break we've been looking for. Larry and Barb seem to be on our side in bringing down my dad and mom. I still don't like it, but they are criminals and must be treated like such. Larry and Barb only know that we are looking for Trey and his companion as a task force. I told them nothing about my relationship. All they know is that we're looking for bad guys. We need to keep that going! Get it? Now, here's what I think we should do. Starting tomorrow, one of us will tail Larry and Barb from a safe distance. They shouldn't suspect anything, for sure. So far, they've run into my dad twice, which is two more times than we have. Everybody on board? Get some sleep, as this is all going to get interesting."

After everybody headed back to their individual tents, Cole pulled his friend Buster aside for a private conversation. "Buster, we're getting close. The other guys are clueless as to what we are planning. If this works out, in a few days, Trey and Patience will be out of the way. We will look like heroes, and both of us will be one step closer to our payoff."

"Easier for you than me, pal. I'm already sick about my part in this," Buster said.

Cole grabbed him by the neck. "Yeah, well, you can't quit now, you jerk. You try and you'll end up just like my folks."

●　　　●　　　●

Morning came quickly for Barb and me, as we were both bushed. We slept well!

After breakfast, I asked Barb, "Where do you wanna go today, sweetie? I'm thinking about Harbor Springs. How about you? We can go over there and walk down the long pier and see if there are any big boats from Columbus. Remember that day?"

Barb smiled. "How could I forget? You almost talked us onto a yacht but couldn't quite pull it off."

"After we've visited the pier, we can eat at the nice restaurant there next to the dock. Should have a great day. You know, there's something else I want to visit while we're up here. It's called the Tunnel of Trees. Have you heard of that?"

Barb hadn't heard of it, but I had picked up a brochure at the rental car place so I knew a little about the place. "It's apparently close by. It runs north out of Harbor Springs and goes clear up to the northern border of Michigan. It's on a road that runs parallel to the lake, and you'll get the idea of the tunnel of trees once we get there. But let's not get ahead of ourselves. We can just do Harbor Springs today and have a nice day there."

The morning was warm and sunny. We walked the pier and then leisurely walked back to the restaurant for a casual lunch. Afterward, we got back to our car and headed on to downtown Harbor Springs, hoping to check out a shop we saw earlier.

As soon as we left our parking spot, Barb said, "Honey, do you get the feeling we're being followed?"

"No, why, sweetie? I haven't even thought about it. Tell me what you're thinking."

"Well, earlier, when we came over here this morning, we made about six turns in a row. I couldn't help noticing a dark blue GMC pickup that kept following us each turn we made. Now, the same pickup is right behind us again. Could be just a coincidence, but I think we're being followed. It could be one of those guys who camped with us. I distinctly remember that one guy has a dark blue pickup."

"I didn't know you were so into pickup trucks, sweetie. What made you notice that?"

"I am into pickup trucks, as it turns out! If this is one that I can recognize, I'll let you know. Let me look in the rearview mirror, and I'll see if I can confirm that. . . Wow, I'm almost positive that is one of 'em. For sure, it's one of those gigantic pickups with seating for four, really decked out! It's got to be one of the guys from the campsite."

"I wonder why they're following us. Maybe they think we are the pathway to finding Trey, as we've found him by accident twice. When we get back tonight, I'm going to say something, because I don't like to be followed, and I don't like to be tied to a criminal in any way whatsoever. Let's just enjoy ourselves for now. If that guy's following us, he'll just have to follow along wherever we're going, and that'll be that."

We enjoyed our day tremendously. The blue pickup was definitely following us. We didn't let it dampen our enthusiasm, and we both agreed that we'd deal with it when we got back to the RV.

Once back and settled, I said to Barb, "I see our friends are back. Looks like Cole is coming to hang up the swimsuits. I'm going over to get to the bottom of things."

"Be careful what you say, Larry, as we certainly don't want to alienate a bunch of cops."

I walked over to Cole and said, "Cole, something interesting happened on our journey today. We seem to be getting more than we bargained for by being camped next to you guys."

"What do you mean?"

"Well, while we were out today, Barb noticed that we were being followed."

Cole looked at me with a puzzled expression. "Followed by what, or who?"

"I was hoping you might be able to tell me that. It was definitely a super deluxe pickup truck, and that's what you guys all have. Barb seemed to think it was a dark blue GMC. Any one of you have one of those?"

"Actually, two of us do, but not me. And I don't know of anybody who should or would have any reason to follow you. But let me check into it."

I decided to be direct with him. "I'd like to know right away, Cole, because I don't want any part of whatever is going on between you guys and Trey."

"Hey, I understand. Once everybody gets back, I'm going to get to the bottom of this, I promise you. I'll try to get back to you this evening after I talk to everybody."

"Okay, that's fine."

Back at the RV, I told Barb, "Well, sweetie, he certainly was open to the idea of finding out who it was. He says it wasn't him, and he certainly didn't know of any effort to follow us for whatever reason."

Clearly less than pleased, she said, "Well, I sure think it was one of their pickup trucks. Otherwise, there wouldn't be any reason for anybody else to be following us. Do you agree?"

"Yep, I sure do. Well, I'll be glad to find out later what he says. I hope he's being honest, because if not, I think we have a problem, and we should maybe think about heading back to Columbus tomorrow, or as soon as possible."

"Wow, I never thought our vacation would become an adventure. Like it or not, we seem to be involved in something more than just a camping trip."

We had dinner in the RV, and we settled in to watch a movie on our TV.

"Tomorrow, is it okay if we head up to that Tunnel of Trees road just north of town?" I said. "Also, maybe we could have lunch at a restaurant that I saw on a brochure? It's right on the lake and it has picnic tables on a terraced lawn behind it. Sounds so scenic. It sits right on a lakefront peninsula."

"Yeah, that sounds like a great plan," Barb said. "That road is not very long, but it takes quite a while to travel because the speed limit is only twenty-five miles per hour. It'll probably end up taking clear to lunch just to get there. That's if we start at maybe eight or nine o'clock in the morning."

"Hey, that should be great," I said. "I'm glad we have this campsite. It's really neat to just relax under the trees, isn't it? Think I'll make a little campfire for us. I spotted some extra wood here that somebody left behind, and I just like the idea of a campfire. We have stuff we can use to make s'mores, I hope."

"Yep, I brought plenty of fixings," Barb said.

I quickly got our fire going, and we were right in the middle of preparing the marshmallows for our s'mores when Cole appeared.

"Hey, guys."

"Hi, Cole. Did you get a chance to talk to your group?" I asked.

"I sure did. Turns out it was one of our guys. My friend Joe Stone was being a bit of a cowboy yesterday. He basically thought that since you guys saw Trey twice in two days, maybe you were going to see him again and you had some connection with him that we didn't know about."

My attitude changed, and it was obvious as I replied, "Well, your friend truly is a cowboy. Seeing Trey was nothing short of a stroke of luck. However, at this point, I'm not sure whether it was good luck or bad luck. At any rate, if it happens again, we're just going to pack up and leave and get out of here because we don't wanna be part of what's going on with you guys. We also don't want to distract your efforts by pulling one of your guys off to follow us. At the same time, if you really think for one minute that we're involved in any way, that's wrong! It would make me angry, Cole! Just tell us now and be straightforward. It's not what we signed up for, and we can just be on our way."

Seeming to be contrite, Cole responded, "Please don't leave on account of what you just said, because I will make sure that you are not in any way being followed or even thought of as part of what we're doing."

"I wanna know if the picture I showed you is the guy you're looking for."

"I can tell you absolutely yes on that."

"Well then, you must know him pretty well, right?"

"That is right."

"Do you mind telling me how you know him? Other than the fact that you're on an official venture to arrest him, which is obvious."

"I'm afraid I can't. I can tell you this, however, he's definitely wanted and needs to be found ASAP!"

"I always knew him as Trey. Is that the same name you call him?"

"No, he is known by a totally different name. That's why I was very confused and interested when you called him that. I think he's using an alias, and perhaps has used it ever since he got here."

"You know he's from the United States, right?" I asked.

"Well, we never knew that for sure until you confirmed it, but we always did suspect it."

"I heard that back in the sixties, after college, he had a job in Dayton. When he left there, he presumably headed to Canada to evade the draft. Lots of guys from my era were doing that, and when I told my friend back in Connellsville that I had seen Trey in Dayton, he said something to the effect of, 'I heard Trey's off to Canada

206

to be a draft dodger.' Just from what I knew of Trey, that didn't surprise me."

Cole seemed pleased. "Well, I guess it wouldn't surprise me either. Ever since he's been here, he's been a bit of a character. He's also managed to become a criminal, both minor and major."

"Oh, you wanna explain that?"

Cole responded, "Well, without going into a great deal of detail, he's done everything from petty theft to grand larceny to attempted murder to now being suspected of a crime that has to do with his daughter and her boyfriend. She was found dead a couple of weeks ago, along with her boyfriend. Trey became the prime suspect in the boyfriend's death. We arrested him and had him interrogated. He explained that he received two hang-up calls from his daughter's cellphone. He went over immediately to check up on her. When he arrived, he found her beaten and dead. The boyfriend was there and near death. To him, it looked like a drug-induced quarrel that ended tragically. He picked up the boyfriend and shook him to the point that he was soon dead. Even though we had Trey—as you know him— in custody, the judge was aware of his good standing in the community and granted bail. He took off with his wife and headed across the border into Michigan. We know he has some property down in this area. Not surprised that you saw him here. Look, Larry, this whole thing has gotten way more complicated for all of us. The only reason I even want you to know this stuff is that I know you and Barb are good people and want what we want, to get him back to Canada."

I had an empty feeling about what he'd just said, but I replied, "Okay, that will help me the next time we talk about him."

Cole left and we were alone with our campfire and our thoughts. I said, "Barb, I don't know about you, but I'm getting increasingly leery of our new friends from Canada. I'm getting the feeling that Trey may be more of a victim than a perp. I do think we were followed and that Cole was both aware of it and probably sanctioned it. I also had to pull hard to get him to give details. What do you think?"

"Yes, I'm thinking the same thing. At first, I had no reason to be suspicious, but these guys have taken so much interest in us, that I can't believe that all they're interested in is upholding the law. It seems there's more to the story than what we know, and Cole's version of events doesn't add up."

Conflicted about what was happening, we got ready for the day's sightseeing. On the way through the Tunnel of Trees, the radio was on with local music and news. An announcer suddenly cut in: "We have a news bulletin just in from Young State Park. A couple was found in their campsite this morning by local authorities after a frantic call to 9-1-1. They were camped by themselves near the back of the park. The woman was badly burned but should recover. Her husband was in a state of shock but not physically hurt. Reports from authorities show the couple was attacked late last night or early this morning. Their tent was burned through completely and still smoldering when police and park rangers responded. Police say the man and woman are lucky to be alive, and they are opening an inquiry into who might wish the couple harm."

"Barb, are you listening to this?"

The newscast continued with a sound clip from a police officer: "This was not a robbery, as their red pickup was found undisturbed and little else was bothered. It's like the perp snuck up behind the couple, assuming they were both asleep in their tent. The assailant then pitched a lit Molotov cocktail into the tent and took off, leaving them for dead. What the perpetrator didn't know was that the husband wasn't in the tent. He was returning from a 'nature call' and saw the fire and explosion. He rushed to the tent and dragged his wife through the flames. She was sleeping in a mummy-style sleeping bag. It had a high enough fire rating on it to save her life. He dragged her out, just as the fire totally consumed their tent. The man and woman are from Ludington. Their names are Bill and Gloria Compton. Anyone with information on this crime should call the Petoskey police hotline. Your information, as always, will be confidential."

"Oh God, sweetie," I said to Barb. "That has to be the couple we saw the other day. I bet Cole or someone in his group did this. They probably thought it was Trey. I'm going to throw up. This is the worst thing that's ever happened. If I hadn't told Cole about this, I'm sure it would have never happened. They're probably realizing that we could connect the dots if we heard the news."

Almost in tears, Barb said, "I'm scared, Larry."

"So am I. We need to do something and do it fast. I have an idea. If you remember, I taught with Trey's sister

Scarlett down at Jones Junior high school, and I think Bill Hughes keeps in touch with her. They taught math together at Jones and knew each other a lot better than she and I did. I'm going to give him a call right now and just see if he still has any numbers for her. If so, I'm going to call her and tell her what's going on and see if she can give us any insight that we might not get from our friends up here. I think that's the best way to approach this. They're never going to know that I've done this, and if Scarlett seems to think there's anything going on that we should know about, then all the better. You agree?"

"Absolutely. I can't wait to hear from Bill and Jean anyway. When you get them, let me speak to Jean."

THE BEGINNING OF
SOME CLARITY

"HEY, SCARLETT, it's **Larry Buttermore**. I hope you're doing well, and I hope you remember me. I don't know if you do or not because it's been probably fifty years since we've seen each other. I know we spent a couple of years teaching together at Jones Junior High School, and those were the good old days, of course. The reason I'm calling will perhaps surprise you. Barb and I are up in Petoskey, Michigan, camping at a neat campground. We have seen your brother, Trey, here. Do you have some time for our story? It's a tad long, but it may be important."

"Hey, I've got all day! Plus, when you're finished, I have a story too. Somehow, I bet they're related." Scarlett, as usual, was very kind about the whole mess. I told her about running into Trey at the restaurant, taking the picture of him, and subsequently meeting Cole and showing him the photo of Trey.

"Larry, can I interrupt for a moment? First of all, it's good to hear your voice. Even though it's been fifty years, I can still recognize it. You were a legend at Jones, and I used some of your wonderful teaching techniques to get me started in my career. Bill and I talked about you often, and I still keep in touch with him. I assume that's where you got my number?"

"Yes, it was, and I hope you don't mind that I got it from him."

"Oh, absolutely not. He's as good of a person as both of us could hope to have as a friend. And I remember you so well. Trey and I don't keep in touch very much, but I did hear from him just a week ago. He told me a little bit about what's going on with him. Here's the story I alluded to. My husband, you may remember, is an attorney here in Upper Arlington, and he and I are trying our best to help Trey. I'm so sorry about you getting mixed up in this mess. And it is a mess, for sure. Cole must be Trey's son, Jared. I think Cole might be his middle name. He lied about his name, but I'm sure it's him, as his wife is Barb, and the kids have the same names he gave you.

"This is just terrible! Trey dropped part of his last name when he got to Canada and now uses Chapel. Trey's companion you've seen him with is his wife, Patience. When my brother called, he explained that he and Patience feared for their lives. He has been in hiding at various places in both Michigan and Ontario. He told me about the brutal murder of his daughter. He and Patience loved her dearly. He also told us that Jared has somehow convinced the police in Canada that Trey is responsible. Larry, he is not! I'm as sure of that as I can be.

"Jared is a modern version of the Prodigal son. He is a money grabber. He has found out something that Trey and

I have been trying very hard to conceal from our respective children—our family's wealth. Dick and I, as well as Trey and Patience, are very wealthy. Most of the wealth is from the estate of our mom's family. We knew that if the kids were aware of this, they might not strive to be successful on their own, but instead just wait for the wealth to pass to them when we die. Jared has plotted to speed up that process. He either killed his sister directly or he had her killed. The boyfriend was collateral damage, if you will. With her out of the way... Oh, Larry, I warned you that this is some incredibly sad and terrible business. To get what he wants, Jared is now on a quest to kill off both parents. It's a plan that he has to finish, as he is in way too deep to back out now. He's apparently a very smart and convincing person too. These guys he calls his 'task force' probably have no idea what's going on. He's got them believing his story that Trey is totally guilty. He needs to be stopped soon—along with this task force—or my brother and his wife will be dead."

I was in a bit of shock from what Scarlett had just shared with me. "So, it looks like my intuition about what's going on with Cole/Jared may be correct," I said. "At first, I listened to him and determined that Trey was a bad guy. But after we were followed, we began to have doubts about things. I did see your brother, for sure. We also saw that he was driving a red pickup truck. That led us to almost getting an innocent couple killed. We were visiting a state park that we frequented years ago with our kids. When we were there, we saw a red truck that we thought might be Trey's. Later that day, we reported that information back to Jared.

The next day, we were riding in our car with the radio on. A news bulletin came on to say that a couple from Ludington were nearly killed when someone threw a homemade bomb in their tent. Luckily, the man wasn't in the tent at the time, and he rescued his wife. After hearing that, we were positive about two things. First, that Cole instigated the attack, and second, that the intention was to kill Trey and his companion. We were terrified. If someone is willing to do something like that, what else might they be capable of?"

"Oh, Larry, your intuition was absolutely correct! Jared is a dangerous character," Scarlett said. I could tell she was worried about Barb and me. I listened as she continued to give me more details about her brother.

"Trey got married in Canada after escaping up there in the sixties, and he's been up there ever since. When Jimmy Carter signed the order that said Trey and others like him would face no penalty or incarceration, Trey was finally able to get in touch with me, which was wonderful because we hadn't even made contact for several years. That was his choice, and I understood it, but I didn't like it because I love my brother. I always have and always will. Through my conversations with Trey, I've come to know a lot about what his life has been like since he fled to Canada. If you have the time, I'll try to give you as much information and backstory as I can. It might take a while, but even the small details may make a big difference in understanding such a complicated scenario."

"I have time, Scarlett, and I'd appreciate any information you can give me," I said, genuinely thankful.

"I'll start with how Trey met his wife, Patience. Trey told Richard and me all about it. It's a real love story, Larry. Trey became a success first as a used car salesman. I know that puts him right up there with the likes of the profession my Richard is in, but Trey was good enough and resourceful enough to parlay it into buying out his boss and owning the dealership and the service business attached to it. Over the years, he longed for a wife and family."

As I listened to Scarlett talk, the vivid story she told made me feel as if I was there in Canada with Trey and Patience the day they met. I settled in to listen as Scarlett filled me in about Trey's history.

TREY MEETS PATIENCE

ONE DAY, Patience walked into the dealership and asked for the owner. One of Trey's guys, cautious as always when someone wanted the boss, asked, "What would this be about, ma'am?"

Patience said, "Well, I've got a complaint."

Still trying to keep things from escalating and wanting to shield Trey, he said, "Maybe I could help?"

Meanwhile, Trey was in his spacious office that had a mirrored two-way window. He watched the very attractive young lady with great interest as she had an animated conversation with the main floor guy. After several minutes, Trey's guy couldn't persuade her to allow him to be the mediator.

"Would you mind waiting here, ma'am? I'll see if I can raise him." He slipped around the corner and into Trey's office.

Trey asked him, "What's going on out there? I couldn't help noticing you with the pretty lady."

"She might be pretty, but she's also upset about

something, and she won't tell me what. She insists on seeing you. I'm sorry, boss."

"No, it's all right. Please bring her in."

Patience was led into the office. The floor worker said, "Boss, this is . . . Sorry, ma'am, I never really got your name."

"It's Patience. Patience Helm."

"Please sit down. I'm Trey. I'm the owner. How can I help you?"

Trey's office was not typical for a used car dealership. When he bought the place, it was one of the first things he changed. He realized that his office would be used for a variety of stuff, often involving customers and negotiations. As such, he thought the room should exemplify the character of the owner and the class of any such office in town. Other than the two-way mirror/window, the office looked like a corporate board room.

"When I heard your name—" Trey began, only to be cut off by Patience.

"I know. I'm surprised you didn't break out laughing. Also, I see you were obviously watching me from your window."

Trey continued, "Well, your name is Patience, right? That isn't the vibe I'm getting right now. But I'm sure you are a patient person. And by the way, my intention for this window was never to use it for spying on customers. Its purpose has always been for viewing the showroom floor and making sure all my guys and gals are on their toes."

"No need to explain. I'm not easily offended."

"So, Patience, what can I do to help? In the past, I would almost always have known you ahead of time, as I involved myself in every part of the sale and service of everyone coming through the door. Recently, as our business has grown, I mostly sit at my desk and run the place. Some days I long for the way it once was. Like now, as I'm afraid I don't recognize your name or your face. I apologize for both."

"Trey, you wouldn't know it anyway. I'm here because of my dad."

"What's his name?"

"Denny Helm."

"You're Denny's daughter?"

"So, you know my dad?"

"Absolutely! He was one of my earliest customers and such a great guy. How's he doing?"

"Not so great right now."

"What's going on with him?"

"Well, this past Monday, he pulled up in front of our house and turned the car off. As he was getting out, he smelled something. All of a sudden, the whole car was on fire. Luckily, we live a block away from the fire station. One of the neighbors saw it happen and called right away. They were able to save our house from catching fire, but the car was totaled and our driveway has a huge black scorch mark on it. My dad could have been killed!"

"First of all, Patience, I'm so sorry. Second, I'm so glad your dad wasn't hurt and that your house is okay. Let me ask you, is this the Pontiac he bought from me two years ago?"

"No, it's a Canadian Ford Explorer he bought two weeks ago."

"Once again, I apologize! As I mentioned before, I would have known about him and his purchase back then. I do know that I want to help. First, please give me the name of your insurance carrier and agent. I'll call them in the morning, and I'm pretty sure we can take over all the liability for this with our dealer policy. Second, bring your dad down tomorrow. If we can't find a suitable replacement on the lot, I'll loan him something till we do. Also, let me send my garage crew up to your place. We deal with soiled cement all the time. I bet we can clean and power wash it back to near perfect. Can you think of anything else you or your dad will need? Once again, I'm so sorry this has happened. Believe me, it's a first. I also would like to have the car to inspect, so maybe we can find out what caused the fire and be able to prevent it from ever happening again."

Relieved, Patience replied, "Trey, I think the insurance people already investigated that and should be able to share it with you. And may I say a big WOW for you and the way you took care of me and all this. Believe me, I came here loaded for bear, if you know what I mean. Instead, you have been above and beyond wonderful. I can't wait to tell my dad!"

Trey was relieved to hear she was happy with the results, and he responded, "How about we make an appointment for the both of you for tomorrow? Would noon be okay?"

"Perfect."

The next day came and went. Trey saw to it that Mr.

Helm and Patience were taken care of and then some. He offered them any car, truck, or SUV on the lot.

"If there's any difference in what the cost is, don't worry about it. I mean that. I feel so bad that this happened, and we are capable of dealing with any deficit. We'll get some reimbursement when our insurance kicks in. That's what it's for. Besides, this will be my first ever claim. Hard to believe, but nothing like this has happened before!"

Over the moon was the response. Patience and her dad could not resist hugging Trey for his generosity and, even more impactful, for his caring attitude. When Patience got her hug in, Trey couldn't help noticing something special. Just her touch and tenderness gave him goosebumps.

Trey had felt a lady's affection before and had frequently been a pursuer of such. After graduating from hotshot used car salesman to owner, he decided that spending time in bars and on one-night stands was no longer considered proper. If he was to be the talk of the town, he wanted it to be for the right reasons. He was now in his mid-thirties and still available, but he hoped that someday true love would find him. He became patient and didn't lust after every young, attractive customer he saw through the two-way mirror in his office.

Patience was different from the get-go. She was definitely attractive, but in a wholesome way. Most young ladies who wanted to be noticed worked too hard at it and were usually obvious. He knew that. Patience also had another quality that set her apart: she was very caring toward her father. This appealed to him more as he thought about it.

Scarlett stopped the story here for a moment to reinforce some important details about her brother's mindset during that time.

"Larry, you have to remember that Trey had been estranged from his own dad for many years. His decision to come to Canada was about much more than just evading the draft. He was aware of the US involvement in Vietnam and read article after article on the opposing opinions from every outlet he could subscribe to. In the long run, he decided, right or wrong, that we should have stayed clear of this conflict. It finalized his decision. He told me he would be leaving, but he never said a word to our mom and dad. He sat with me at my dorm in Columbus for several hours before he took off. I wasn't as firm on my own take, as I simply hadn't thought about it like my brother had.

"After listening, I said to him, 'I am not sure of everything you're telling me, brother, but I love you and will miss you. I'll do my best to let Mom and Dad know that you love them dearly but fear they might talk you out of your decision. Please call me as soon as you get where you're going. I need to hear that you are safe and sound.'

"We parted with a loving embrace, not knowing if and when we would see each other again. It was particularly sad for me, as I was younger, and Trey, despite his noticeable faults, was still my big brother, my protector, and my hero. It would be many years before I was able to hug him again. And from that day forward, our dad and mom led their lives thinking they had no son, as they didn't fall on the same side of the politics of the war, and they felt that Trey simply was a draft dodger."

"Wow, that must have been tough for both of you," I said. "However, I feel as if I'm getting to know Trey better."

"It was very tough, Larry. It was a tough time for families everywhere. But back to the story…"

I settled in to listen some more as Scarlett picked up the story of how Trey and Patience came to be in love.

A ROMANCE BLOOMS

ABOUT A WEEK AFTER Trey finished taking care of Mr. Helm and his daughter, a customer came in and asked for the owner.

"Sir, I heard what you did for Mr. Helm. I need a car and would like to think I would get treated the same way if anything like that ever happened to me."

"Oh, how did you find out about that?" Trey asked.

"Didn't you see the article in today's paper?"

"No, I guess I haven't read it yet today."

"Well, when you do, you'll be patting yourself on the back. I bet I won't be the last person who comes here for a car after reading about you and how your compassion made one family's nightmare a blessing in disguise. Now get busy and sell me a car!"

After the customer left, Trey went to his office and sat for a while with the biggest smile on his face. He had grabbed the *Gazette* from its spot on the waiting room table and found out what the guy was talking about. The paper, being local, had a human-interest column. It urged people to write in concerning real-life stories from the town. He had never really read it much before, sort of considering it a gossip column. This particular day, there were two pieces—the one about him and another piece. Trey was glad he was the one receiving the praise, as the other column was not going to do the butcher shop a block from his dealership any good. The piece on the butcher shop involved a loyal customer who had come in and was given some chicken breasts that were taken home to be cooked up that very evening. The customer found the breasts to be ripe and unfit to be served. The store was open till 7:00, so he decided to take them back. Apparently, there were multiple witnesses to what happened next. As the customer was explaining the situation, not yet angry and just looking for a satisfactory resolution, the butcher lashed out. "Get out of here and don't come back. I've seen your kind before. Now get out!" That short (not) sweet little article could quickly and easily ruin the shopkeeper.

The shopkeeper's brother turned out to be the guilty party, but he was the owner, and the reputation of any business, but especially any small business, must be at the forefront of any message the store sends out.

After Trey read both articles, he was so appreciative of the effort someone had exerted to say kind things about his business. In order to get into this column, the writer had to be willing to identify themselves along with their telling of an experience. In the case of his column, he saw the writer's name was Patience Helm. Once again, he got goosebumps.

He knew it was important that he took care not to come off as patronizing. He just wanted to get to know her better. She was a few years younger than him, but not so much younger that them getting together would seem strange. He wanted to call her, but what would be the pretense? Would she see any wrong motive if he called and talked to her? His desire to know her better quickly outweighed any apprehension, and he found her number and dialed it up. He was hoping she'd answer. He wasn't sure if Patience worked or not, as she had been able to accompany her dad on a weekday to get the car matter settled.

What bad timing, he thought when her dad answered. Trey had rehearsed his initial conversation with Patience, sort of like a football team "scripts" its first few plays. Do (say) what you've practiced till the flow of the game (conversation) gets into its natural flow.

"Is this Mr. Helm?" he asked when he heard the male voice answer the phone.

"Yes it is, and who might this be?"

"Oh, it's Trey calling from Burchfield's."

"Hey, how are you doing? I can't tell you how much I like my new Overland. It has so many features that I haven't begun to master, but I love it."

"Well then, why don't you make an appointment? We have a young man from the local community college here who knows more about car technology than you and I put together. I just hired him last week. I'd love for you to come in and be his first victim—I mean, client." Trey laughed at his own joke.

"Fantastic, will he be in tomorrow?"

"Yep, he gets in at 4:30 after his last class, and he'll be here till 7:00."

"I can make that work. Oh, by the way, I've done nothing but rattle on since I picked up the phone. Did you call for anything special?"

Almost afraid to ask, Trey was ready to say it was just a courtesy call and leave it at that. But at the last minute, he plucked up his courage and said, "Well, I actually was hoping to speak to your daughter."

"Oh, I see."

Mr. Helm's tone indicated he was funning a little and trying to make Trey squirm. It was working.

"She's at work, Trey. She's a teacher down at Longfellow. How about I tell her you called and suggest, if you want me to, that she call you back. How does that sound? Oh, by the way, she gets home around 3:15, so if she calls, it will be later than that."

Trey could tell that her dad was not at all against her calling him back, but he wanted Trey to have a bit of anticipation, if and when she did.

"Please tell her this is my late night at the store, and I'll be here till seven."

With both parties satisfied that the phone call accomplished its mission, they hung up.

Later on, a call came through that made Trey's heart skip a beat.

"Trey, this is your new best friend, Patience. My dad wouldn't let up till I called you back. Now, don't get me wrong, I would have called anyway. He just thought that sooner would be better than later."

"Well, I like your dad even more now than I did before, which was a lot! How are you doing?"

"I'm just fine. I had a couple of parent-teacher appointments after school. They were scheduled ones, but I'm always a little stressed beforehand, as I never know how they will go."

"Did they go okay?"

"Well, this one little guy keeps flirting with me to the point of embarrassment. I was looking for ways I could soft-sell his parents that their dear son, although not rare for a fifth grader, goes way past the centerline and has embarrassed me in front of my class."

"Wow, so if I ever flirt with you, please let me know in plenty of time, as my parents are clear down in Detroit, and they would be mortified!"

"You're very funny. Do I sense that you are flirting with me now?"

"Maybe, just maybe. I did want to thank you profusely for the piece you wrote about us in *The Gazette*. I'm pretty sure I've sold six cars because of it. I mean that. Plus, I get many interruptions from folks waiting to pick their cars up next door. It's harder than I thought to wear a halo, Patience. I can't really split the commissions on six cars, but would you consent to going out to dinner with me sometime? You can bring Dad if you want."

"Wow, a dinner date with the most popular bachelor in town. Not sure I can handle that! I'll say yes, and you can decide when and where later and give me a call. That way you have time to reconsider if you want. Also, no offense, but my dad will not come with us. I'm quite sure of that."

"I'll pick out a nice place and call you soon, okay?"

Even though Trey wanted this to be the outcome, he was surprised and pleased that she made it so easy. He made reservations at an elegant little place one of his tire vendors had taken him to earlier in the year. He liked that it was quiet, and he also liked that he didn't expect to see any of his customers there. Trey was anything but backward, but his date with Patience made him squirm.

The night of the date, Patience wore a red top with thin spaghetti straps and a navy-blue skirt that made Trey have a hard time not staring when he picked her up.

"Is Dad here? I'd like to say hello."

"That's nice. I'll get him."

Patience soon returned with Mr. Helm, who eyed Trey with a fierce scowl. "Hello, young man. So, where are you taking my daughter, and when can I expect her home?"

Patience rolled her eyes. "Oh, Dad . . ."

Trey responded naturally with no hesitation. "We're going to the Eagle's Nest. It's out on the lake, and I'm hoping they'll have an outside table, as it's about as beautiful as a night could be. Oh, and as far as what time, you tell me, and I'll have her back safe and sound."

"You're a good one, Trey. You two have a wonderful evening."

"You handled my dad just right," Patience said once they were in Trey's car. "He's a very protective one, and since Mom died, even more so."

"I hope you'll tell me more about your mom later. I'm sure she was quite the lady. Have you ever been to the Eagle's Nest?" Trey asked.

"No, but a few of my teacher friends rave about it. Should be a great place."

When they arrived, the hostess at the podium told them that although they had a reservation, a table on the deck was highly desirable and would require a wait of about fifteen minutes.

"What do you say, Patience? We can sit at the bar till they're ready," Trey said.

"Hey, fifteen minutes will pass in a flash. I'd sure rather be out there tonight. The view of the lake back here is stunning. Maybe we'll even get to see a sunset," Patience replied.

The meal was wonderful. Trey was surprised that she was not a picky eater when she ordered a filet, medium rare, a baked potato, and a salad. He had to ask her if it was okay with her if he "copied," as that's exactly what he had intended to order. Trey asked if she would like anything to drink.

"What do you like?" he asked.

"I sort of like wine, but you decide."

"Wine is great. Are you fond of Merlot, or maybe a red blend?" Trey inquired.

After settling on Merlot, they milked it, and the moment, enjoying both to the hilt.

"Oh, look, Trey, we get to witness a Canadian sunset! Isn't there a song about that?"

On the way home, they made easy conversation, and each of them knew that this was not going to be their last date. Nothing had ever felt more right for either of them.

"Do you think your dad would mind if I kissed you?" Trey asked when they got back to her house. "I know it's our first date, but—"

She quickly solved his dilemma as she leaned in and kissed him in a way that sent shivers up his spine.

"I had a wonderful time, Trey. I hope you did too. Will you call me?"

He had a hard time catching his breath after that kiss, but he managed to say, "Oh yeah." He would definitely call her again.

During the next few months, Trey and Patience's relationship grew from an almost childlike puppy love to much more. In his youth, Trey had been a player. His buddies, especially in college, seemed to have the same opinion of dating. Get what you can, get what you want. If you don't get it, move on until you do. Trey left a trail of short stints with the girls he dated. As was the case with many of his guy friends, the sex part of dating was considered a dangling carrot. He specifically remembered one of his frat brothers saying, "Hey, don't worry, she'll stop you when she wants to, so keep going till that happens."

Trey and his buddies supposed (right or wrong) that these same conversations were happening in the girls' dorms as often as in his chapter room at the frat. It was a different era and the awareness of today simply didn't exist in the '60s. OU was something of a party school by reputation, but girls almost always lived in dorms that were off limits to guys and had curfews that were set by the school.

This brought on a phenomenon known as "parking." The car seat became the '60s version of the apartment of today. The car seat was the place where stuff happened—after-dark stuff. The car seat was where the hormones of the young were released, and where touching and exploration went on that couldn't happen in the light or in public places. Kissing led to feeling, which led to…more.

For the most part, if a guy and a girl became serious, this became a nightly ritual. The places to park were well known and yet secretive. It had to be a place where it was somewhat secluded, of course, and dark, and where the campus or Athens police didn't patrol. The patrolling of such areas, or lack thereof, was both by commission and omission.

As most guys learned, girls controlled the show. Most were protective of what they considered the ultimate prize, and guys couldn't do much about that. Guys often talked of eventually getting married as a way to receive a license for finally going "all the way." Sad as this was, Trey followed such a path in his dating life until he came to Canada.

Having settled in a fairly small town once he got to his new country, Trey realized that it wasn't hard to have one's reputation tarnished. The available population of single, eligible guys and gals had shrunk dramatically from his days as a BMOC (Big Man On Campus) at OU and from his bar-hopping days in Dayton.

He'd also had enough of the lifestyle. His desires had morphed from one-night stands to a growing desire to find the right person and settle down. Could Patience be the one? As they grew fonder of each other, they both had ample opportunities to jump ahead in terms of satisfaction. They weren't kids. Even though Patience still lived with her father, Trey now had a nice luxury condo with a king-sized bed.

Trey talked freely about his past. In his transparency, Patience could see that he was clearly different now than he was when his "stories" took place. Sensual kissing and touching kept both longing for more, but neither let it become anything that a cold shower couldn't take care of.

"What about your dad?" Trey asked at one point, after they'd been dating for a while and their relationship was progressing toward serious. "I know you love him, and I do too. If we decided to marry, what about him?"

"My dear, don't worry about Dad. His brother in Sarasota has been asking him for years to come down there. He lives in a luxury mobile home complex that has everything from a pool and clubhouse to nightly activities. Thanks for caring, but that will simply not be a problem. The only reason he is even still here is because he finds it necessary to look after his baby girl."

After hearing that her father would not be left with a problem if they got married, Trey's entire demeanor shifted.

"She's the one!" he began to tell anyone close enough to him to be interested in his love life. In order to keep his intentions as secretive as possible, he slipped over into Michigan to buy his lady's ring. With a select few jewelers in Sault Ste. Marie, all of whom he had sold at least one car to, he opted not to offend one over the other, plus keep the purchase from his locals until he decided on the perfect time.

Ring in hand, Trey made plans to take a trip to see Mr. Helm at a time when he knew Patience would not be home. She was in school all day that day, so the timing was perfect.

He called Mr. Helm to let him know he was coming.

"Mr. Helm?"

"Trey, good to hear from you. You must know by now that my daughter doesn't get home till about 4:00?"

"I do. I'd really like to come up and talk a bit with you."

"I think you could figure that I will be here pretty much anytime. I am retired, you remember?"

"Yes, sir, I'll be up in about a half hour. See you soon."

While he traveled, Trey rehearsed his words. He wasn't sure he would get any resistance, but he also didn't want to be a klutz about it. After all, Mr. H. would hopefully become his father-in-law, and if this moment went badly, he had a feeling he'd never live it down.

Denny Helm greeted him at the door.

"Come in, fine sir. Can I get you a beer?"

"Nah, I have to go back to work," Trey said.

"So, what's on your mind? I hope it's nothing serious," Mr. Helm said.

"Well, it is serious, but in a good way, at least for me. Mr. Helm, I am totally in love with your daughter and would like to ask for her hand in marriage. I know how close you are, and I wanted to make sure I had your blessing if I do this. I bought a ring yesterday, so I'm totally invested, if you know what I mean."

"Come here, son—give me a hug!" the old man said, tears in his eyes.

"Dad—may I call you that?"

"Of course."

"Patience will hopefully be surprised by this, so don't

you spill the beans, okay?"

"You have my word," Mr. Helm said.

"Also, we talked about a possible future together a few weeks ago. I asked specifically about you. She told me that you would be fine and would probably feel unshackled by her moving into a new season of life. She said you have a brother in Sarasota and that he's been wanting you to come and live with him for some time. Is all that accurate? I ask because I would have no problem with you joining us when we are married. I have an extra—"

"Let me clear the air, Trey. I'm thrilled that you care about me and my future, but what Patience told you is totally true. I would gladly move to Florida. I'm just sorry it didn't happen sooner. But you know what they say, good things happen to those who wait."

As he drove back to the office, Trey could barely contain his excitement. Soon he was on the phone with Patience.

"Hi, sweetie, are you busy?" he asked.

"Nope, just leaving school to do a few errands on the way home. What's up?" Patience replied.

"I know Saturday is going to be one of the prettiest days of the year. How about we do dinner at our favorite place?"

"The Eagle's Nest?"

"You got it. I'll see if I can get us a reservation at 7:00 for our favorite table on the deck."

"Sounds wonderful!"

Trey and Patience had been back to their favorite spot many times since their first date. Everyone there knew them on a first-name basis at this point. A quick call to the manager secured the reservation.

Trey also asked the manager, "Will you do me a favor and set up a few special requests for us?"

"Yes, for sure, sir. What's the occasion?"

"Big surprise, but you'll have to wait till Saturday, just like me."

On Saturday, when he picked his Patience up, Pops answered the door.

"Wow, you clean up pretty good, son. Special occasion tonight?" With that, Dad winked at Trey, and the evening was on.

Scarlett seemed a little surprised. "You didn't tell me to get dressed up."

"Hey, you always look better than me. I just wanted to come a little closer to your classy looks."

"Flattery will get you everywhere, my sweets!" she exclaimed with a laugh.

At the restaurant, it didn't take long for Patience to get the feeling that something was up. The tablecloth had been changed out from the usual red-and-white checkerboard to white linen. A candle was in the middle, and a bottle of champagne was being cooled.

"What's going on? Did you just win the lottery? Please tell me."

Next, she found the love of her life on his knees beside her chair.

"Patience, I've loved you ever since I laid eyes on you. I can't and don't want to get the vision of your face out of my mind."

Pulling out the beautiful navy-blue velvet box from his

jacket, Trey looked into her eyes.

"Will you do me the honor of marrying me and becoming my wife, forever?"

"Oh yes, Trey, I thought you'd never ask!"

"I think that's the same thing your dad said," he told her with a chuckle.

Naturally, all eyes on the deck were aware that something special was happening. First one person and then everyone began clapping. Smiles and tears flowed like the champagne. It was an evening to remember.

As they sat in the driveway that evening when he took her home, it was hard for them to imagine what had just transpired.

"Sweetie, can we just call off work and get married tomorrow?" Trey asked her.

"Trey, I know it will be hard, but I also know we have to plan and have a perfect wedding. I hope you agree!"

It was his turn to display his mock disgust. "Oh, okay, I guess I agree!"

It was July. September was always the most beautiful month of the year in southwestern Ontario.

"Would it be all right if we have an outdoor wedding, darling?" she asked.

"Any place in mind?"

"Yes. How about Pancake Bay? It was probably my favorite picnic spot growing up. Mom and Dad packed us a picnic almost every Sunday, and after church, we would drive over there and stay till dark. The beach is always so peaceful. I bet we can set up stuff for free, and it's close enough for all our friends to drive to. I've always loved that spot. It also faces west, and if we had the wedding in the early evening, we could set up tables and easily have the reception right there. Complete with a Canadian sunset, right?"

"You read my mind," Trey responded. "I didn't grow up here, but I understand completely why you chose it."

The wedding day was perfect. A "Chamber of Commerce" type day. The dress was casual. Khakis and a white dress shirt for the guys. Yellow sundresses for the ladies. A long, white, strapless dress for the bride. The setting was almost surreal it was so beautiful, as evening seemed to calm the wind into a light breeze. The only sounds seemed to come from the waves lapping the shore.

"You did good!" Trey told his soon-to-be bride. "I can't imagine a more beautiful spot to tie us together. A destination wedding that cost little and took us all less than a half hour to get to!"

"Thanks, my sweets. But why am I still nervous?"

"Don't sweat it," he told her. "I am too, but I chalk it up to anticipation, not nervousness!"

"Anticipation of what?"

"Honey, don't make me blush. I've longed for this moment and all the moments from now on, ever since you first kissed me."

"Now I'm blushing too. Can I kiss you again, right now?"

The wedding and reception went on to perfection. Trey had made a reservation at a super quaint inn that was only a mile down the road. He told the innkeeper that they would likely check in around midnight and asked if that would be a problem.

"Hey, you guys are lucky, as my wife and I like to watch Johnny Carson before we retire, so we will be up. Enjoy your reception, and we'll see you when you get here."

The inn was on a point of land that anyone would covet as a place to build. Their room was one that looked out over Lake Superior and had a sliding door to a little deck. The owners were delightful in their welcome and assured the newlyweds that breakfast would happen when they got up and that there was no rush. They even suggested that they sleep in.

Trey asked his new bride, "Honey, did you get a chance to take a breath through the evening?"

"It took about an hour to do the ceremony. My nerves began to calm when I saw you standing at the beach waiting for me. I looked at you and felt chilled but calm."

"Hard to believe we've been married for several hours now," Trey said as he stared at her with a huge smile on his face. "Unpack, sweetheart. I brought some champagne I bought special for tonight."

"Okay if I change into something more comfortable?" Patience asked.

"Oh yeah, please do."

Their room had both a slider and a huge, many-paned picture window facing the lake. They could leave it open with no fear of anyone peering in on their first private moments as a couple. Sitting in front of the window facing the lake, with the moon full and casting a glow on the water, Trey and Patience sipped the champagne and looked at each other.

They had been with each other many times, but not like this.

Her change to something "more comfortable" was significant. The material was soft and sheer and, as planned by its designer, provocative. Trey tried his best not to stare. Every inch of his body now felt different. He tingled from top to bottom. Patience felt the same thing, but with the added heat and a bit of self-awareness that comes from revealing yourself to your lover-turned-husband.

"What do we do now?" Patience said.

This broke the silence, as they couldn't help but giggle at what Patience had just blurted out.

"I think we'll figure it out." With a smile, Trey got up and came around behind her. He slipped his hands over her shoulders and began to slowly move them to caress her front. She soon was guiding them to places they had both dreamed of. He gently picked her up and carried her to their marriage bed.

After 3:00 a.m. had come and gone and they had spent moments together that were sheer bliss, he asked her, "Are you glad we waited?"

With a dreamy smile on her face, she answered, "Oh yeah."

They drifted off to sleep and sweet dreams.

Morning came early for Trey since his body was on an automatic alarm clock. He waited patiently for his bride to wake, but by the time she did, he was beside himself with anticipation.

"You're finally up, sweetie," he exclaimed when her eyes opened.

"What time is it?"

"Oh, it's only nine."

"I never sleep that late."

"Could have fooled me. I've been up since 7:00. I got us a pot of coffee. I'll be on the outside porch. You take your time and join me when you're ready."

"Don't look at me, please!" she said shyly, as she covered herself with the sheets as she got up and walked away from him toward the shower.

"You have a nice butt."

"I told you not to look!"

"You're beautiful front and back, and I can't help it. You better get used to it."

"Okay, okay!"

Later, on the porch, they enjoyed each other's company and had no trouble making the day come alive with easy small talk.

"What are our hosts going to think? They surely have breakfast ready," Patience said.

"I hoped this might happen, so I stopped over earlier and said maybe lunch would be a better option," Trey replied.

"Oh, did you really?"

They spent most of the morning under the covers and intertwined in each other's arms.

A MOMENTOUS CALL

"I HOPE WE GET ALONG **as well forever as we did today,"** Patience murmured as they held each other. "A lot of my teacher friends say that things go downhill from day one in a marriage."

"Not going to happen!" Trey responded lovingly. "You know why? Those sad statistics are mostly due to not talking beforehand and spending ninety percent of their courtship lusting after each other instead of loving after each other."

"Who told you that? They must have been very wise."

"Nobody. I guess it was just me talking to me, as I was like that for many years. I came to the realization that it couldn't and wouldn't be how I would approach my bride if I were ever lucky enough to have one."

The next day, they packed up and began the rest of their honeymoon. They made a long drive to Toronto for night one. They had dinner at an outdoor Italian place that one of Patience's friends had recommended. They spent two days there and then went on to Niagara Falls.

"I know everyone goes to Niagara Falls, so don't laugh, Patience."

"Hey, I'm not laughing. My dad and mom came here for their honeymoon. They said they only had fifty bucks to spend, and they still had five dollars left after three days there, and they even got to have dinner at the Seagram Tower. I smile every time my dad tells me about it. Can we go there?" she asked.

"Of course. I want to do what you want to do. The only agenda I have is that we both agree on everything. By the way, I want to go on the *Maid of the Mist*. Are you okay with getting soaked a bit?"

"Yes, I was hoping you'd say that, as my dad and mom always regretted that they didn't do that. Without credit cards, I don't know how people got along. They had that five dollars and knew they had to get gas and lunch on the way home, so they felt sad but didn't let it get in the way of the wonderful time and memories."

"It's too bad that we have to stay on the Canadian side, but I still can't chance going over the border. I never felt like a fugitive, but the crossing here is probably the most watched one, at least in the east. If they check and have my stuff on file, my freedom could end in a heartbeat."

"I know, sweetie. Hopefully someday, the US will find a way to forgive. You are not a criminal, my love. I don't mind that we can't cross."

"After we see everything you want to in Niagara, I'll let you in on a little surprise. I trust you brought your passport?"

"What? Where? I did, but I didn't pack for much more of a trip. Where are you taking me?"

"You may have noticed that I packed an extra suitcase. I talked to your dad, and he slipped enough clothes, undies, and stuff for us to fly off for a few days to a place he told me you've always dreamed of. I'll give you a hint. It's an island."

"Oh, Trey, you don't mean Bermuda, do you?"

"Yep, your dad said that you have dreamed of going there since you were little. I must admit that I have always thought it would be a perfect vacation spot. We drive back to Toronto and leave tomorrow morning. How about that? What do you think?"

"Totally like a dream. How do you think of everything?"

"Hey, you only get married once!"

Marriage suited both of them. In early 1975, Patience shared the best news with Trey since she had accepted his engagement ring.

"We're going to have a baby!"

"Are you sure?" Trey asked.

"Of course I'm sure, you big dummy."

"When?"

"I'll have a bump soon, and the baby will arrive around June."

"Can I hug you, or will that hurt?"

"You're so funny. Of course you can hug me!"

"Have you called your dad?"

"No, but let's do that this evening. I'll start by saying, 'Is this Grandpa Helm?' I can't wait to hear how long it will take him to get the message."

"You are bad! Be sure and put him on speakerphone, as I want to be bad with you."

"Trey, are you okay with having a boy?"

"Of course."

"That makes me smile."

"Oh man, can't wait till he grows up. Tossing a ball, hockey, tennis, hiking. Let's not get too far ahead, though! First we need to pick a name, right?"

"I thought about that too. I've spent lots of time since I found out in those naming a baby books."

"Any favorites?"

"Actually, yes."

"Well, I'm letting this one be one hundred percent your choice. I'm too excited to be rational anyway. I'd probably call him Johnny Carson Chapel," Trey joked.

They both started laughing.

"Well, he will have the same initials with the names I've chosen. How about Jared Cole?"

"Works for me. It has a nice ring to it. Besides, he'll be the perfect child no matter what!"

"I hope Dad can afford to come up for a visit since you still can't go to Florida. What a crock."

Something else significant was happening that would change their longing. Just as the draft and its implications made Trey's mind up to come to Canada, Jimmy Carter was elected to replace Gerald Ford. Any new president comes in with certain things on their agenda, good or bad, that are born out of dreaded campaign promises. For Trey, one item on Carter's agenda came as a total and wonderful surprise. On January 21, 1977, shortly after his inauguration, Jimmy Carter stepped up to a mike and declared that the hundreds of thousands of young men who fled to Canada were now free of any penalty and could return to the US.

One day, after baby Jared had been born, Patience came from the den into the kitchen with tears in her eyes.

"Trey, did you see what just happened on TV?"

"Tell me."

"I'll give you a hint. What have you been asking for, praying about, ever since you first met me?"

"You mean kissing you ten times a day, every day?"

"No, silly. How about the word *amnesty*?"

"What?"

"Yep. I'm sure we can get the details on the 6:00 news. Jimmy Carter is our new best hero of all time. He's freeing you, us, to be able to go over without sneaking. Now we can plan a vacation as soon as our baby is old enough and not have to make Dad travel."

"That's unbelievable! I've been here over ten years. I supposed many times that I'd never get to go back, legally. I hope my folks and my sister have heard. Above all, I hope they will take me back. It's been hard on me. I hope they longed to take me back and haven't forgotten our promise to always love each other, no matter what. I suppose thousands of guys my age feel the same and feel like they will live out the Bible story of the Prodigal son. I'm going to call Scarlett. I know she still loves me. I hope she will tell me a way to get my folks back in my life."

Scarlett interrupted the flow of the story again to tell me how meaningful that phone call was to her. "Larry, in 1977, I was living in Upper Arlington. I had a successful career as a math teacher, had a prominent attorney for a husband, and we'd welcomed two beautiful children. Our parents were living in Michigan, and they were in their early sixties and dreaming of retirement. When Trey called me, I was shocked and overjoyed. I knew he had to be careful about how much contact he had with family in the States, not wanting to jeopardize his new life. But I had missed my brother dearly, and I was so glad to learn of all the big developments that had happened since I'd last talked to him."

I could tell that Scarlett was getting emotional remembering this phone call, so I encouraged her a bit and then was quiet so she could continue on with her story.

"Sis?" Trey asked, hesitantly.

"Trey, I bet you're calling about the story that has been on the news all week."

"Yep, I've been a little stressed ever since I heard."

"Why?"

"Well, I know you'll take me back, but what about Mom and Dad? They haven't said boo since I left."

"Trey, I'll call them tonight and take their pulse on all this. I hope they understand that you always loved them, and that the decision to give up maybe more than you gained was a difficult one."

"Thanks, Sis! You can tell them that besides me, they get a beautiful daughter-in-law and an even more beautiful grandson!"

REUNION

TREY AND PATIENCE spent a few days in great anticipation. They had no idea how to even imagine the outcome. What if his parents had written him off for good? Three days passed before Scarlett called back.

"Trey, they want us all to meet at the lake house next Saturday for a family reunion."

This house had been built by Trey's grandparents for the purpose of being a family gathering place. Because of their untimely death, that dream was never fulfilled. It passed to Trey's parents, but because of Trey being estranged all those years, and Scarlett being fairly distant in Ohio, it rarely got used.

"They started to cry when we talked, and they can't wait to see you and meet Patience and Jared!"

"Now I'm going to cry. You have just helped melt away over ten years of anxiety. I can't wait to hug you."

Their entire family met at the house on Lake Charlevoix. Trey and Patience were the last to arrive, even though they lived the closest. Crossing the border was the challenge, as even though Trey's status had changed, it seemed the border people didn't get the memo regarding amnesty. A phone call or two at the crossing squared everything.

Pulling up to the house was something of a revelation for Patience. "This place is like a resort, isn't it?"

"Boy, I'd forgotten how incredible it is. My mom's parents built it before they passed."

"You never told me much about them. One thing is for sure, they had some serious cash!"

"That's partly why I never much mentioned them. I so appreciate that our family history includes stuff like this, but I always felt that I didn't want it to get in the way of my own ambitions and success."

"I get it completely! Anyhow, if I ooh and aaah as we walk around the place, don't laugh at me. Also, won't I sort of stand out as a bottom feeder in the midst of all the things your family has achieved?"

"Are you kidding me? Please don't say that or even think that. You're anything but! Once my parents and sister spend a minute with you, they will see why I was smitten."

"Oh, it wasn't because of my beautiful body?"

"Funny! Besides, Scarlett is also a teacher, and I'm certain you two will hit it off."

The greetings from everyone were just what Trey had hoped for. Warm and wonderful words went back and forth, and the conversation was never one bit forced. The long years of separation melted away. Jared Cole—nicknamed J.C.—was an additional heart warmer. After a sumptuous cookout-type feast, the girls decided to retire to the screened porch with little J.C. It was a perfect evening for it. The two overhead paddle fans gave off a soft breeze.

Patience had nothing to worry about. She became family in a heartbeat.

"So, son, let's go out and start a fire and sit by the lake. I want to get back all ten years before I allow us to head in for the evening," Brad said to his son.

"Thanks, Dad. I do too, but I hope you will give me more than one evening. What about Richard?"

"Oh, he can come with us. He's been like a second son to us. We have no secrets, and he's a very secure guy. He'll do nothing but add to our conversation. You know I was kidding about our talk, don't you? Maybe two are due."

For the first few months, Trey's parents couldn't get enough of the reunited family. They either met at the lake or made the trip up to Sault Ste Marie to see Trey and his family. Scarlett was busy, and she lived farther away, but she came as much as she could.

Soon, Patience was pregnant again, and a baby girl made their life and family complete.

"Trey, honey, do you like the name Paige?"

"I love it. Where did you come up with it?"

"I thought about this baby being another page in our story. I saw the spelling in my book of names that I had back when we were picking J.C.'s name."

Trey thought the name was especially perfect, as he felt they were starting a new chapter of their lives with his family back in it.

GROWING PAINS
AND A TRAGEDY

IN THE EARLY YEARS, **the kids were easy and good. They** were smart, kind, mannerly, and everything their parents could hope for. Then Jared turned thirteen and Paige eleven. That year, everything seemed to change. Paige became a snot. It's hard to imagine who and what influences the young mind. She began hanging around with two girls who were Jared's age. Their parents were neighbors that Patience and Trey knew. Because the girls were older, Paige looked up to them. It was shocking that one- or two-years of difference could mean so much. But it always does, especially with girls. Both the girls were already filling out and wearing makeup. One even smoked. They started asking Paige to stay over a few times. Little parties, seemingly innocent, began to happen each weekend. Paige would come back and start questioning her mom and dad's authority. After a while, it turned up a notch, and she would talk back and become belligerent at any mention of it becoming a problem. And it was!

Jared, at just thirteen, was a man child. He was bigger than his dad already. He quickly developed a temper. He and Trey rarely saw things the same way. One evening Jared came home drunk. He came into the kitchen and started swearing at Patience when she confronted him. She knew she couldn't handle him physically, but she also knew that he had crossed a line between parent and child. She first told him to go to his room. When he just laughed at her, she told him she would be calling his dad at the dealership.

"Go ahead, you bitch," he responded.

Patience called Trey, and he was soon beside her at the house. Jared must have thought better of his actions and took off before his dad arrived, because by the time Trey arrived, Jared was nowhere in sight. This gave Trey and Patience some time to think about a proper course of action.

"How could this happen?" Patience asked, tears in her eyes.

"Sweetie, I hope it's just a phase! The teen years are hard."

"Boy, so do I. If not, the future will not be bright for them or us. I feel that we need to get a handle on them now rather than later."

"Agreed. For now, let's cool down about what happened. Jared still loves us, I'm sure. He probably is somewhere now, regretting what he did and said, realizing it was the booze talking and not him. He's got one major thing going for him. He's really good at hockey. He's already on a good traveling team. Maybe we can talk with his coach and ask him to do everything he can to keep J.C. on the straight and narrow."

Jared eventually came home, and his parents said nothing to him about what had happened. He went straight to his room. Not ideal, but both parties seemed to defuse.

What happened over the next few years was hard for the parents to watch. They tried a lot of different approaches. Sometimes they just gave in and showered the kids with stuff. They gave them trips, cars, credit cards, all in hopes of them being more responsible.

When that didn't work, they pulled back and they became super strict. Because the kids were still living at home, Trey and Patience thought this approach would work. Apparently, they pulled back too hard. When they did this, it was almost like what happens to an addict. Both kids suffered withdrawal-like symptoms. They became totally non-communicative with their parents and acted out in increasingly harmful ways. Jared would often get sent home from school for fighting and other malfeasance. Paige threatened to run away and at times seemed suicidal.

When Jared turned twenty-one, he left home, and Paige wasn't far behind. But soon they started doing more mature, adult-type stuff. Jared enrolled in a local law enforcement school and soon graduated. It took his dad's influence and endorsement to make it happen, as his teenage years left a few bumps and scrapes on his résumé. Had his dad not been so connected, the chances that he could have made this move would've been very low.

Paige got a job and a boyfriend. She asked if Mom and Dad would front some money for a deposit on a place for them to live. They happily helped, hoping it would help her settle down.

For a few years, all the bad stuff seemed to be behind Jared. He met someone at a local dance. They dated and spent time at each other's homes. Her parents liked Jared a lot. Trey and Patience were thrilled that their son seemed to be getting his life squared away. Soon they were engaged. She was soon pregnant with Jared's child. Had this happened a generation before, the outcome could have been much different, as being "knocked up" took on a much more ominous tone back then. Jared and his girlfriend moved in together, and both sets of parents were supportive.

Paige and her boyfriend lived at the edge of the city in a secluded little cottage. It seemed like things were on the way back to good for the Chapel family. Jared became a police lieutenant in Sault Ste. Marie. His wife was able to stay at home with their young son, Cole. Paige became an assistant manager at a prominent ladies' clothing store. Her boyfriend worked as a server at the Eagle's Nest.

In late June of 2000, the family was beset with an unspeakable tragedy. Trey and Scarlett each received a phone call from the Michigan State Police. Their parents were on a short trip to a mall in Bloomington Hills. They were at a red light when a drunk driver came through and hit the car at high speed. They were killed instantly.

"Nothing could be done to save them, son," the officer said to Trey.

"We tried to revive them," a sweet female officer reported to Scarlett.

And just like that, a family that was torn apart, then put back together, was once again torn apart.

The drunk driver was a young girl whose parents were unaware she had ever taken a drink. She was unhurt. She was eighteen at the time.

Scarlett and Trey were grief-stricken. Scarlett had been as close as a sister with her mom in her adult years, and she was also "Daddy's Girl." Their absence left a gap in her life that felt impossible to fill.

Trey had re-earned his place in the family, as he was given total grace by both their dad and mom. Over twenty years had gone by since their initial reunion. Those years were, by their own admission, blissful. They lived for their children and grandchildren.

The girl got off with no jail time. Her sentence would be cemented in her mind forever, though, the inescapable fact that she had made a mistake that cost two wonderful lives.

The parents had a will, a trust, and a living will. They were in their eighties but had still been quite active and together at the time of their accident. They had meticulously planned their own funerals, so the kids had very little they had to make decisions about. It would be held at their church in Grosse Pointe. They didn't expect to pass together, so each had separate requests, right down to the hymns to be sung.

They had lived in Grosse Pointe long enough to have a large circle of friends. At the calling hours, Trey and Scarlett dutifully met and greeted well over a thousand friends, neighbors, business associates, and church members. The line was out the door and around the entire block. Fortunately, the weather was bright and sunny and in the seventies at both the showings and the service.

Because the parents and kids never lived in the same communities as adults, Trey and Scarlett were somewhat surprised at the outpouring of people, most of whom they had just met. They would soon realize that their parents were pillars in their town, their church, and their greater circle of friends. They had accomplished much and contributed much.

"Sis, we lost them. How could that be? They were many times more special than we even knew."

"I know. Time after time, a person would tell me how one of them had helped them recover from regular stuff like changing a tire, to major stuff like helping with bills and debts. We have a lot to live up to, Trey."

"For sure."

Both Trey and Scarlett had no trouble pursuing the driver's family, and their insurance company, for damages. Richard, Scarlett's husband, handled all of this. Because they were already wealthy, the unneeded windfall from the settlement was mostly used to benefit their church with a new organ and to establish a special scholarship at U of M.

The rest of their estate went to their family, to be equally divided between Trey and Scarlett. Richard was a Godsend in this process, as it involved many and varied accounts, and assets both financial and real estate. They had a modern art collection that was auctioned off for over two million that neither Trey nor Scarlett had known about.

In short, Trey and Scarlett had life-changing wealth bequeathed to them. Both agreed they would give it all back in a heartbeat to have their parents back alive.

Once a year, Trey and his family planned a reunion with Scarlett and her family. The place for this reunion was always the cabin on Lake Charlevoix. The two families always kept the ownership of this property in a trust, as that's how their mom and dad wanted it. The fewer people who knew the ownership, the better, they all agreed. This, they hoped, would keep the next generation from thinking of it as anything but a blessing.

Scarlett had met a family when she first started teaching who provided her with a firsthand look at what could happen when kids see a family's wealth from a different perspective. She met regularly with the Clancy family. They presented her with quite a nice opportunity that she was allowed to pursue as a teacher. She tutored two of their four kids. The Clancys were wealthy, owning several companies around the Columbus area. As Scarlett became more attached to the kids, the parents treated her and her husband like family.

"Scarlett, we have a beautiful cabin in the Hocking Hills. We want you to use it and enjoy it. We love taking our kids there, and yet don't really get full use of it, as we're always so busy."

Scarlett and Richard loved the Hocking Hills area of Ohio, as it reminded them (mostly her) of the time spent in Pennsylvania. Taking full advantage of such an offer took a while to digest, but finally Mr. Clancy gave them confidence that saying yes was the right answer, period.

A visit was in order, and a beautiful weekend was spent at the cottage in Hocking Hills. It was more like a beautiful rustic home than a cottage. Inside, it had a great room with a floor-to-ceiling stone fireplace and open beams and expansive windows looking out over the wooded terrain. Above, there was a balcony around one entire side of the building, and that housed four bedrooms, each with its own bath.

The property included around forty acres of wooded hillsides with streams and paths, and being there was like being in a dream world. So, over time, Scarlett and Richard and their children, as they came about, were able to visit this cabin several times a summer because the Clancys simply made it clear that they wanted them to use it. The Clancys weren't using it to their advantage as they would like to, so it was a win/win for everybody. Eventually, the kids from the Clancy family were out of school and on their way to college, marriage, business, and adulthood.

Mr. and Mrs. Clancy still liked hearing from Scarlett, and they kept in touch for quite a long time afterward. During one conversation, Scarlett asked them if they still had the cabin.

"Oh no, we don't have it anymore," Mr. Clancy said.

Incredulous, Scarlett asked, "Why? Seems like your kids will miss out on their childhood memories of time spent there."

Mr. Clancy replied sadly, "Well, we decided five years ago we'd sign it over to our children. We hoped they would continue to use it as a family compound and enjoy it like we did. Scarlett, once they discovered it was worth a substantial sum if you sold the timber and the mineral rights for the property to some corporation, they had little interest in keeping it. Most of the beautiful forty acres went that route.

Then they sold the cabin and the remaining property to one of their Upper Arlington friends.

"The popularity of the Hocking Hills made the property value increase many times over what we paid for it when we bought it. Let me just say that they got a lot of money for it. We were disappointed as parents because it isn't what we would have dreamed for the outcome. We always assumed, even though there were four different children, that they'd have four different families and that they would split the time and enjoy the property like we did when we purchased it back in the day."

Scarlett paused again in her storytelling. "Larry, after hearing what had happened to the Clancy family, Trey and I became concerned that the beautiful place on Lake Charlevoix that we had inherited, that we had been blessed with, might cause the same result with our own kids. We wondered if the children knew the monetary value, would it become nothing but an asset, nothing but a potential source of money to them once we had passed? So we took great pains to tell the kids a little white lie as they grew older and were still visiting the property. The lie was that we just rented the cabin, and that the owners themselves were gracious enough to reserve it for us once or twice a year every year during the period we were able to go."

"I don't blame you, Scarlett. I see exactly why you made that decision," I said, encouraging her to go on with the story.

"Yes, well, in the end, the secret was found out, and our worst fears were realized," Scarlett said.

I felt uneasy as she continued telling the story. It was about to take an unfortunate twist...

COULD SUCH A THING
HAPPEN TO OUR FAMILY?

AS JARED GREW OLDER, he decided to ask Dad and Mom if he could bring a friend to spend time with them during their reunion. At first, it didn't sound like too good of an idea to the parents, but they eventually gave in and allowed Jared to invite one of his pals to come along. This seemed like an innocent gesture, but later on in life it proved to be the beginning of a quest by Jared to know more and more about that piece of property.

"J.C., that place has got to be worth a lot of money," his young friend said to him upon return from the reunion trip.

"What do you mean?" Jared said, puzzled.

"Well, it's right on the lake. It's huge. It's a beautiful cabin, and you guys have it every year. I'm surprised that your parents tell you that they rent it. I bet they own it, and I bet your aunt is involved in the ownership. I think your parents are richer than they tell you."

As a moody young teen, this wasn't lost on Jared, although he didn't dwell on it. But over time, as he grew older, he poked around and poked around. He kept asking his parents about their holdings, their properties, and how much money they had. It was a conversation that became very uncomfortable for Trey and for Patience, but they didn't put two and two together in a very good way, and they thought nothing more of it than just a young boy thinking ahead.

Jared was now a young married man with a family. His job as a law officer was secure. He had seen a lot for a man so young. It was a given in his line of work. He had lived through tremendous swings in his relationship with his parents. One thing kept eating at him. He realized that his parents were wealthy, likely wealthier than they ever let on. They were generous enough with him and his sister, but not really, not to the extent that he eventually convinced himself they should be.

He wanted what they had, but he didn't want to go through the time and effort they had put in to attain it. Plus, his in-laws were constantly bugging him. They also realized the wealth his parents must have, and they were wondering why their daughter had to work. They had recently remarked, "Jared, you and our Barb should be living in a big house on the hill! Don't your folks have a trust fund that you can tap into?"

In the meantime, Paige and her boyfriend—nicknamed Squeaky—had taken a dark turn. When she was younger, Paige had become fascinated with cigarettes and beer. The two slightly older girls she hung around with were allowed to partake in both, and their liberal-thinking parents believed it was their decision what they wanted to do with their bodies. Trey and Patience were unaware this was happening at the time. As the two girls got a little older, they started using marijuana.

Paige was introduced to it, and she liked the feeling it gave her. For the early part of this journey, she was able to disguise it from her parents, and when she left home, she even managed to keep it from her employer. Then things changed. When she was at a party with her boyfriend, he talked her into trying cocaine. She was soon addicted.

They were constantly using. He somehow kept his job. She was soon to lose hers, as she would come to work stoned, or come late, or not at all. Her boss felt compelled to tell her dad, since they were longtime friends.

Trey and Patience were mortified that they had not known what was happening with their daughter. "Sweetie, we have to do something, and soon!" Trey told his wife.

"I agree. The first thing I think we should do is drag her home, away from that creep she's with," Patience said.

Trey wanted to move quickly to save his little girl. "What do you think we should do to get her home? She should be at the cottage right now. Squeaky is still probably at work, bartending. Let's go see her and get her back with us. Maybe she'll even agree to a rehab situation. How did this happen?"

They hurried over to confront their Paige at her place. After knocking multiple times, they decided to look in a window. They saw her sleeping or unconscious in a chair.

"Trey, we've got to break in. This is worse than I thought. Poor girl."

"Agreed!"

They tried and found that the window they were looking through was actually open. Trey crawled through and let Patience in. Paige was in a stupor. After some anxious moments, they managed to revive her. It took her several minutes before she realized her condition.

"Honey, we came to see you, and you wouldn't answer the door," Patience explained. "We were concerned and let ourselves in. We've come to take you home until we can figure out a plan to help you get back on your feet."

By this time, Paige was fully coherent and indignant. "I don't need your help! Nothing's wrong. I was just taking a nap. I'm fine. Please leave!"

"Paige, we know you lost your job," Trey said, trying a different approach. "We also know why. We don't blame you. We blame Squeaky, or whatever his name is."

"Leave him out of this. Please leave, as you are doing nothing but pissing me off. I don't need you two. I never have and never will!"

Crestfallen, they looked at each other and realized they had lost their daughter. Their little girl was nowhere in sight, despite the fact that they were looking right at her.

•   •   •

Meanwhile, Jared decided on a plan. He had his eyes on a prize. The prize was one he could only get if he inherited it. He considered that his parents were not old, and that asking them for money now would probably not fly. He decided his parents would not participate in his selfish wishes if he went to them with his thought, so he ruled out asking. He had a sister to share with as well, which was a problem he couldn't lose sight of.

The prize, he concluded, was worth a lot. He surmised three things. First, he would someday become a multimillionaire. Second, he didn't want to wait. Last, he didn't want to share this prize with his sister.

The prize would probably make him the wealthiest person in town, but once in hand, he would blow the small-town life for someplace where he could escape any critiques that would certainly come in Sault Ste. Marie. A place like Vegas, or possibly Miami, appealed to him.

To make all this happen on a timeline he could live with would be a daunting task. He would have to "get rid" of the other participants. That would include his parents and his sister. To eliminate them from getting his prize would have to mean killing them, having them killed, or having them somehow die by accident. This would have to be slick with little or no risk of any guilt falling at his doorstep.

One thing he learned as a policeman/investigator was that it's easy to make tracks, but much harder to cover them up. In the hundreds of cases he'd been on, he'd used this fact to trip up most offenders, as the tendency was that they hadn't thought through their plans to fruition, to the end game, and getting away with it. He would not be caught, as he would plot every move, think of every possibility, and cover every base.

He also decided that he needed an accomplice. Two sets of hands and eyes would be better than one for what he was plotting. He decided on a guy he once helped through some rather minor scrapes with the law.

Buster was caught stealing from his dad's business. Dad had him arrested. Jared was on the case. When he interviewed the young man, Buster convinced Jared that he was stealing because he felt his dad was withholding money he thought he had earned from a recent job he did for the company. Jared became sympathetic and helped minimize his sentence to a few hours of community service. He encouraged Buster to become a volunteer cadet in the local organization connected with the force. A few years of exemplary service there, and Buster wanted to become a law enforcement officer himself. It didn't come easily, but he was eventually accepted. His past record was minimized because of his service as a cadet and because Jared stood for him as a character reference.

Once sure that Buster would be interested, Jared told him, "Remember, pal, you owe me. Now you and I are going to do a project together. Once you accept, it'll be a win-win for both of us."

Buster listened to a little of what Jared wanted before saying, "So, I'm generally a don't-give-a-shit guy, J.C., but I'm afraid I can't begin to know what makes you tick. You're saying you'd pay me fifty-k to help you with your plan? And that you'll only reveal what you're up to if I sign a contract that says I follow what you tell me, when you tell me, go where you tell me, and swear everything to total secrecy?"

"Buster, that's it, pal. I'm going to find someone by the end of the day. I have lots of flunkies who won't be critical like you. You in or out?"

Buster was curious but cautious. "That's a lot of money. It's more than I'm making now in a year. Can't you give me more?"

"More money?" Jared screamed, furious at the audacity.

"No, more information."

"Look, last chance. In or out?"

"In."

"Okay, Buster. By the way, where did you get such a dumbass nickname?"

"Okay, what? My dad's name was George, and mine is too. My parents never liked the damn name but also felt I should be named after good ole dad. Buster came up when I started getting in fights at school. It stuck."

Within a few days, Jared had his plan in order and told Buster it was time to meet for phase one.

"I have the first part of my plan ready to go. We are going over to pay a visit to my sister tonight. She's shacked up with her boyfriend. They are so screwed up on crack these days that the whole thing will look like a spat gone wrong, way wrong."

Buster was incredulous, staring at Jared as if he had grown a second head.

"We're going to off your sister? I thought you liked her. What about Squeaky? He's a big dude. Won't he be a problem?"

"Look, you signed up for this, now don't give me any shit. That's why I chose you, and that's why you're getting big bucks. Just meet me at the Pub at 9:00."

"What's all the stuff in the back seat, J.C.?"

"Cleaning stuff."

"What are we cleaning?"

"You'll see."

•　　　•　　　•

Later that night, they arrived at Paige's cottage. They made entry easy by not locking their door.

"Buster, take these gloves and put them on."

They opened the door and walked right in. Paige was clueless as to why they were there, never imagining for a second what her big brother's real motive was.

"Hey, Jared. Hey, Buster. What are you guys doing here?" she asked meekly.

"Never mind. Both of you sit on the sofa and listen closely."

Jared took out a short, stubby club that he had used in his police work many times. With one fell swoop, he clubbed Paige on top of her head. She slumped over and made no sound. Her boyfriend was next. Squeaky stared at his longtime mate and started bawling. Then he recognized the pure evil facing him and started to plead for his life.

"Not going to happen, Squeaky. You got my sister into these drugs, and I never got to thank you properly, you sonofabitch!"

What unfolded in the next few minutes was both sickening and hard to watch (for Buster). Jared knew that his initial blow to both was well placed and strategic enough to kill. He must have hit Paige twenty more times with lesser blows. Then he turned to her boyfriend. He used the club on him as well. He made sure his initial hit there was not a killing blow. He issued several more hits and threw him down to the floor.

By this point, Buster was suddenly scared for his own well-being. "What the hell just happened here?"

"You saw it, now don't act stupid. I wanted you to come along to witness this, pal. Now get out to the car and get the cleaning stuff. We will leave no trace when we leave."

Terrified, Buster cried, "You are sick! Is that why we put on rubber gloves before we came in?"

"Sorry, you're in this now. Just keep doing what I say and keep your f***ing mouth shut."

Jared and Buster did two things. Jared had him pick up Paige and manipulate her hands and nails to put some nasty gashes on Squeaky's arms and face before replacing her on the couch. Then they did a thorough cleanup of anything that might implicate them. Jared made three quick calls to his dad on Paige's cell phone, saying nothing, then hanging up.

It worked perfectly, as Trey knew something was wrong and headed there immediately.

Two days later, Jared and Buster had coffee and a short meeting before heading to the station.

"Hey, man, the plan worked to perfection. My dad came in and saw the carnage. Just like I hoped, Squeaky was about to croak when he got there. The crime scene I set up in my mind played perfectly. He thought that Squeaky did the deed on my sister. He was out of it, but still breathing. My dad picked him up, shook the shit out of him, and dropped him back to the floor. He then, just perfectly on cue, called the police. I made sure I would be available to take the call. I got an officer and an investigator to join me, then went there, only to find my dad, Paige, and Squeaky. I acted all upset at the sight of my only sister brutally beaten to death. Her beloved boyfriend was dead as well, leaving my dad to explain what he thought happened."

After taking the call from his father the night of the terrible event, Jared responded. Once inside, Jared and two other officers found Trey holding his beloved daughter in his arms.

"How could this have happened? What could have made this bastard druggie kill your sister, my precious Paige?" he sobbed.

"Dad, look around. They were using tonight. That sometimes goes haywire and sets people off. Were either of them alive when you got here?"

"Yes, but it was the wrong one. He was still breathing when I got here," Trey sobbed.

"What did you do?" Jared asked.

"What did you expect me to do? I picked him up and started yelling at him, 'Why did you kill my daughter?' I shook him hard, and he mumbled something, started gurgling. I couldn't stand it and threw him to the floor."

"Well, looks like you finished him off. He's way dead now. Why don't you go home? There's nothing you can do here. Plus, you'll have to tell Mom."

Trey, totally in shock, left, dreading arriving back home. He had told Patience where he was going and that he'd report back as soon as he knew everything was all right with their daughter. When he got home, he had to share the awful news.

"Honey, something terrible has happened," he said to Patience, words he never wanted to have to deliver.

"What—just tell me that Paige is okay."

"Sweetie, she's not okay. I found her badly beaten, and by the time I got there, she was already dead. It looks like she got into some sort of violent argument with her boyfriend, and he killed her. I guess she was able to fight him off some, as I found him near death. He mumbled to me that he didn't hurt her. I pleaded for him to tell me who did, but he died in my arms."

"No, no, NO!" Patience shrieked as she fell into Trey's arms and sobbed till she was too numb to continue.

The next day, Jared, along with two other investigators, showed up at Trey and Patience's home. One of the two officers took the lead in speaking.

"Mr. Chapel," he said, "you're going to have to come with us to the station."

"Why? I told you everything I know last night."

"Sir, we're going to have to book you and arrest you."

"You've got to be kidding me. For what?"

"Well, sir, second-degree murder."

Jared was standing behind the main guy talking, and his dad thought he could almost detect a smirk as he was led away.

•　　•　　•

Later, at the coffee shop with Buster, Jared was beside himself with glee. "This couldn't be better, Buster."

"Not for me, sir. You have me by the balls, and I can't believe what is happening. You really think they're going to convict your dad?"

"Hell yes. He shook old Squeaks to death in a fit of rage. That's what the definition of second-degree murder is."

"Yeah, but your dad is such a stand-up guy. He's been around the city for years. He could parade in a thousand people for 'character witnesses.'"

"We'll see. I'm going to talk to the prosecutor and see if a case can be made to have him held without bail. I think he and Mom could be a flight risk if not. What a hoot. My dad, a flight risk. So far, we have the perfect setup. Get him behind bars and then have an 'unfortunate' situation happen while he's locked up. Then two down and one to go."

"Are you talking about your mom?" Buster asked, horrified.

"What? She'll be the easiest of the three. A grieving mom and wife ODs on sleeping pills? Piece of cake!"

"I want out right now. I'll take my lumps for my part so far. I don't even want a cent. I would never be able to spend it. I feel so dirty. Just don't ask me to go any further."

"What about your family? You don't want anything to happen to them, do you?"

"You bastard, you wouldn't!"

"Don't cross me. We have more work to do."

Despite Jared's warning that he thought his father might be a flight risk, the judge allowed bail, based on the fact that Trey had no prior record and had a business in the community, along with a solid reputation.

"He doesn't appear to be a flight risk to me," the judge insisted.

Grateful for the opportunity to regroup and look into how they could effectively have the case investigated, Trey and Patience tried to form a plan. Despite how badly they didn't want to believe it was possible, they suspected Jared had something to do with it.

"Honey, I saw Jared when they came to arrest me. Not only did he not come to my defense, but I'm also sure I saw a smirk on his face. What would possess my own son?"

Trey pleaded with the local officials to do more DNA testing to find out what they suspected—that someone else from outside committed this crime. It would lead them through a minefield, as Jared had already used his law enforcement influence to stymie any progress.

In addition, the investigators found Trey's prints both outside and inside the window he had crawled through on his earlier visit, when he and Patience came over and tried to lure Paige back home. This was an unexpected windfall for Jared.

"Why are you even listening to my dad about further investigation of Paige's cottage? I was in there at the outset, and it was apparent what happened. Squeaky killed my sister in a drug-induced rage, then my dad arrived and saw what happened and killed the bastard for taking his daughter from him. Open and shut. We dusted for prints and had forensics do preliminary DNA testing with no other stuff to go on. You even found his prints there, didn't you?"

His argument worked, and his influence helped. Little more was done to investigate the crime, as it was already "solved." Trey, however, was sure that he needed more stuff investigated. He knew he hadn't killed Squeaky, and he wanted to know exactly what had happened to his little girl. He hired a private investigator and found an independent DNA testing firm. The cottage had been locked down for the week that followed as an active crime scene, but it was no longer in that state, and Trey had a key.

•   •   •

After a day or two, Buster was beside himself at what he'd somehow gotten into.

"So, if you're giving me fifty thousand for helping you, where's the money coming from? You killed your sister. She certainly didn't have any money. You didn't ask me to rob her place. I don't understand!"

"All you need to know is that you will get your cash, but not until everything is done. Secrecy, man! We need to keep vigilant until all the dominoes fall," Jared said.

"So, what's next?" Buster said reluctantly.

"You've worked on cars, right?"

"You know that. I even spent some time at Burchfield's in the shop area. I know a thing or two."

"Good, 'cause we have a little fixing to do at my dad's house tonight. He has been leaving his car out. I think he needs a little 'brake work' done."

"What's that going to accomplish?"

"Think about it."

Much to Buster's horror, they sneaked over to Trey and Patience's driveway to do a quick and easy snip-snip on their car's brake lines.

•   •   •

Trey and Patience were under a lot of scrutiny after the charges were filed against Trey, but they still had many loyal friends in their corner who were sympathetic. While the charge was serious, their friends all thought that if/when the case made it to trial, a jury would find him innocent and rule it something like "justifiable homicide."

Trey and Patience decided to take a much-needed break and set out for their favorite watering hole for a burger and a beer. Within a short distance, Trey realized that the car was not acting right. He quickly lost control and ended up in a ditch. Luckily, they never got up to speed, and the damage to the car was light. More importantly, they were not hurt.

"Sweetie, we could have been killed. Our next turn would have been to swing onto Second, and we would have been going full speed. We would have crashed and been injured or even killed." Trey's face was white at the thought of what could have happened to his wife.

"I know, honey. What could have happened? You just drove the car earlier. Was anything wrong then?"

"Nope, this car was fine! I think this was a setup, Patience. Someone wants us dead. I hate to say it, but I think Jared is out to get us both. It's hard to believe, but no one else would have any reason to want us dead. Patience, before I jump to any conclusions, I'm going to call Ben from the shop. He's as good a friend as I have. I'm sure we can make him see that this is a setup by Jared. If he can come get us, I'll bet we'll find that something was tampered with that made this happen."

"Why don't you call the police too?"

"Well, if my suspicions about Jared are correct, I think that would be a bad idea."

"Yeah, I see your point," Patience agreed, starting to cry softly. How had this happened to both of their children, to the life they had worked so hard to build?

Ben soon showed up with his four-wheel drive Jeep and pulled the car out and towed it back to the shop. After looking it over for them, he reported back, "Sure enough! The brake lines were cut. Who would do such a thing?"

"Ben, I won't tell you, as I'm not certain, and I'm trying not to jump to conclusions, but I think both Patience and I know who did it."

"Wow, what are you guys going to do?"

"Ben, I want you to tell no one about this. I really fear for our lives. I'm going to take that red Chevy pickup that came in last week and pack it up, and we are going to leave town. At least till this whole mess gets straightened out."

"I know nothing, Boss!"

"Thanks, Ben."

Trey and Patience were both shaking in shocked disbelief.

"Honey, we need to leave tonight. Otherwise, I'm of the opinion that Jared will somehow have us dead very soon. Looks like he'll stop at nothing. We need to pack the truck and get started as soon as we can. I want to do another thing before we leave. Have you ever heard of a burner phone?"

"Yes, but only because I've watched lots of episodes of *Magnum P.I.*"

"I think we can trust our friend Thad."

"You mean Thad who owns the cellular store by our dealership?"

"Yes, I'm pretty sure he can get us a pair of phones and won't tell anyone."

"I know his wife as well. We've played cards together for at least two years."

Mission accomplished. Thad was immediately on board and sworn to secrecy.

"I think we should head for a safe place," Trey told Patience. "We can camp. I packed enough equipment to do that. I also stopped in the office and extracted enough cash from my personal safe to keep us going for at least a few weeks. The safe was something Rick Burchfield showed me when I took over. It was so cleverly hidden that I decided to leave it in my personal office when I remodeled it."

"I feel so vulnerable, honey. I trust you and agree that if we stay, we have no chance. Such crap!"

"Patience, we'll head across into Michigan. The border folks are probably not yet on any alert that we are moving. If that goes okay, then we need to get across the Mackinac Bridge. Once again, if the Canadian authorities knew we were in Michigan, they could put up a blockade at the bridge. Once past that point, I have three or four remote campsites I know of, and we can move more freely. No doubt we need to get started, and just pray Jared hasn't thought as far ahead as we have."

"Okay, let's get on the road."

GETTING INVOLVED

AFTER MY LONG CONVERSATION with Scarlett, I went back to the campsite and relayed everything to Barb. We decided together that Trey and his wife were likely the victims. I called Scarlett back and asked her, "Do you think Barb and I can be of any help here?"

"Let me talk to Richard and get back to you. Since Jared and his Canadian crew somehow think you're a possible conduit to finding Trey, maybe there's a way to turn the tables on them. In the meantime, see if you think they are still following you. If so, I think we can take advantage of that. I'll get back to you after I talk to my husband. Also, if it's okay with you, I'm going to talk with Trey and tell him about our conversation. He's supposed to call us soon. When I last talked with Trey, I encouraged him to get an untraceable burner phone. He can then call me and Dick and get outside counsel that otherwise could be used to find him if he kept using his standard cell phone."

"Good thinking, Scarlett."

"Thanks, Larry, that way he can try even harder to

stay low, knowing that you may be our 'mole' in the hole, if you will."

"I think I'll do the same. I don't know how Jared could trace my phone, but he does know my full name. With his police connections, he probably could get my number pretty quickly if he wanted it. The best part of this is that Jared never revealed why he (they) were hunting Trey. He also never told us that he was Trey's son. I think both of those omissions will allow Barb and me to move about freely, as what he doesn't know will work perfectly and give us a chance to help Trey and Patience get out from under this deadly plot. That's fine. Who knew that we'd have such drama from a week in Michigan? I'll look forward to hearing from you."

After a nervous day or so, we heard back from Scarlett.

"Hey, Larry, it's Scarlett. Hope you're doing well, surviving this mess. I talked with Richard and, most importantly, I talked to Trey. He and Patience are at our camp that my grandparents owned over in Lake Munuscong. He's safe over there. None of our children, his or mine, ever knew about that place, and I don't think Trey was followed. If so, he'd be dead by now. I think the burner phones for both of us, plus Trey and Patience, will prove to be our way out of this mess. We thought about a plan and want to run it by you and see what you guys think about it. More importantly, are you willing to get involved or would you rather just flee the scene and get back to Columbus and out of this mess? We think it'll work, though, but none of us want to put you in any danger."

"I'm more than happy to hear you out."

"We need to draw Jared into a trap, and that trap would be one where you would be involved as kind of like the bait. Where have you guys been that there might be a public place that could prove to be helpful to us? We have talked at length with a bunch of different agencies. They tell us that if we could find a place that was public, such as a bar or restaurant, we should be able to set a trap for him. Then you guys could be used to draw Jared and his fellow officers to the place. It would be ideal if it were somewhat remote, yet visible to the road. If it would be along the shore, that would be ideal, as the lake side of it would be sort of a natural boundary that would keep down any escape routes."

I thought for a moment. "Well, there's this one restaurant up north of Harbor Springs. Barb and I took a sightseeing trip through what's called the Tunnel of Trees. It's right on Little Traverse Bay. We spent some time there the other day. It's got a long shoreline and a beautiful piece of land that might be a place where we could do something like the so-called trap you have in mind."

"Does it have a wooded area around it or any place where we could hide the police from Petoskey, the state police, and the FBI that are all going to be involved in this? Richard and I have been in contact with those people, and we know that they'll cooperate with us, and we're pretty sure they are convinced that Trey and Patience are victims here and that Jared and his cohorts are at fault. I call them that without knowing if any of them know that they are actually involved in this. It's very likely at least some of them honestly think they're just doing their jobs. My guess is that maybe one or two of them are in on this, and the rest of them aren't. Nevertheless, right now they are still the bad guys and have to be treated as such. So, if we could somehow give Jared some false information that would draw his crew up to that restaurant, perhaps that would be the trap we need to catch him. We would let him think that he was going to ambush Trey and Patience, and therefore have everything in place to get rid of the final two pieces of Jared's plot. In the meantime, the authorities would be hiding, and they would turn the tables on him and his guys at the end of this scenario. So, do you think you could help us with that, Larry, and do you think Barb would go along with it? I know it's dangerous, and I also know that you guys certainly don't have to be involved."

"Scarlett, at this point, we're already fully involved, and we're not going home until we see that Trey and Patience are safe and that his bastard son and his cohorts, if they're involved, are caught. So, what do you think we should do?"

"Larry, I spoke with the police department on Petoskey. They don't want you to be seen directly in contact with them. They suggest that you agree to meet with them at some location that Jared would not be in any way suspicious of. While there, they will brief you on as many details as you need. They will confirm your identity with cameras, and you will ask any questions you might have. That way, you don't just need to trust what I'm telling you. Can you think of such a place?"

"Yes, we have to confirm our rental car tomorrow, as we are now extending our stay. If that sounds good, I'll give you the location, and you can set it up with them. I have a 2:00 appointment there."

"That's perfect! Unless they see a problem with that, you won't hear any more."

The next day went smoothly as planned. At the rental car office, the lead officer made contact with me and briefed me on the plan they were trying to put in place.

"Larry, I'm so glad you and your wife are cooperating with us. We originally thought of just doing a sweep of that campground you guys are in. That way, we could minimize any chance of Trey and Patience being harmed, as well as you two. Then we talked it over. If we did it that way, we'd have to be one hundred percent sure of Jared's plan and Trey's innocence. We are only ninety-nine percent sure, if you know what I mean. That led us to needing to bring Jared into a trap. If he's guilty, then he will respond to any way possible to get Trey and Patience killed or captured by his group. Larry, here's what we think would work. You need to tell Jared that you were on this trip yesterday through the Tunnel of Trees, and you just stopped at this restaurant. While there, you once again saw the red pickup truck, and you think maybe Trey and his companion might be working there or perhaps staying there, since it's also an inn. If that's done innocently, it should convince Jared that it's a possibility, and he'll want to check it out. Hopefully, he'll think it's the right possibility, and that should get his whole crew up there tomorrow, if you tell him. If somehow wants you and Barb to go along with this plan and also be there, we think that's okay. Every one of us will have the pictures we take of you and Barb today, with us. It will be scary, but just go along with it. Here's my personal cell phone number. If you are asked to go, just call me. We'll alert everyone that you're going to be there as well and to make sure they don't harm you in the process."

That evening, back at the campsite, I passed by "Cole" and stopped to speak, like I always did.

"Hey, Cole, how's it going? What have you guys been doing? Have you had any leads, or have you been getting any closer to catching up with the guy you're looking for? I hope you are, because I think he's still on the loose, and that concerns me. Scares me a bit, and also scares my Barb. We want to stay up here, but we don't feel very safe."

"Hey, I understand, Larry. I don't feel very safe either, as long as this creep is out there, and we want to catch him."

"Well, I might be able to help you guys."

"How so?"

"Barb and I were up through the Tunnel of Trees yesterday. Have you ever heard of that?"

"Oh yeah, we try to take that in every fall because the leaves are incredible."

"Well, we saw the red pickup truck again. We even think we saw Trey and his companion in a restaurant that's up there. I tried to get a good look at him, but I don't know if he suspected me or what. He kept making sure his back was to me. I don't know if that was purposeful or accidental, but nevertheless, I never did get a great look at him."

"Okay, Larry, that's good information. I will check it out tomorrow, for sure. You know, I was thinking, since you have this magnetism toward Trey, maybe you can be part of our group and help us catch this guy."

"How can I do that?"

"Well, not really sure, but maybe before we leave tomorrow morning, if you're still at your campsite, we can talk a little further about that. Maybe I can talk with my buddies tonight and see what they think."

THE TRAP

"HEY, BUSTER, you know this guy from down in Columbus who thinks he sees Trey every other day? I don't know if he's for real or not, but I think we should make him part of our plan to catch my parents. I'm also getting a little concerned that the rest of our group might catch on one of these days. You and I are fully invested in our plan. The other guys are just doing this because of their loyalty to the cause and to me. They would not be pleased if they knew what was really going down."

"I don't want that to happen to you, Cole. Plus, I'm still planning on some serious money when all this crap is over."

"Yeah, yeah, yeah, Buster, I understand. I'm getting a little antsy too. We need to get this thing over with. So, let's tell Larry and Barb that we want them to come along and help us set things up when we get to this restaurant. I know where it's at. I've been there several times with my family. I know it's on the left side and right on the bay."

"It's a beautiful place, but we are not even sure Larry's assumptions are for real. We do know that he's led us to a false alarm already, and we had to cause some collateral damage for that couple down in Young State Park."

"Hey, shut up about that, Buster, you know that had to be done, and so far, we didn't get the blame for that."

"So, just tell Larry that we want him to go with us, and when we get up there, we'll give him further instructions," Buster said, feeling empowered now. "I think when we get up there, we should just plan on Larry and Barb sitting in their car. We'll surround their car so they can't get out, and if they prove to be snitches, then we can deal with them without them ever getting away."

"Buster, I'm impressed! You're not as dumb as I gave you credit for. So, when we get there, if the red pickup truck is there, we're going to surround the place. We've got eighteen of us. That should be enough. Once we find out if it's really Trey, we take the place over. We arrest him on behalf of the Canadian Provincial police. We need to make sure everyone is in uniform today."

"He's supposed to have a woman with him, according to Larry. You know it's gotta be your mom. Once we have them, we get them in one of our cars and get them back to the camp and we can deal with them there. I'm of the opinion that if this all goes as planned, we need to just take them out on a boat, tie them to a couple of cinder blocks, gag and bind them, and push them overboard and let them be found five years from now, or never, in the middle of Lake Michigan."

"Buster, that's the smartest thing I've heard you say to date! That sounds like a plan to me, too. Whatever we do, we don't want to get caught, and we certainly don't want to draw too much attention."

"We won't, because once we make an arrest, it'll look like it's just something that we've been working on for a long time. Unfortunately, it's true. We'll have a nice campfire tonight. We'll invite Larry and Barb over again, and we'll see if we can't have some good fellowship and act like everything's totally cool."

"All right, let's do it. I'm going over to see if they're there."

Five minutes later, he found Barb and me outside on our camp chairs.

"Hey, how you guys doing? You know this thing with Trey has gotten out of hand, and I'm so sorry that all of this has kind of ruined your vacation. But...we're pretty close to catching this sonofabitch, I think. We would like you to come with us tomorrow to the restaurant to see if it really is Trey. Then we're going to be able to arrest him, and at that point, we'll thank you guys and let you go on your way. It will probably take a little time to process him and then head back to Sault Ste. Marie with him in tow, and certainly that is something that both you and I wanna get done, right?"

"Yeah, I guess so. Sounds like a plan. What are you going to do, by the way, when you get up there?" I asked.

"Well, there's a bunch of us, so we can surround the place and poke around and see if we can find them. Once we find them, I'll identify them, and then we'll arrest them. If it's not them, we'll simply find out, be on our way, and continue our investigation. And also, we'd like you to come over this evening. We all hope this might be one of our last evenings here, at least for this trip. We'll have us a cookout and cook up some steaks, and you can just have a big evening with us and be our guests. How's that sound?"

"Well, sounds pretty good, actually. We're really just about out of food in our RV anyway, so that works well for the both of us."

"Should be fun," Jared said. "It's a nice evening. It's warm and not too humid, so we'll see you later."

"Well, he took the bait," I told Barb. "I'm pretty scared, but we've got to keep with the plan. I'm going inside to call our Petoskey guy on his cell, so he'll know that we will be there. Come in with me. We can just pray. Pray that nothing goes wrong, and that no one gets hurt. Okay?"

"Hope the plan works!" Barb said, her voice high with nervousness.

THE STING OPERATION

WHEN THE NEXT MORNING ARRIVED, it was a very bright, sunny, beautiful day, and a plan had now been hatched to catch Trey and Patience. A second plan was also in place to trap Jared and his cohorts and get them where they belonged—in jail—or at least some of them, if not all of them.

"So, we all drive up the Tunnel of Trees road again?" I asked.

Jared (Cole) said, "Hey, there's a straight road that goes up there, and another straight road that goes off to the left. That allows us to avoid the Tunnel of Trees, which takes about an hour longer. There's no sense in sightseeing today, as our purpose here is anything but sightseeing. That work for you and Barb?"

"Yeah, we knew about those roads too. We took them back the day we went up there ourselves because the trip up took so long. When we were done, we realized there was another way to get back and just took it. You're right. It takes about an hour or less to get back than it did to get up."

Jared was the leader of a caravan. At the turnoff to the

left, he pulled all of us over and explained some things to Barb and me as well as to his team.

"All right, so we're getting close now. What we're going to do is this: there's a big clearing up here just about a quarter of a mile from the building. We're going to all park here and walk in. Larry, we want you and Barb just to stay here. Park your car in a way that you can be comfortable, and at the same time, if anything happens down there, that you'll be safe."

"It seems like you're blocking us in, Cole. Is that correct?"

"Well, I didn't realize that, but it does look like that, doesn't it? That's not our intention, but let's just leave it like this, and we'll certainly come back and give you the update when we're all done with this. Trust us, we've done this on-foot kind of thing before, and we think it's in your best interest to leave your car where it's at."

After getting us set up to where we couldn't much move, Jared talked to his men.

"Okay, now, let's fan out and get this place surrounded. The red pickup's right there in the parking lot, so either Trey's here or somebody else with a red pickup is."

As they closed in, he pulled Buster aside. "I hope it's Trey, and we can kill the sonofabitch and get his body into Lake Michigan soon!"

Once on the restaurant property, Jared announced, "All right, so how many doors? Let's walk around and see how many doors this place has before we do anything special. I don't think there's anybody here who is suspicious of us yet. I don't even see anybody. It's too early in the morning for a lot of traffic. Most of the people who come here come for lunch, and that's not happening for a couple of hours. Let's get started."

They proceeded one door at a time until there was just one door left. As they opened it, Jared shushed them with a hand signal.

"All right, let's get in there and see— Oh shit, there's my dad and mom!"

"Are you sure you're not seeing things?" one of his men whispered.

"Yeah, I'm sure! Now he's got his back to us, so we're going to sneak up on him. Somebody grab him. The lady there with them is definitely my mom. I'm sure of that too. So, we got what we came after, so now let's just make sure we can do this clean. There's one other person in this room. I don't know who they are, but they're an innocent bystander. I hope we don't have to do anything to harm them, but if we do, we do."

Trey and Patience had been coached to be as passive as they could possibly manage. Act as if they had been caught and were providing no resistance.

Buster sternly said, "Mr. and Mrs. Chapel, you're under arrest. We're going to read you your rights and cuff you both. Do you understand?"

Trey and Patience complied and were led toward the door. Jared finally appeared in front of his mom and dad. They looked him in the eye, and he dropped his gaze, knowing that he would soon find a way to execute them both.

"All right, we got them where we want them," he said. "Now let's get them back to camp. Once we're back outside the building, one of you will get one of your trucks, and we'll put them in the back. We'll wait by the entrance."

Soon all eighteen were outside, along with Trey and Patience. A surveillance team watched to make sure all were accounted for. Once done, a small army of local officers and K-9s and vehicles came from the north side of the restaurant.

The FBI agent in charge used a bull horn and announced, "All right, listen up. This is the FBI. We're here to arrest you. Hold up your hands where we can see them. You're all under arrest!"

"What do you mean we're under arrest?" Jared demanded. "What the hell for?"

"For openers, murder. Murder, attempted murder, and other assorted crimes."

One of the innocent officers, blindingly following the plan, said, "But, sir, what are you talking about? Are you arresting all of us? Do you know we're policemen? We're from Canada."

"Sir, at this point, we're going to arrest you all, and then we will find out just who's who and what's what!"

"My wife and kids are going to kill me if they think I'm going to get arrested. How can a policeman get arrested?"

"Sir, don't cry," the head agent said. "We're almost positive some of you aren't involved and some of you are, so we'll figure this out as we go, but at this point, you're all under arrest."

All of a sudden, Jared pulled a gun out from under his pants and began shooting. He tried to shoot Trey, and at that moment, gunshots rang out from multiple directions and police started swarming everywhere.

Jared was badly wounded in the parking lot. Everything fell quiet. One of the officers who just got arrested, offered, "You know, I somehow knew he was involved in something bad here. It's just the way he acted. He seemed more interested than all of us put together when it came to getting his dad arrested and getting him taken care of. I don't know if anybody else is involved, but I'm sure not! I just feel so bad that everything like this has happened. I know that we've already gotten some innocent people killed, and gosh, I'm just glad that this is going to be over."

"Yes, so are we," the agent in charge said. "The FBI has been involved for several days on this, and we're glad it's come to an end. Sorry that we may never quite know exactly why Jared was so insistent about all of this, but we'll be trying our best to find out. Right now, we need to get fast medical attention to Jared. He's got a wife and kids, and we also need him alive in order to get any answers. By the way, you all probably know Larry and Barb. We know they're here somewhere. Let me ask you guys, where did you park? You obviously parked somewhere and walked over here."

Mustering up his courage to do the right thing, Buster said, "Sirs, can I tell you something before we go any further?"

"Of course, what is it?"

"I am so ashamed. I've been in on this entire terrible crime from the get-go. I was promised a large sum of money, and I had to sign a contract to get at it. He required that I sign the contract before I found out what we were doing, but I had no reason to think I couldn't trust him. Jared then started his spree. After he killed his sister and left her boyfriend for dead, I felt trapped. I saw how violent he was and feared for my life from then till now. I can tell you anything you want to know. I am so glad no one else got hurt or killed. Jared should be hanged from a tree for what he did. These guys with us trusted him as a leader and believed all along that his dad and mom were the enemy. Men, I'm so sorry! Officer, please arrest me."

Buster's statement was able to clear the rest of the men. The Petoskey police part of the contingent went back to the campsite and explained to the unsuspecting families what had just happened. They also explained that their husbands and dads would have to be detained for questioning, probably overnight. Barb and I got a call from the Petoskey officer saying that everything went as planned, except for Jared's part.

Relieved, we waited patiently to be unblocked so we could get back to Petoskey. One of the innocent Canadian officers showed the Petoskey group where our car was.

"I think Jared really felt they were part of a trap and he was probably planning on killing them too. Their car's blocked in. You should find it right away. It's a green SUV, probably a rental car."

So, the trap worked. Jared tried and failed to commit suicide by cop, even though this was obviously his intention. Trey and his wife were traumatized, but they were secure. Barb and I were emotionally beaten up but secure as well. And the story is sort of an all's well that ends well tale.

But that's very shortsighted because Jared wasn't just a man who committed terrible crimes. He had a family, a beautiful family he would not be able to come back to for a long time, if ever. Their dad, who they thought was a good guy, wasn't. Her husband, who she thought was a decent man, wasn't. Now they would be going through life without a husband, without a father, and they would have to pretty much start over and make a new life for themselves.

Trey and Patience would also need to rebuild and start a new way of life. Perhaps they would be kind and become part of the life of Jared's wife and three kids. Trey and Patience were all that was left of their family.

Jared was life flighted to Petoskey. He stayed under maximum surveillance and eventually recovered enough to face his charges. He was tried in both Michigan and Ontario. He was eventually imprisoned in Canada and served a life sentence.

Buster was arrested and booked as an accessory. He had a long road back, as he had to face charges in both places. He became the chief witness in Jared's crimes and was given a lesser sentence for revealing his role in the plot. He served his time, and when released, he left Sault Ste. Marie, moving to Nova Scotia to be with his younger brother.

The rest of the young officers were never charged. Each was questioned. It became clear that they were being good citizens and officers and had no idea what Jared's sinister nature held.

NOW WHAT?

AFTER A FEW DAYS of intense investigation, Trey and Patience were free to go.

"Is it okay if Patience and I meet Barb and Larry?" Trey asked the FBI officer in charge.

"Of course. We had to question them as well as you. They're back at their RV. I can reach them by cell. I feel sure they will come down."

"Thanks so much!" Trey said.

After hearing that Trey and his wife would like to meet with us, I asked, "Honey, are you up to this? I think we must do this before we leave. We're both traumatized right now, but so are they. It should be cleansing for all of us."

The station had a nice private reception room, where a much-needed conversation took place.

"Larry," Trey began, "I don't know how or what to say that would express how my wife and I feel right now. I hope somehow we can repay you for your kindness."

"Trey, you guys have been through enough. My Barb and I need to get back to Westerville and some normalcy.

How about I give you my number. We plan to come back here in the fall. Maybe then we can get together and talk about our adventures."

"That would be great. We have so many questions. Have a safe trip, and we'll be in touch."

Two months later, my phone rang. "Larry, Trey here."

"I know who you are, Trey. Remember, I know your voice. That's what got us here, right?" I said with a chuckle.

"How about you join us at our cabin on Lake Charlevoix? You don't have to schlep your motorhome unless you want to. The weather up here is currently in the throes of Indian summer and is just beautiful. Plan on staying a week if you can."

"We can do that. We'll be there Friday evening, if that's okay?"

"It's more than okay. I've invited my sister and Richard. I hope that's okay. You all played such a wonderful role in saving our lives. We want to celebrate! If you can, arrive about 5:00. We can enjoy a cookout and hopefully a beautiful sunset."

"Can't wait! Please give me your address so I can put it in my GPS."

"It's easy: 1 Belle Lane, Charlevoix, Michigan."

The trip was easier this time, as driving an SUV is a piece of cake compared to an RV. We spent a lot of time on the trip reliving our previous adventures.

"Larry, as I view this whole story, I can't help seeing God in it. What were the chances that we'd be in the same restaurant with Trey and Patience? Further, that you would recognize his voice, then have the chutzpah to confront him, take his picture, and get out alive?"

"You make it sound like just that! Then we ended up at our campsite with none other than their son. Once again, a God thing!"

"Then the picture you took catches Jared's eye, and our adventure is off and running!"

"Well, it all worked out, thankfully. You and I were able to survive it, and we saved Trey and Patience's lives. I do feel sorry for them, for sure, as they should be totally joyful right now. I'm sure they are full of mixed emotions because of the fallout of losing most of their family. I pray for time to heal them as best it can. Well, we're almost here. Wow, look at the pillars and iron gate to their place. Ready, sweetie?"

As we pulled up in front of the grand cabin, the whole family warmly greeted us.

"Larry and Barb, welcome to Lake Charlevoix. The weather has cooperated, and we should have a great week. Let's get your bags, and we'll show you to your suite."

"Wow, this place is something. I love Lake Charlevoix. Your view of the lake is a bit different than the one we've seen, as we mostly were only at the restaurant by the drawbridge."

"Glad to hear you like that, as we will be dining there tomorrow evening."

"Is that your boat, Trey?"

"Well yes. Scarlett and I inherited this place and the yacht when our parents died. Our grandparents passed it on to our parents. By the way, I hope you like boats, as we will be doing some sightseeing around the area in it. It's big enough to go anywhere, and even stay overnight. We'll just be taking day trips. It will give you a perspective of the area that most people don't get to see."

"Can't wait," I responded, and I meant it.

"For now, let's get ready for dinner," Trey suggested. "Afterward, we will sit around the campfire and get reacquainted."

We had a delicious dinner of steak, baked potatoes, and salad. Dessert was Pennsylvania-oriented with warm rhubarb pie and vanilla ice cream.

"So, before we get too far along," I said, "please tell us how things ended up with the arrests and with Jared's family."

"Good place to start," Trey said. "So, Jared was able to be released from the hospital shortly after being shot. He recovered enough to be questioned. After a very short period of trying to shift blame, he admitted everything. He had an accomplice, one of the young men you met. I'm pretty sure the guy will get off with a light sentence, as he did not kill anyone, and the prosecutor felt he was under stress from Jared to comply or die. He helped Jared clean up in the aftermath at the cottage before I arrived. I never saw either of them there, but they were outside when I got there. Jared had it set up. He and his buddy broke in and found Paige and her boyfriend on the sofa. Buster, the accomplice, held the boyfriend down while Jared brutally beat and strangled his sister.

"Patience and I could hardly stand to hear this, but we knew we had to. Once he knew Paige was dead, he turned his attention to the guy. He thought he was dead, and they did a thorough cleanup and waited outside. Somehow, they knew I'd show up, and they would then have someone to throw the blame on. They got me arrested, and that's the beginning.

"As the investigation wore on, I could see two things developing. First, they really wanted to pin the whole thing on me. I was there and I had motive. The way they described it made it logical. I arrived and found my daughter brutally murdered. Then I saw her boyfriend and assumed he did the deed. I took my wrath out on him and soon he was dead as well.

"The police were unable to locate any other evidence of an outside assailant, and I was arrested. The second and far more disturbing matter was that birds of a feather flock together. Jared wanted me to be arrested. At every turn I made, trying to have someone else from the outside take a closer look, he and his cronies—I only refer to them that way because they were under his influence—thwarted me and my efforts.

"Also, his accomplice, Buster, was a young man he had helped get out of some minor scrapes. He offered a lot of money to him to be part of his sinister plan. He told the investigators that if I would have been kept in jail, the plan was for me to have an 'unfortunate accident' while incarcerated. Once that happened, Patience would meet a similar fate. He would see that she would be cast as the grieving mom and wife, and then she would die of an 'accidental' overdose of sleeping pills.

"All parties to his evil plot would be quickly out of the way with zero suspicion of him being responsible. This part got thwarted, as I was able to get out on bail. Jared fought to have me remanded and detained before my trial. I think had I not been such a well-known part of the community, the judge would have complied. So, getting out made me a flight risk to Jared. That's when the real fun began. I had a near death mishap in my car when Patience and I tried to go out for an evening. Once again, my connections paid off, as one of my faithful employees at Burchfield's helped rescue me, and we found that my car had been rigged in an attempt to have a fatal accident. I told Patience that we needed to use some tactics I learned well, in my early years up here. I knew how to get over and back from Canada to Michigan without getting caught. I also knew that if I could do this long enough, that maybe Jared and his evil plot would be recognized. I was right, but I had no idea how bad it really was.

"Jared knew I'd run across the border. He luckily didn't know how or where. He had been to this cabin as a kid, and he figured we'd be somewhere in the area. To make matters worse for us, he formed the group of guys you encountered. We had no idea that this so-called 'task force' was in place. We were scared to death, but we knew we had to keep moving in hopes that he wouldn't find us. We took the red pickup truck from the dealership when we left. I felt it would blend into the Petoskey/Charlevoix scene, and we could pack it with camping gear and other essentials for our flight. His Barb and his two girls were with him and his buddies when you met up with him. Luckily, Cole Jr. was down in Philadelphia, as he might have inadvertently gotten involved if he'd been home.

"Bottom line is that Jared was convicted of his sister's murder, as well as that of her boyfriend. The terrible collateral damage of the couple at Youngs State Park also fell on him. He will be in prison for life with no chance for parole. That is justified, but terrible for Patience and me, as we still can't believe this has happened. His wife and kids are okay financially, as Jared and Paige both had trust funds they never knew existed. Such a shame, as they never lacked anything, and yet Jared's greed led to all this mess. Well, that leads me around to answering your question, so will you then start to unravel your part in all this for me?"

"Thanks, Trey," I said. "Before getting too far along, tell me one thing: when I confronted you at the restaurant, did you know who I was?"

"Well, I remembered your name and that you were someone I knew back in the day. If I saw you on the street, I wouldn't have known you from Adam."

"Any idea what you said that would make me positive that your voice was one I could be sure of?"

"No, please tell me. All of us, including Scarlett, would like to know."

"Okay then. I only ever met you twice after high school, right?"

"Wow, you must have quite a memory!"

"I do, but it was something you said at both instances. Plus, the way you said it both times sealed the deal. You'll probably laugh, but if you hadn't said it, you'd probably be dead instead of entertaining Barb and me. It's what you said when I called you Trey and totally startled you. Your reaction was, 'No, but what the f***'s it to you anyway?' When we met in the bar in Dayton fifty years ago, the only difference was that you admitted you were indeed Trey, but both times, "What the f***'s it to you?" cemented your identity. I'm sure you said no this time as you were hiding your identity, right?"

"Wow. So, me being me paid off big time. I don't much talk like that anymore, do I, Patience?"

Rolling her eyes, she agreed. "Trey settled in and became a very good citizen when he found me. I wouldn't have it otherwise."

"When I thought you had taken a picture of me, I was sure you were somehow involved with the plot to capture us," Trey said. "That's why I was about to smash your face and your phone."

"Looking back, I thought I handled that little episode with as much aplomb as a scared rabbit could! Do you remember what I said?" I asked.

"Yep, you said, 'Don't flatter yourself, pal,' and that you were taking a selfie. Pretty quick thinking. Why did you want a picture in the first place?"

"Remember Dave Gillott? I couldn't wait to send him a text with your mug shot and tell him that I had met up with you again. When I saw you in Dayton, I called him immediately, and we had a good laugh. He also told me then that you might be heading to Canada. When I saw you at the restaurant, that seemed plausible, as we were pretty near Canada."

"So, then what happened, Larry?"

I recounted the events up to the point of hearing the news about the couple from Ludington and their unfortunate fate. Trey and Patience both piped in, "We heard the same news, but never connected the dots, as we didn't know what you guys did."

"I understand. It was at that time that I remembered your sister and our Jones Junior High connection. I figured my longtime friend Bill Hughes would know how to get in touch with Scarlett. I just knew by this time that there was a strong chance you were fleeing for your life, and not because you were guilty of any crime, as Jared would have us believe. Fortunately, I was able to get Scarlett's number from my friend Bill, and I reached her that evening. By the way, where were you guys hiding? You must have done well, as you had a ton of folks looking for you."

"We were actually pretty lucky," Trey said. "Through the years of learning every nook and cranny of the area's geography, we had some places no one knew about. We could go over and back because, well, just because we could. There's a very narrow place at the western edge of St. Joseph's Island where I made a duck blind a long time ago. I had a kayak stored in it, and we could cross over to Neebish Island and get easily to Barbeau."

"Sounds like you had a plan," I said, impressed with how well he had thought things out.

"Yes, Larry, a survival plan. We had a tent, some food, some cash, and we just needed time. I called Sis, and she told me about you. Even then I marveled at the connection. How this whole thing was put together so well. How you were so blessed to have a talent for hearing a voice and remembering it for all those years."

"You sound like a guy who might even admit to this all being a 'God Thing.'"

"Oh, we both do, Larry. Too many things that happened simply can't be coincidences!"

"Is it also a coincidence that the name of your boat is *Over and Back*?"

"Now that *is* a coincidence. My mom's parents named it. We now have it, but it does fit, doesn't it? Tomorrow we'll take her out and go over and back with no one looking over our shoulder!"

With the storytelling out of the way, the week was amazing. Barb and I became fast friends with both couples. A date was set for the next year to get together again. Scarlett and Patience found out that Barb had been a teacher, and they began to get together on the phone and through Facebook. Richard and I bonded, and we each became clients of the other.

Trey and I couldn't get enough of each other. We talked often and shared stories of our past. We were surprised when we soon realized we had much more in common than we ever would have thought.

CLOSING AUTHOR'S NOTE

BY READING MY STORY, you certainly picked up on the fact that the beginning took place during the Vietnam conflict. The two main characters, Trey and I, offer a perspective on the time period.

As I finished writing, I began to see that this time period was one where there could be many perspectives. You, the reader, only saw two of them here. One was Trey. He chose to become a draft dodger. He never went to Vietnam and instead went to Canada. While he became a productive citizen of that country, the only conflict he had to endure was being estranged from his family for about ten years. All the while, he was forging ahead, establishing himself. He found a mate, started a family, and never looked back. After 1977, President Jimmy Carter pardoned him, with no preconditions, and he was free to return to the United States. His family took him back, and even though his life was not perfect given what happened with his family, the outcome had nothing to do with the Vietnam conflict.

Then there's me. I sought out and got a deferment. I did nothing wrong, but I presented a different perspective than Trey's. I worried often that this break that I guess I earned would be pulled out from under me, as it was early on when my initial "Marital" deferment was pulled. I dwelled on it less as time went on and counted it as a blessing. I went through life and never got drafted. I still have my draft card, and it remained 1-A throughout my life. I caught a huge break. I never went to Vietnam.

Recently, I saw a great little illustration on the internet. It showed a can of Raid wasp and hornet killer with a man picking it up, looking it over, then taking it to the checkout area. He decided to ask the young lady working there a question.

"Is this stuff good for wasps?"

She looked it over and quickly handed it back to him.

"Oh no, sir. It's terrible for wasps. It kills them on contact!"

Laughable, but perfect as an illustration of perspective. A bit later, I was scheduled to teach at a weekly church service we offer at an assisted living facility next to our church. I used the lesson learned in the Raid story and added to it several Bible-based thoughts and came up with a talk that was very thought-provoking. I used the story of the Prodigal son from the Bible. In this story, there are three main characters, a wealthy father and his two sons. Short and sweet, the younger son is extremely selfish and foolhardy. Even though he knows he will eventually inherit his father's wealth, he grows impatient and asks for it immediately. His father grants it, and the son is off and running. He just as quickly squanders it all and finds himself living in squalor and realizing that the pigs he is tending to are better off than he. In desperation, he decides to go back to his father, ask forgiveness, and request a job as a menial servant for the family he once was very much a part of. When his dad sees him from far off, he treats the son's return with great joy. He throws a feast and party and welcomes his long-lost son with open arms. Everyone seems happy, except for one. The older brother can't believe any of it. The good brother who stayed on and worked daily and never asked for anything special, now has to watch his no-good brother get all the attention and a feast to boot.

The story clearly showed three very different perspectives.

After delivering this message at Feridean, I went next door to our regular church service. It was then that the parallels and perspectives set me on a path back to my story and the unique timeframe called the Vietnam era.

Sitting right in front of me was my dear friend Bob Kuhn. He and his wife began attending a small group that Barb and I met with on Tuesday evenings. They were one of the newer and younger members of our group, but only by a few years. Our group was always doing some kind of a study. Usually, we studied from the Bible and occasionally from a book or video.

I couldn't help noticing that Bob was very emotional if a subject somehow related to death or suffering. He would often break down and even cry. He would tell us about his Vietnam experiences. It didn't take a lot to realize he had been through a lot, and much of that has stayed with him.

I also knew his perspective on that time period would be very different than my character Trey's and my own. I never talked with him about it but decided it would be a good place to start. I was thinking of incorporating some interviews into an epilogue portion of this book (although those plans would eventually change). My biggest fear was that he would think less of me if he knew I had been deferred and that I never had to go through what he did. Nevertheless, I asked if I could interview him. He accepted, and I was able to meet with him at our church after a meeting. I recorded it on my phone and learned a lot in a hurry.

After my time with Bob, I decided that more interviews would be an appropriate way to pay proper respect to those men and women who actually served in Vietnam. My plan became to talk with one person from each of the four major service branches. I knew at least one from each, so I pursued them as soon as I could. Each one gave me a deeper understanding, and each one added immensely to what I hoped to accomplish.

Some of those interviews have been woven into the fabric of this current book, but as I did more interviews, I realized there was more content than I could fit in a small section of *Over and Back*. I've decided to publish those interviews as my next book, coming fall of 2023.

In that book, you'll read my second interview, and through it, meet my friend Gus Shackson. He was a frat brother and classmate at Otterbein. After being in AFROTC

while at school, he joined the USAF. It was great to recon-
nect. He lived in Florida at the time. We did the interview
by phone. I would have much preferred a face-to-face at his
place, as it was winter. Sadly, I found out that Gus passed
prior to the publishing of this book.

Next came another church friend, Bill Cooper. I knew
from some stuff Bill posted on Facebook that he was a Navy
guy and that he had served in Vietnam. I called, and we
soon met at a restaurant in Sunbury and had our interview.
It turned out great!

John Keir was a guy I worked with over thirty years
ago when I was a store manager at a well-known furniture
store in Columbus. I knew he lived in Westerville but hadn't
talked to him for years. Somehow, I knew he had been in
Vietnam. Someone had told me about him having a tough
time with his health because of Agent Orange. I almost
gave up on talking with him, as the number I found for
him proved to be old. I decided to try one more time and
connected. I'm glad I did, for two reasons. He was a Marine,
which allowed me to have someone from each branch. And
second, I was able to spend over two hours with him, and
his story was truly riveting.

As with many projects, this one began to take on a life
of its own. I'm an Otterbein University Alum. At my annual
"O" Club golf outing, I was a volunteer. I had a lot of down
time, and during one such time, I introduced myself to
Wendy Roush. I knew who she was but had never really
talked to her. As we chatted, I told her about the book and
the interviews. She told me that her cousin was an Otterbein

grad and had been killed in action. I knew his name right away! He was a year older than me, but I had met him many times on campus. She suggested that it would add a lot for me to have the perspective of a family who lost a loved one in the conflict. She was insistent, and I agreed with her. She soon had his younger brother get in touch with me. We met for lunch in Granville and had a great talk.

"Larry, my brother's wife passed away a few years back, but they had two daughters before he passed. Would you like to talk to them?" he asked me.

"Wow, that would be interesting for sure."

I soon spoke to his oldest daughter. She revealed that her dad and mom exchanged reel-to-reel tapes back and forth, and that she had a 30-minute tape that I could listen to.

Now I had a second Air Force interview. Why not keep going? As it turns out, I did a total of eleven. All but the last one were people I either knew personally, or who were recommended to me. The last one was quite by accident. I was shopping in my local Kroger store and happened to be in the same aisle with a guy wearing a Vietnam Vet ball cap. I noticed him and wanted to at least tell him thanks for his service. I also decided to ask what branch he served in.

"Army Special Forces," was his response.

I could tell he had an interesting story but didn't pursue it any further. He seemed genuinely pleased that I asked, and we parted ways. I finished shopping and was on my way to my car when it struck me. I had to go back and tell him about my project and ask if he would be interested. After a resounding yes, we exchanged names and phone numbers.

I called him that evening and found out we were neighbors just six minutes apart. I visited him a day later, and the whole experience was well worth our time and effort.

I hope you gleaned both value and enjoyment from reading *Over and Back*, which combines history with mystery, fiction and real-life experiences, to bring you differing perspectives. And I hope you'll check out my next book, through which I'm sure you'll learn as much as I did by reading of these men and their families and their varied experiences while serving in Vietnam.

ACKNOWLEDGMENTS

FIRST AND FOREMOST, I want my efforts to bring glory and honor to my Lord and Savior, Jesus Christ. He inspires me daily.

In the acknowledgments section of my first book, *Switch Hitters*, I found it easy to give credit. I had a built-in cheering section, including my wife, Barb, and my children. I also had a few special friends who inspired me to finish it.

Unrealistically, I felt that my first effort would be a bestseller, that I'd now be famous, have written several more books, and... None of those things happened. Just over ten years have gone by. I'm now retired, and my Barb passed away in 2016. The pandemic hit. I was cooped up and needed something to do to keep me motivated, and this book was a product of that. I guess I am a storyteller. This book is a story, for sure. I got it in my head and I couldn't put it down until it was done.

My first book was what I termed "Autobiographical Fiction." My publisher was not amused, as they knew I'd made up that category for my own benefit. This book is a novel, but it contains many people and incidents that are real and from my past. I'm claiming it is not much different than *Switch Hitters*. Besides, the storyline begins in the sixties and moves through to present day. If you knew me back then, you probably wouldn't remember what was true and what was fiction. If you read the more recent parts, how could you trust me anyway?

Here's a bit of trivia from my first publisher that should prove my point. *Switch Hitters* had about twenty-five characters. My publisher asked if any were real. I admitted that all were either totally real or I used a real name and made up a storyline for the character. They immediately told me that I had to get a written permission slip from each. What a bummer, I thought. I wanted to be done! I ended up loving it, as I had to speak to each of the people featured in the book. I knew how to get in touch with most, but a few I needed help with. My brother Bob helped me a lot there. Harry Cochran was a real guy. I featured him and his family prominently, but in a totally made-up way. I dreaded that he would think ill of this and would not sign on. Instead he did and became my biggest booster. One of my other main characters was Chuck Lohr. At the time I went hunting for him, I sadly found that he was deceased. Bob reminded me that his wife was the sister of one of my other characters. Once I reached her and explained to her that Chuck was portrayed as a hero, she was thrilled. She also became a true advocate of my story. After I finally got all the names accounted for, the book was published. Afterward, many, if not all of the characters asked me, "Did I really do that?"

I feel the same way about this book. No one should be embarrassed by the way I've portrayed them.

I have a few friends I've remained close with for years, and these are the same folks who have constantly spurred me on. Dave Gillott has asked me many times when I was going to do another book. Bill and Jean Hughes shared many of the real family memories that this book includes. Bill Blaine, a fellow author and true friend, met with me recently and was the same encourager now that he was then. By the way, he is twenty years older than me. He and I did our first book in 2009. He has since written at least six more!

After I finished *Over and Back*, I needed to get an editor. One of my friends, Dave Eaton, suggested I talk to his daughter-in-law, Brittany. We met. She read the manuscript and announced that she thought it was worthy of being published. She also recognized that it needed help. She hooked me up with her friend Emily.

"Emily is part of a publishing house and she can help."

I have since been using the services of Emily and her staff to polish the story and get it published. Thank you, Brittany and Emily; my main editor Devon; and my wonderful tech supporter, Clair. Fran Barker (Fran Barker, Photography) graciously took an updated picture of me for the book.

ABOUT THE AUTHOR

LARRY BUTTERMORE **is** a retired but extremely busy resident of Apple Valley, Ohio. He grew up in Connellsville, Pennsylvania, and came to Ohio to attend Otterbein University. Larry became a published author in 2009. His first book is called *Switch Hitters*. The book is an example of autobiographical fiction, drawing on memories of a childhood softball team he was on. In 2019, the COVID pandemic had him at home with lots of extra time. Over and Back went from a loosely organized story to the novel you now possess. Enjoy!

If you'd like a special, personalized sticker to put in the front of this book (perfect for gifts!), Larry invites readers to reach out to him directly via email at larrybuttermore@gmail.com.